THE EMPEROR'S SHADOW

A Phoebe McCabe Mystery

THE AGENCY OF THE ANCIENT LOST & FOUND
BOOK VI

JANE THORNLEY

RiverFlow

THE SHADOW OF THE EMPEROR

The Agency of the Ancient Lost & Found, Book 6

PROLOGUE

Pompeii, AD 79

THAT MORNING I STOOD OUTSIDE MY DOOR AND SAVORED ALL THE FRUITS and flowers with which the gods had sowed the earth and the good fortune they had bestowed upon my head. I had much for which to be thankful. An orchard hedged with flowering trees and a back garden alive with brilliant color and running water as well as a fine and richly appointed domus, that was the world I lived in now. Though it was not solely mine, I shared the benefit.

My life couldn't be more removed from my days of servitude to the goddess Vesta when I lived in comfort but with little freedom. Who would have imagined that I, placed into the goddess's service at an early age, would one day be in command of such a magnificent villa?

"Mistress?"

Wrenched from my reverie, I turned. It was Lucius, one of the few slaves that had been with me since my release from the Vestals, a good and trusted man. He was of dark skin and born a mason in Egypt before he had been brought in slavery to Rome, and I had always felt a kinship. We were of a similar age. He knew things the others did not. "Yes, Lucius, what is it? Is Juno all right?"

"Juno is fine, mistress, though the tutor did not arrive again this morning and the young mistress now reads her Greek in the scriptorium."

It was good that the girl remained diligent with her studies but she must have a tutor as I could only school her in so much. Cato Servius, the best I could locate with experience schooling the children of noble families, had let me down again. He had been with us but for a month.

"What has gone amiss with Servius this time?" I demanded. "Are my coins not as good as any other?"

"They are, mistress," Lucius hastily said to appease me. "I have checked the town and it seems that he has left, his bags piled on a mule heading for Naples."

"But why no word to me?"

"Because he left in haste after yesterday's rumble. I hesitate to say this again, mistress, for I know that you have little patience with the news, but I must keep you informed."

Ah, yes. One thing about this man that I had yet to alter was the fear that appeared to lodge in his heart. Every corner held a monster, every bird an evil portent. I watched him twisting his hands, thick-knuckled and well-used to hard labor across the years, though I had lessened his duties of late. "Just come out with it so I can be about my day."

"It is said in town that the earth shakes beneath our feet too often now and that soon the gods will spew their fury upon our heads. Many citizens like Servius have left or are preparing to leave. Mistress, once again I implore you to consider that we do the same."

My gaze flew up to the cloudless sky, to the tangle of birds flying overhead. Leave paradise? I had been entrusted with this villa and with the girl who would someday inherit the world. We had no place to go that would nurture her in the manner with which the fortune had been provided to me to ensure.

I sighed heavily. "Has not the mountain rumbled many times in the past, Lucius? Have we not had a massive shake but years ago where all citizens had to run for cover and then rebuild once again? As I have said many times before, we cannot leave for we have no place to go."

"We could return to Rome," Lucius said. "Now that the Emperor Titus rules, it is said to be a more just place."

"More just than what, Lucius? No place is safe for such as me and none are just. That which has been granted me to nurture lies here. Now go into town and tell the soothsayer that I will visit her soon."

"Yes, mistress." He bowed his head as if awaiting his execution.

"And pray to our gods. Remember where our fortunes lay. You better than any of the others know the truth of my words. I have taken a vow to her and you to me and must trust in the gods to protect us as they have many times before. Now, be off about your duties. I will hear no more of this."

Besides, I had other things to consider just then. I must find another tutor and quickly for I could not have that girl spending her days roaming about when there was so much left for her to learn. But first, I must pray for our continued protection.

Leaving the garden, I quickly retraced my steps through the frescoed rooms of the vestibule toward the atrium. I passed many servants along the way sweeping the leaves from the mosaics, cleaning the braziers, polishing the brass. Was it only my imagination or did they each shoot me a worried glance as if gauging my mood? Why was everyone so on edge? We had lived with a rumbling mountain all our lives.

I would light a flame and send a prayer before checking on my young charge.

In a corner of the atrium, surrounded by the garden frescoes we loved so well, stood a most magnificent altar to our household gods: the Lares, and, always, to Vesta. Their little statues greeted me each morning. Before them I would make my daily sacrifice of wine and fruit but on this morning I would add something more precious—a pearl from the great queen's hoard—and light a candle that they might protect our domus with continued good fortune.

I carried the pearl with me always. Many others I had used to pay for larger expenses for even the monies I had been given would not last forever. The pearls, however, were bountiful and held much value. Carefully, I took the creamy orb from my stola and slipped it beside the statue of Vesta. *Pray protect our house, great mother. I give you this pearl to prove my devotion.*

Striking the flint, I lifted the flame toward the alcove and reached between the figures toward the candle. "Protect our hearth and home, O mighty ones," I said aloud. "Keep us forever safe just as you have done these many years."

But as the flame reached the wick, it flickered, and went out. I stared. Never had that happened before.

"It is a bad omen, mistress."

I swung around. "Why are you not at your studies, Juno?"

She was now fourteen years old and ready to be wed. Fair of face and slim of figure, she had attracted the eye of many suitors but not yet the one I desired. It was not wealth I sought for the girl, but status. Her future husband must be ambitious, from a good house, and be favored by his father for public life. Now that I had one in mind with the dowry to secure it, I need only wait for the father to arrive before I could secure the match. My one goal in life, a mission entrusted to me down two generations, was to prepare this girl to rule the world.

True to her advanced learning for which I paid much to maintain, she answered in Greek. "I weary of studying the same script day after day. I'd hoped that we could take a walk, perhaps to the baths."

Down to the baths to catch a glimpse of Marcus Priscus, she meant, for we had a bath room of our own and had no need to use the public facilities. Juno had caught glimpses of the young soldier at the games and now those thoughts heated her blood. There could not be a more unsuitable match and she knew it. She was destined for another and it mattered not her wishes in the matter.

"Not today, Juno. Instead, we shall proceed for a quick walk to see the soothsayer so she can remind you once again of your destiny. Quick, fetch your palla."

It was but an impulse on my part, thinking that to visit the soothsayer and hearing the old woman speak again would settle this general unease once and for all. Whatever the wisewoman said would be proclaimed about the villa and put the servants at ease. We could not afford this distraction when there was so much to be done.

Wrapping my red woolen palla about my head and shoulders while the girl left her head bare, we stepped forth and headed down the walk. Always, I preferred to leave the villa with my head covered so as not to draw prying eyes to my person, but Juno was young and marriageable. Her head must remain uncovered. Even if I wished it otherwise, she would likely resist as she did with most things.

Today, I planned only to proceed to the soothsayer and to be quick about it. No hesitation as we strolled past the market stalls, no lingering to admire the wares that had recently arrived by ship or from Rome, though Juno was eager to touch the baubles and stroke every length of fine fabric, as always.

"Enough," I chastised as we strode along. "Do not dawdle." I loved the girl, of course I did, but I knew that too much softness on my part would only turn her headstrong nature in a direction we could not afford. Though her mother had been a Vestal Virgin, still Eros rode in her blood—that had to be curtailed no matter how I detested the role I must play—custodian as well as guardian.

The streets were crowded this morn, many wagons lumbering along the cobbles laden with household goods. I could see the line trailing out from the sea gates all along the Roman road.

"The citizens are fleeing, mistress. Why do we not follow?"

Suppressing my fear, I said: "Because your fate is not to be a follower but a leader." Taking, the girl's hand I tugged her from the traffic into one of the narrow thoroughfares.

"How can I lead if I am dead?" she demanded.

So headstrong. So opinionated. It is a delicate balance to school one to be both strong and obedient. How could I not squash this endless rebellion without damaging her spirit? Juno knew only part of her destiny, but not enough perhaps. What rewarded me in the future only plagued me today. "Enough! Stop such foolish talk. To die young is not your fate for you are destined for great things."

Or so I desperately hoped. The empress had decreed it; the Vestals had struggled across the years to make it so, and now I was tasked with the final piece. Surely all this good fortune could not end so abruptly when we were so close to the prize? The haruspex would settle all. She would tell me the news for which I would pay her dearly. Today, I would double her price to divine from the liver of a slaughtered cow.

The haruspex lived on a side street behind the Stabian baths not far from a bakery. Usually, there were many crowded about the stall purchasing loaves but today we passed only a handful waiting nervously about.

The priestess's domus was small but well-appointed. Many paid for her services in kind, either through artisan trade or in goods. Some brought her food by the cartload. It was said that when a petitioner brought a liver for her to divine, he would often bring her a large piece of the animal upon which she could dine. In my case, I always paid in coin and the woman seemed glad of it.

"I don't wish to listen to this old hag go on and on," Juno hissed as we approached the gate. "She always says the same thing: I am to be the wife of a great man and be the one to steer his ship behind the throne. Why is it that no one asks what I want?"

"Hush! This woman was once a Vestal from Rome and deserves your respect."

But respect did not come easily to one so young, or one so convinced that she knew better than her elders. Before I could say more, the soothsayer appeared. Usually so serene, today she was dashing out the door, her palla hastily thrown over her head, with her servants carrying bundles of belongings on their backs trailing behind.

"O anointed one, did you not receive word that I was to visit this day?" I asked, surprised.

The soothsayer stopped and gazed at me, always unsettling with her rheumy white-scaled eyes. "I sent Lucius away to tell you that I would not be receiving today or any other day. Did you not receive word?"

"I took another path," I explained, "but please remain long enough to read for us. My young charge grows restless and must be soothed."

"Today no one is to be soothed, they are to be warned. I am leaving Pompeii this morning—now, in fact—and suggest you do the same."

"But I cannot! You know I cannot," I exclaimed, scurrying behind her, sacrificing my dignity for my desperation. Juno followed behind, watching the exchange with her quick sharp eyes. Together, we all piled down the steps out into the streets. "Please, take a moment to scry for me, I beseech you. I have brought coins enough for a cow's liver and could pay more, if you desire."

Outside on the road, a passing cloud had cast a pall over our heads but I hardly noticed. The soothsayer turned to face me, her expression as dark as the sky. She was older than I by many decades and had never been forced to do manual tasks and yet still her body stooped. "You do not need me to read for you, mistress. Look up for once and use your eyes instead of your desires. Vesuvius tells your future if you have the will to listen."

With that, she turned to climb into her litter, her slaves easily lifting her frail person into the chair, and in moments she was trundling down the street toward the main roads, leaving me to stare after her.

"Did you hear that, mistress?" Juno demanded beside me. "The old woman speaks the truth for once! I can see it with my own eyes. If you will not listen to reason, then why must I listen to you? I am away and nothing you can do will stop me."

I tried to grab her hand but she was too quick for me. In seconds, she had disappeared into the press of people now trudging down the streets toward the gates and, for one blinding minute, I knew that I had failed.

I

On a dreary London day deep in the heart of an equally gray November, I hopped the tube for Pall Mall to meet Rupert Fox for lunch. Let me just say that Pall Mall, the traditional stomping ground of the very rich, was not a street I usually visited. The St. James area, with its embassies and clubby addresses, rarely lured me over.

Mostly, I just worked at my computer in our agency offices off King's Road, cross-referencing missing art with international registries and Interpol databases, every day the same. My one big outing was my biweekly hand-to-hand combat practice, which at least got me out of the flat. When not on a case, I lived a dull existence. I liken my life to how sailors often describe oceanic sailing: one part terror mixed with three parts long stretches of sameness.

Evan was on a case and Peaches away in Jamaica. My godfather and gallery business partner, Max, was off to France on a textile shopping expedition with our office manager, Serena, his girlfriend, leaving the gallery in the hands of Serena's daughter-in-law, fledgling fashion designer Jennifer. More about that later.

Anyway, I was convinced that Rupert's invitation had been a ploy to cheer me up or, at the very least, to distract me. Granted, I was anxious. Evan could only be tracking down my nefarious ex, which involved significant danger and might explain why I hadn't heard from him in days. Of course I worried. Who wouldn't? Add to that the fact that I couldn't stop thinking about the man who had become my official "boyfriend" and of how little time we actually managed to spend together now that we were a couple.

When I exited the Charing Cross station minutes later, I remembered the countless times I'd been ferried across London by Evan in the comfort of Rupert's limousine while he masqueraded as his father's chauffeur. Of course, I didn't know of their true relationship at the time. Still, I'd seen more of him back when I was under suspicion of international art theft myself than I did now. There's the irony. Apparently, being a person of interest back then made it the good old days.

So, Rupert had chosen the Royal Automobile Club headquarters as our lunch venue, but why? Because he wanted to wow me by the grand entrance, exemplary service, fine food, and floral bouquets festooning the polished foyer? Or did he have an ulterior motive entirely? My bet was on the latter. My friend was a great automobile enthusiast as was his son but he knew that I couldn't tell a Porsche from a Peugeot. To me, cars were notable by color alone. I was particularly fond of the green kind.

The moment I stepped through the door, an impeccably uniformed man— dark navy, brass buttons—descended upon me with courtesy glinting off every fastening. One needed a reservation and to be invited by a member. One did not just walk in off the street looking for a quick burger with a side of fries.

After mentioning Sir Rupert Fox, the demeanor slipped into a more gracious welcome and another young steward escorted me up to one of the bars. He explained while en route that there were multiple lounges and to watch my step as I climbed the carpeted entry. Perhaps the fact that I was garbed in one of my art knit wraps and wearing an otherwise nondescript pair of velvet pants with a turtleneck meant that I required walking lessons.

Okay, so I was being testy.

Mostly men sat in the leather seats drinking and chatting, the conversation seeming as revved and engaged as a sleek automobile zipping around a track. No doubt they were negotiating business deals or otherwise lubricating the social wheels of the upper echelons. One glimpse of the glossy silver sports car on display on the grand landing didn't improve my mood.

Rupert was waiting for me dressed in sartorial splendor as usual—Savile Row tailoring in a subtle gray-green tweed with a crisp white shirt paired with a blazing chartreuse tie. No doubt matching socks were tucked into his polished loafers.

"Rupert!" I exclaimed.

He rose to greet me, bestowing an air kiss to each cheek as he ushered me into the seat across from his. "Dearest Phoebe. What a delight it is to pry you from the office for a touch of social discourse at last. Now that I am partially retired, I rarely have the opportunity to see you as often as I'd prefer."

Rupert had retired from Interpol and now only worked when the Agency of the Ancient Lost and Found required his services.

"I'm happy to see you, too, Rupert, but why here?" I beamed at him.

"I believed you would enjoy a change of scenery, of course, and the food is top-notch. Sad to say that I no longer drive late-model cars myself but recently purchased a four-year-old Rolls-Royce Silver Cloud. One must economize where one can. Did you chance to see the Aston Martin on display? Oh, I've taken the liberty of ordering you a glass of fine chardonnay to help you to unwind and one also for the guest I hope will arrive shortly." I took a breath to protest but he stopped me with a smile. "One glass will not put you awry," he told me.

"Yes, it will," said I, but didn't put up much resistance.

The glass arrived along with a bowl of mixed nuts and potato chips, the kind one imagines the chef preparing in the kitchen moments before your arrival. Nothing mass-produced here. I drove into the snacks first followed by a sip of wine. Delicious. The knots in my neck began to loosen as I resolved to enjoy the moment.

"So, what's happening with you these days, Rupert, and who is this mysterious guest you've invited? Have you heard from Evan?" That last question just slipped out. Blame the wine.

Rupert fixed me with gimlet eyes framed by his incredible bushy eyebrows, which consistent grooming only managed to contain but never tame. "I am finishing the last of the renovations at my country estate, which I'm relieved to say are nearly complete." He'd decided to ignore my inappropriate question—fair enough. I wasn't supposed to know the intricacies of Evan's Interpol assignments even if they affected me both emotionally and physically. "Tedious business that with all the endless costs to acquire building materials in this post-pandemic climate. Prices have risen exponentially—"

"So, you must be glad to have that done," I interrupted. "I know that Evan must be in pursuit of Noel so I can't help but worry. Hope you understand, you being his dad. Is it back to Sardinia, do you think? He probably doesn't tell you any more than he does me."

Rupert scooped up a few nuts with the silver spoon provided and placed them in a little dish. "As I was saying, the ability to acquire certain bespoke items has become a gauntlet run of negotiations and under-the-table payments that drive me to distraction."

9

"Sardinia, then, or maybe back to Sicily? I know there was some speculation that Noel has been hiding out somewhere in southern Italy."

"Now I have dispatched my household to my Belgravia home for a spot of rest and to connect with friends."

I gave up. "Like me and this mystery guest you've invited?"

Rupert checked his watch—nothing ordinary there, either, but I didn't know my watches any better than I did my cars. "Precisely so, but I am not personally acquainted with the man. He contacted me by phone, as in the landline variety, Monday last, and requested our services. He said he had a case that might interest us. I do hope that the chap deigns to come."

"If he has a case for us, why not go through the agency website? Why call you at home?"

"I have no idea but I expect all will be explained. He did claim to be a bit of a fan of the agency and had heard of my exploits in particular and I couldn't very well resist an opening like that, could I? I suggested him meeting us here and told him that I would bring you, the illustrious Phoebe McCabe."

"Great," I murmured.

"I thought he'd be thrilled to meet at such an auspicious location. Nevertheless, I detected considerable reticence when I named the locale, to the point of him suggesting we meet someplace less visible."

I looked up. "Someplace invisible, then?"

"Don't be glib, Phoebe. But really, who wouldn't want to dine at the Royal Automobile Club headquarters?"

"Maybe a veteran walking enthusiast? Joking. Don't scowl at me. What do you know about this man, anyway?" I asked.

"Very little except that he works as a volunteer at a museum where he claims there have been some irregular goings-on."

"Like hanky-panky in the Etruscan exhibit?"

Rupert glowered. "You are in rather an odd mood today, Phoebe."

"Sorry. Anyway, please carry on."

"The man, a one Markland Rodgers, said only that he had experienced some unaccountable goings-on at his museum and he thought that we might be the ones to find out the answers on the sly. He originally hesitated to bring the matter to anyone's official attention. If he can solve it without fuss, all the better, though a few of his colleagues are also aware of the anomalies."

I looked up. "What kind of anomalies?'

"He wouldn't say."

"Did you check him out?"

"Of course. A Markland Rodgers has been working at the museum for several years."

"Which museum?"

"Sir Bentley Broadhurst."

I gasped. "Sir Bentley Broadhurst, my absolute favorite museum in the world?"

"Well, that's a bit rich, Phoebe." Rupert's caterpillar eyebrows collided on his brow. "There have been many museums that have engaged your attention in our line of work over the years but this is the first time I've heard that Sir Bentley Broadhurst's was a favorite."

"It was among the first museums I spent any time in when I moved to London because it seemed, well, almost cozy. I love it to bits." Okay, so the wine was talking by then but my emotional draw to the most magnificent house museum in the world was absolutely true.

Sir Bentley Broadhurst was a nineteenth-century lawyer (1750–1839) and an enthusiastic collector who bought three buildings in Eaton Square to become his offices, home, and personal museum to house his magnificent collection of mostly ancient artifacts and art. He positioned each piece with an artist's eye, playing off the elements of ancient art and architecture one against the other to illustrate the striking beauty of the whole.

Rooms were opened up with upper and lower floors viewable from different angles with careful attention paid to light sources that were curated through stunning window features. In short, the man was a genius, making history seem more accessible, human, and completely alive. "I can't imagine an anomaly happening at the Broadhurst museum."

"Neither can I," Rupert remarked. "Nevertheless, this Markland Rodgers chap insisted that strange events were occurring on the premises."

"Like what—talking statues, spectral presences, missing art?"

Rupert leaned forward. "Phoebe, I said I did not know. Besides, I do not believe in spectral presences. That's entirely your interest, hardly mine." He looked up. "He told me to look out for a man wearing a red scarf and here comes one now wearing a rather dreadful example. What stitch is that —garter?"

I turned to watch a tall man of medium build approach dressed in a navy sports jacket over a white T-shirt, jeans, and sneakers complete with said woolly scarf wrapped several times around his neck, everything a bit worn and crumpled. Of average looks, he had a pale pleasant face with a fuzz of short gray hair and kept his eyes fixed ahead as the steward led him toward us.

Rupert got to his feet as did I and a flurry of handshakes and introductions followed.

"It's very good to meet you, Sir Fox, and you also, Phoebe McCabe. Your reputations precede you, as they say." His grip was firm despite his mild appearance.

Markland sat down smiling, his eyes finally resting on our faces, each in turn. Sky-blue eyes, direct, shrewd gaze. "I admit to hesitating on meeting you here and thought at first to suggest a pub somewhere but dining at the club is a treat, too. I certainly can't afford places like this on my pension."

"You are here as my guest, dear chap," Rupert said while beaming in pleasure. "Happy to treat one of Britain's indispensable volunteers. You did say that you volunteer your services?"

"Yes, at the Sir Bentley Broadhurst Museum," Markland said. "I retired as a curator from there five years ago but now I'm happy just to help out part-time."

"A noble cause," Rupert said with a nod. "What would England do without her volunteers? And it was while you were engaged in your selfless service that you noticed something awry on the premises, as I understand?"

"Exactly. It's the most damnable thing and I really can't figure it out. I'm hoping you can help."

"You've come to the right place, I assure you."

"What exactly is going on?" I asked, eager to discover the reason for our meeting, but at that moment a steward whispered into Rupert's ear.

"Our table is ready," Rupert told us. "Shall we proceed into the dining room?"

The dining room could almost be described as palatial, at least the gold-embossed baroque interior with its painted ceilings and murals gave every impression of a royal abode, fitting enough seeing as the Prince of Kent was the club's official headman.

We were seated at a table by the window, every glass and piece of cutlery gleaming in the light, and presented with a large, stately menu while I appreciated the huge floral bouquet that dominated the central space. Imagine the price of dahlias and chrysanthemums in November!

"May I recommend the sole meunière?" suggested Rupert. "It's exemplary and I know just the wine to accompany it."

We agreed and once our orders were taken I just wanted to get on with business. Gazing at the man across from me, I watched as he unfurled a snowy damask napkin onto his lap. "First, let me prepare the staging to these events. Are you familiar with the museum?" he inquired.

"I've been many times but there's so much to take in that every visit is a new discovery," I told him.

"Isn't it just?" His eyes met mine. "In order to better understand the extraordinary occurrences that have been happening of late, let me explain how we guides work. Each day, one of us is in charge of a room or a group of smaller areas such as hallways and corridors during our shifts. We are there to answer questions from our visitors as well as to ensure that no one tampers with or otherwise touches the exhibits. Because Sir Bentley Broadhurst specified through an Act of Parliament that objects remain positioned in the museum exactly as Broadhurst designed it, the artifacts are more accessible to visitors than most museums, which is both its charm and its vulnerability."

I nodded. "That's one of the reasons I love it so much—I feel as though I'm walking through time itself with no barriers to partition me off."

"Something which Sir Bentley wished to achieve through lighting and staging. The man knew what he was doing. He was a master of theater, among other things. In any case, those of us who work there, especially those who have been at it as long as I, have come to know the displays intimately. We stare at them every single day, sometimes for hours at a time. We notice when an object shifts position."

Our lunches arrived before us, looking delectable in every sense. I leaned forward. "Shifts position?"

"Moves, maybe by mere centimeters, but moves nonetheless. Several artifacts have shifted position and none of us is responsible for the act. It appears to be happening almost every night."

"But, dear man, surely the facility has excellent security systems in place?" Rupert protested while simultaneously carving out a tasty morsel.

"Absolutely—the best—yet no alarms have gone off nor have cameras detected anything unusual."

"Surely you're not implying..." Rupert hesitated to utter the words. "Something of a supernatural nature?"

Markland lifted his hands. "I have no idea, which is why I contacted you, Sir Rupert. I hear that your agency is the best for such detective work. I've recently alerted the higher-ups but so far nothing has been resolved. As long as everything is accounted for, no one is unduly concerned. Nothing's been stolen, after all."

"Do you think that a theft may be in the offing?" I asked. "I mean, the museum is filled with priceless treasures."

"Indeed it is, but the museum owns nothing like the crown jewels or works by some Renaissance master," Markland pointed out. "There are a couple of fine Turners and a range of diverse antiquities Broadhurst picked up on his grand tour combined with others he acquired through auction—valuable, irreplaceable, even, but not something that might attract a thief. The more precious objects are frankly unwieldy, like Pharaoh Seti IV's sarcophagus, for instance, or the Hopley vase, neither of which can be simply pocketed."

"One would need a forklift for the sarcophagus," Rupert remarked as if actively considering how to remove the object. "And possibly a crane," he added.

"Yet, somebody appears to be looking for something. Any chance we can spend a night in the museum to check things out?" I inquired.

"Absolutely not," he said mildly, shooting me an appraising glance. "That would be completely against security protocols and I could be prosecuted for even suggesting such a thing."

"But you didn't suggest it," I pointed out.

Picking up his knife and fork, he nodded. "I didn't, did I? Why not pay the museum a visit on one of our candlelit tour nights. Book for an exclusive evening and experience the museum in the manner in which Sir Bentley would have entertained his guests. The next event is this Thursday beginning at nine p.m. I'll be on duty that night. I'll send you the link. The sole is delicious, by the way." He dug into his meal with satisfaction.

2

"Phoebe, you can't possibly be considering what I believe you're considering."

Rupert and I stood in the club lobby waiting for the cab to arrive after he insisted on dropping me off on his way home. Markland had already left.

"How else can we figure out what's going on inside that museum?" I whispered.

"Allow me to make inquiries through the proper channels and, if need be, formally engage our Interpol affiliations."

"And how long would that take—a month, two? Seeing as nothing has been stolen, I doubt Interpol will be too interested and we can't even contact Evan to pull the strings. Meanwhile, somebody's up to something and we need to discover what before a priceless object goes missing."

"Nevertheless, those are the proper channels."

"Since when did you worry about 'proper channels'?" I whispered.

"Since I matured or, at the very least, since I partially retired and realized that doing otherwise unleashes far more complications than one needs at my tender age."

"Stop sounding as if you're hobbling around on your last legs. You're a mere spring chicken in the great barnyard of life at sixty-four. Don't tell me that you're turning into some supercautious fuddy-duddy?"

"Fuddy-duddy!" His look of effrontery was almost comical.

I patted his arm. "Sorry. That wasn't fair. It's just that you know better than anyone that the best way to get things done is to skip the permission stage and go directly to hopeful forgiveness. One way or the other, I'm going to get into the museum to stay the night and I'm hoping you'll come with me. We need the distraction."

He didn't say much after that except to make pleasantries about the new hybrid cab we were in. The cabbie did the talking, anyway. Most London cabbies were philosophers or political analysts, depending on the day and whatever was hitting the news at the time. This one had plenty to say about the British labor strikes and American presidents. He also added a mournful tribute to the late queen.

I jumped out of the cab at our gallery-cum-office and waved Rupert good-bye. We were to stay in touch by text between today, a Monday, and the days leading up to the museum's Thursday night opening. There was planning to be done, research to get under my belt. Rupert still hadn't agreed to participate.

When I opened the gallery door, Jennifer was nowhere to be found.

"Jenn?" I called.

"Back here."

I followed the sound of her voice to the back storage area now expanded to include a mini lounge, storage, and office space. Two long legs were popped on the coffee table, the face hidden behind *British Vogue*. "Hi ya."

"You're supposed to be watching the gallery, Jenn."

The magazine lowered. "I am." She pointed to our closed-circuit TV in the upper corner, which covered every angle of the gallery. "Nobody's entered for hours, Phoeb. It's, like, sooooo dead around here. We should have Monday closing. Lots of places do that."

I glanced at the screen. "Max knows that if even one person drops in and buys a carpet, it's worth paying operational costs." That was a direct reference to her exorbitant salary since Max paid his girlfriend's daughter substantially more than minimum wage and expected her to earn it.

"Yeah, but I'd hear the bell if somebody entered and it's not like anybody can steal anything, anyway, right? Those carpets are kind of hard to peel off the wall and alarmed besides, don't you think? And all the smaller stuff is in locked cases so, like, theft-proof."

"Nothing is theft-proof but that's not the point. Max wants you to mind the gallery, Jenn."

Sighing, the blonde Gwyneth Paltrow lookalike unfolded herself and got to her feet, every inch garbed in the latest fashion, this time full high-waist trousers with a matching cropped jacket. She was dazzling, as always, her outfit accessorized with some original twist, which today happened to be a silk scarf worn as a bandeau beneath the tweedy fabric.

"Any word from your internship with that designer?" I asked as she slipped away with a model-perfect glide.

"Not yet. Soon, I hope."

As if on cue, her cell rang. "It's him!" she squealed, holding up her phone.

"Good luck. I'll just leave you be." With that, I exited the room and stepped back into the gallery. I desperately hoped she'd get the job. I knew from her sketches that the young woman had talent with the kind of edgy verve that could stand out from the fashion wannabes.

For a moment, I just stared into the gallery space with its three-story ceiling, admiring the colors pulsing off the carpets that hung bathed in the halogen glow. Max and Serena liked to stack them one on top of the other with every alternative piece just touching the floor. They were like textile paintings composing the brilliant intricacy of cultural design.

It was just by luck that I caught the dull gleam of something metallic far across the room at the foot of one of our magnificent sixteenth-century Persian Safavids. Those carpets didn't have beading or any kind of embellishments so what was that about? Probably a bit of foil that escaped the morning sweep, not that Jennifer actually did any sweeping.

I crossed the space half thinking that I needed to get up a bit earlier to run a dry mop around the floor, a loving task I used to do before the agency business took over.

Stopping at the carpet, I gazed down at what looked like a burnished gold coin sticking out from under the fringe. Surely not. Seconds later, that's exactly what I held in my palm: a Roman coin with the head of a woman and the name *Augustus* visible despite the wear. Flipping it over, the second side featured an image of a badly rubbed figure seated on a throne. I knew a genuine Roman coin when I saw one but why was it half-hidden on the gallery floor?

Turning, I darted back toward the storeroom just as Jennifer was exiting.

"I got it! I got it! I start next Monday."

Great. Max and Serena would return on the weekend.

"That's fantastic, Jenn!" I hugged her and stood back while she performed a happy dance, hers being almost ballet-like in grace despite the high-heel pumps.

"I've got to text Mom and tell Marco! They'll be so excited."

"Oh, they will. You do that. I'm just going to go through the security tapes. Can you keep an eye on the gallery?"

But Jenn was speed tapping into her phone by then—no, skip that; she decided to call instead, all the time keeping her back turned to the gallery.

I gave up and locked the door, putting up the CLOSED sign on the window before diving into Max's office to hit Replay on the security recordings.

Those recordings were overwritten every seventy-eight hours and I was almost positive that Jennifer hadn't gone through them in the past six days since Max and Serena left. Usually footage reviews only happened in the event of suspicious activity, which was rare. Since the carpets were all alarmed, a suspicious activity would need to be an attempted robbery or damage to one of our priceless textiles.

As I feared, the hard drive registered that the last seventy-eight hours had been erased and partially recorded over. Unless the coin had managed to land in its spot over the past twenty-four hours, I was out of luck.

I scanned through the recordings, including the night when the gallery lay bathed in infrared lighting, finding nothing out of order. I saw myself leaving to meet Rupert late the next morning, noted the three people who had entered the space before and after, including the postwoman, Sylvia; Mr. Peabody, who paid us a weekly visit just to admire our carpets; and a young couple who hastily exited once Jennifer told them the price of the Chinese Ming imperial dragon carpet they were eyeing. Jennifer was right: business was slow.

I hastily posted a picture of both sides of the coin and dispatched it to Rupert along with information about where it was found. He got back to me within minutes.

Rupert: *Extraordinary. Someone must have dropped it.*

Me: *Dropped it halfway under the hem of one of our Persian beauties? That doesn't sound likely.*

Rupert: *Perhaps the person in question inadvertently kicked it under the carpet after accidentally, and quite carelessly, I might add, allowing it to tumble from his or her pocket. I suspect that he or she carried the item as a kind of talisman, a rather common event these days. People can grow attached to these kinds of things.*

Me: *Do you know anything about this coin generally?*

Rupert: *If it names Emperor Augustus, which it does indeed do, the woman's head must be his empress, Livia, though Augustus never minted any coins with his wife's head from his seat in Rome. The coin most probably hails from one of the provinces and I'd estimate the date possibly circa AD 2 to 13.*

Me: *Okay, thanks. I'll just keep it until the owner realizes it's missing and comes back to the gallery looking for it.*

But it struck me as strange. Why would anyone remove a valuable coin from their pocket in a carpet gallery in the first place? Unless, I reasoned, they had pulled out something else and dropped the coin by accident. That had to be it. Nothing else made sense. Still, it struck me as odd. I tucked the coin into the secret compartment of my carpetbag and forgot about it. I needed to focus on my upcoming night in the museum.

Downstairs in our renovated basement lab and office area, the official flagship agency headquarters, I busied myself with researching everything I could about Sir Bentley Broadhurst. That involved skimming multiple books including a description of the contents penned by the gentleman himself. By the time evening rolled around, I'd exhausted every avenue available to me and decided to visit the museum myself the next day.

That left an evening of knitting periodically interrupted by checking emails on my agency superphone. Evan was still off-grid, something he did when his mission was considered top-secret. I sent him messages hoping for a response but nothing came. Why was I the only one who fretted when that happened?

Peaches texted to say that she'd met a new man in Jamaica and, unless something interesting happened back here, she was staying on for a while. Peaches avoided the cold whenever possible and I had no doubt but that her new guy was hot. As for Nicolina, all was calm in Rome so far, and Zann, our newest member and head of the US division, was off tracking down a missing heirloom in Atlanta.

The next morning, after assuring myself that Jennifer was truly minding the fort, I took off for the Broadhurst. As it turned out, Markland was not on duty that morning and I took advantage of studying the museum piece by piece without interruption. Occasionally, I'd ask one of the knowledgeable guides something but I mostly wanted to wander undisturbed.

Actually, I was seeking something worth stealing and though there were plenty of priceless objects to choose from—paintings by Turner and Sir Joshua Reynolds, priceless Greek and Etruscan vases, rare books and illuminated manuscripts—not one object stood out as being something so attractive as to be worth the risk. Of course, if the thief was working on behalf of a collector, anything might be on his hit list, but unless he planned to heist multiple objects at a time, I couldn't see how it would be worth the effort.

Many of the pieces were casts of original ancient sculptures, though there were plenty of authentic bits of Roman and Greek architecture and culture, including cinerary urns, cornices, pieces from a Greek altar, and a pilaster capital, placed throughout the exhibit.

Broadhurst arranged artifacts so that their decorative features played off against one another rather than grouping them together in a common theme. How the light touched the objects was critical to the master's design and he crafted unique window features to do just that. I particularly loved gazing out at the Obelix Court, which formed a square courtyard viewable from multiple rooms.

And the man loved a bit of theater. The Prior's Cemetery was more staging than a real tomb, though pieces of genuine monastical ruins abounded. Since Sir Bentley also included a cast of his late wife's cat, Lady Fluffy, one couldn't take things that seriously.

I wandered from the replica of the majestic Apollo bathed in light from the windows designed to spotlight the god in all his splendor right down to the fig leaf that wasn't big enough to hide so much as a fig let alone an appendage. Then I moved on to the Sepulchral Chamber in the basement where the imposing alabaster sarcophagus of Seti IV dominated the lower level. It was by far the architect's most prized piece, and at the time he purchased it from the British Museum for two thousand pounds sterling, nobody yet knew who had occupied it let alone deciphered the hieroglyphics covering its surface. That would come later.

In other words, the museum was layered, detailed, and fascinating. It would take more than a few hours to do it justice but at least I had refreshed in my mind as to the general layout. I sent a message to Markland asking which particular objects had been tampered with and paused long enough to reread his response: a cork model of a temple dedicated to Apollo, the ruins of which were located in Rome, and two Roman cinerary urns. That these objects were all Roman couldn't be a coincidence.

Retracing my steps, I studied each urn but there were six, all in excellent states of preservation with not one more valuable than the other. I wasn't the expert on Roman artifacts, that was more Rupert and Nicolina's domain, but I knew the basics. And the cork model probably held little monetary value at all. It was also apparent by the size of the urns, which stood about two feet tall and at least twelve inches in diameter and mostly made of marble or alabaster, that moving them wouldn't be easy, especially since the prime specimens were balanced on a thin ledge suspended over two stories. Why even attempt to steal one of those? Roman funerary urns were relatively common. I left totally baffled.

By the appointed night at the museum, I still hadn't heard from Evan but was determined to stop worrying and to stay focused. Rupert had agreed to attend the event but not to stay the night, citing his bad back. It's true that he was slowing down these days, either by choice or physical concerns, I didn't know.

Additionally, he reasoned, I needed somebody on the outside to monitor the screens, which actually made sense. My plan was to use one of Evan's new apps to transfer the museum's security circuit onto our private monitoring system. That way the camera feed for each room would show only on our monitors. Rupert had agreed to stay up long enough to keep watch on his computer while I was still inside the museum based on the two-pairs-of-eyes-are-better-than-one theory. Besides, my tablet's thumbnails were so small I could miss something.

Everything works via technology these days, making the most efficient systems of the nonhuman variety. Though in the Broadhurst's case, a live guard did remain on the museum premises overnight; he spent his active hours monitoring screens from his office where he could also operate lights, power, and everything else with a press of a button. But the security screens wouldn't register anything abnormal that night because the real feed would be patched onto my system. Even my movements inside the museum wouldn't register, leaving my biggest worry being physically bumping into the guard during his rounds. That is if he even did rounds.

By the time Thursday night rolled around, Markland had broken off all communication. I tacitly understood that for him to be in any way involved in what I was about to do could bring criminal charges down on this head so I'd pretend not to know him accordingly. My plan was to remain behind after the night visitors exited and then to leave in the early hours once I'd hopefully found the truth behind those amazing moving artifacts.

We arrived at the Sir Bentley Broadhurst Museum at the appointed time of 8:30 p.m. to join a small group of about thirty museum enthusiasts lining up for the event. By then, the November skies had darkened enough over London to show a candlelit museum to its best advantage.

The door person scanned our tickets and we stepped into the candlelit hallway, a setting that probably approximated how the rooms must have appeared during Sir Broadhurst's days. Apparently, the man, a noted member of Victorian society and a star among those who augmented their collections by poaching artifacts from ancient sites, often held informative soirees in his home. He was known to have led his guests from room to room, much as we would be guided by Markland that evening.

Unfortunately, Markland was not immediately visible. Even by nine, when the event officially began, there was no sign of the man.

"Where is he?" I whispered to Rupert as we accepted our glass of wine from the tray in the main salon where our tour was to begin.

"I have no idea," said Rupert. "Perhaps he's on one of the other levels preparing to take over as we progress?"

That made sense. For the first hour, I enjoyed the effects of the candlelight flickering over the art and artifacts, in the way the museum used uplighting to enhance the surfaces of ancient cornices and carvings, positioned as they were one above the other like a fabulous orchestra of shadow and light. The guide, Susan Brooks, was as lively as she was informative and, at certain points, another guide joined her, a man, but not Markland. By the time we reached the gloomy basement exhibits, I was beginning to grow concerned.

Slipping up to Rupert, I whispered: "Perhaps he decided to vacate himself in case he got caught up in our investigation?"

"Perhaps," he replied. "I shall just make a few casual inquiries of our hosts to see if our man did, indeed, take the night off."

We were nearing the end of the evening when Rupert had his answer. Holding me back as we filed out of the Picture Room to make our way toward the museum exit, the guides dousing the candles as we went and switching to electric light, he whispered: "Phoebe, we've been had, I'm afraid. Though a Markland Rodgers did indeed work here as a guide for many years and volunteered for many more, he was not expected in tonight because he is believed to be quite dead. He died four years ago in a sailing accident. His body was never recovered."

3

I stared. "But I thought you checked him out?"

Rupert adjusted his tie. "I assure you that I made the necessary inquiries, though not perhaps as thoroughly as I might have when working for Interpol, yet I had no reason to believe the man wasn't who he said he was. In any event, I suggest we abandon the whole plan immediately. We are obviously being set up for reasons that allude me."

"If somebody set us up, I want to catch the bastard red-handed. I love nothing better than to double-cross a double-crosser. Besides, what if he's planning a heist tonight thinking he'll pin the blame on me? If we walk away now and something is filched, I'd hold us responsible since only we are in the position to stop him." I stood firm in my conviction. "No, I'm confident enough in the agency's technology to beat the rotter at his own game. I'm going through with it."

"Phoebe, please don't be foolhardy. Being accused of an art crime is no small thing given our reputations, especially if this rotter, as you call him, does indeed plan a crime tonight. We hardly have the agency resources galvanized to stop him at this late juncture and are better placed to alert the authorities to the fact that we have reason to believe that someone may attempt something nefarious against the museum's holdings this night."

I waited for him to catch his breath. "Rupert, just go through with your end of things, please. Leave the rest to me."

Susan veered back into the hall to usher us along. "We're just about to check everyone out," she said with a grin. "I do hope you enjoyed yourselves." The guide glanced from Rupert to me, obviously picking up on our rather heated discussion.

"Oh, I just loved it!" I gushed. "But I'm going to have to leave now to catch the tube. Mind if I bolt ahead?"

"No, of course not," she assured me. "Just be certain to have my colleague check you out."

Which I did, of course, exiting just ahead of the others while keeping an ear out for Rupert's collapse in the hallway behind me, which occurred at the appointed time of 10:05. Rupert was nothing if not punctual.

The moment he hit the floor in his feigned faint, I knew the museum would essentially lock down. I immediately used my cell phone to divert the security system, unlock the doors, and cut the power, in that order. I needed the dark to slip back inside past the employees, now in chaos.

One of them was on the phone to emergency services, one of them was presumably off looking for the power supply, and the other two were kneeling over Rupert, including one administering mouth-to-mouth resuscitation.

They were all too preoccupied to notice the black figure slip through the shadows into the salon and toward the back of the house. By the time, I switched the power back on I was safely tucked away behind the prior's headstone deep in the bowels of the house, which was where I planned to remain until everything quieted down.

Hidden in the shadows, I watched the events unfold on my tablet with my wireless earbuds attached. Rupert began to recover, huffing and puffing while citing a tendency to swoon at the least provocation. High blood pressure, he insisted. No need for an ambulance, he assured them. Would they mind calling him a cab? Meanwhile, the security guard was in earnest conversation with Susan, standing conveniently below the front hall camera.

"It's happening again," he complained. "Can we request that electrician to come back and fix this electrical issue once and for all? We can't go having the power just up and black out like that with no warning like, can we? Don't those fellows have to guarantee their work or something?"

Susan nodded in agreement. "I've alerted the director, who assures me that she'll put in another requisition first thing in the morning. In the meantime, let's hope the power withstands the night without any further interruptions. What I don't understand is why the generator's giving out, too. It's practically new."

"I've taken a look at the thing and it seems to be working fine," the guard assured her.

So there had been other recent outages? Curiouser and curiouser. That couldn't be a coincidence. Now more than ever I was convinced that somebody was making a move on the museum, maybe Markland-who-wasn't-Markland.

I settled down to keep watch on each of the twenty security screens showing as thumbnails on my tablet hoping that Rupert would soon return home to take over. Meanwhile, the guides removed all the remaining candles and did a once-around the museum. The guide who came down to the crypt area bypassed my spot entirely and, rather than looking in every cranny, seemed fixed on ensuring that all the treasures were exactly as the team had left them. Since all the guests had electronically checked out, presumably no one expected stowaways.

By eleven p.m., the museum was locked down for the night, all but the security man had left and he was upstairs sitting in his office keeping an eye on the screens, which would register nothing but another tranquil night at the museum.

Rupert popped on my screen at around 10:45.

"Nice bit of swooning," I whispered.

"I could rather do without the mouth-to-mouth intervention, I assure you. These days, one has to be careful with whom one makes lip contact."

I filled him in on the conversation I'd overheard regarding previous power outages.

"That sounds to me as if someone besides ourselves has been playing with the circuitry. Evan once remarked that aspects of our systems might soon hit the underground market."

I considered that for a moment. "Well, we can't worry about that now. As of this moment, we're in control of the security feed and that's all that matters. Ready for a long night?"

Rupert sighed and held up a glass. "A dram of fine scotch shall make the wee hours pass more divinely."

I had no such pleasant soothers but I didn't find hanging out in a museum at night all that unpleasant. Granted, I was in a spot that magnified Broadhurst's most Gothic touch of theater—arches from monastical ruins, genuine headstones, more funerary urns, and even a skull with a hole in it propped on a shelf somewhere in the dark behind me—but I didn't find that spooky so much as amusing.

Though I was open to certain kinds of spectral encounters, I didn't believe that objects in museums as a rule held enough of their original owner's energy for said owners to stage a comeback. Otherwise, I enjoyed playing around with the infrared feature on my superphone until I could see the features of the ominous chamber more clearly.

The museum did have some night lighting, specifically spotlights illuminating the dome visible from the street, but since the guard wouldn't see anything abnormal, I decided to take a stroll. I wandered through the catacombs and into the Sepulchral Chamber, thoroughly enjoying having the museum to myself.

"Phoebe, what in the world are you doing?" Rupert whispered.

"Stretching my legs," I told him. "Keep watching the screens, please. Is the guard still at his post?"

"The chap appears to be keeping an eye on things while playing solitaire."

"Good. I'm just going to see if anything is afoot."

By then it was 1:15 a.m., and I figured that if anyone intended a theft, it would probably occur between the hours of one and three a.m., statistically speaking. I was mostly focused on what a criminal might target. Certainly Seti's sarcophagus was the museum's prime holding but also unmovable as we'd already determined. Still, I gave it a pass just in case.

After detecting nothing unusual on my scanner app, I slipped past the magnificent piece and gazed overhead at the layered artifacts and architectural objects rising up three stories under the museum's centerpiece, the grand dome.

Broadhurst had placed the sarcophagus so that one could look down into it from the landing, the same landing that held the statue of Apollo plus the grandest of the urns balanced along the ledges above my head, everything monochromatic shades of marble and stone with touches of gold. In the daylight hours, the area was lit by natural daylight like some kind of fantastical multidimensional periscope.

So what would a thief target? I thought as I looked up. The non-Markland fellow had indicated the cork model of the Temple of Apollo and two urns that had once held the ashes of some deceased Roman. I could see those urns from where I stood. Though we couldn't believe anything that man had told us, why single those out?

A sudden thought struck hard. "Rupert!" I whispered. "Both the objects Non-Markland had told us about were Roman and so is the coin I found on the gallery floor!"

"Forget that for a moment," he whispered back. "Something's afoot on the floor above your head!"

My gaze shot upward and, for a second, I caught the flash of something red. I bolted for the stairs.

"Caution, Phoebe! The guard is on the move."

I didn't care about that; I cared only about catching a thief in the act. I took the stairs two at a time until I arrived at the third floor where I sprung down the hall toward the dome area.

"Definitely of the human persuasion," Rupert was saying in my ear, "dressed in all black with a ski hat pulled over his head heading toward the back of the house."

I had just reached the balcony under the dome when my eyes landed on the statue of Apollo on the opposite side. Impossible to miss the fact that the majestic god now wore a woolly red scarf and held an equally vibrant red envelope in his outstretched hand. I scrambled toward him.

The statue had to be at least twenty feet tall and on a pedestal, too, making the only way for me to pluck that envelope from his fingers being to swat it off. Using my scarf, I took several jumps up to flick it from the god's fingers, successfully managing the feat just seconds before the guard shouted at me from across the balcony.

"Halt immediately!"

I had just enough time to pocket the envelope before the alarm went off.

❧ 4 ❧

There's nothing more humiliating than being grilled by the Metropolitan police as if you were a common thief, or worse, a common thief wannabe.

"As a member of the Agency of the Ancient Lost and Found, I wasn't there to steal, I said, but to catch a possible thief. Surely you've heard of us?" It was all I could do to keep my voice even as I gazed across at Chief Inspector Helen Drury. Contrary to common misconceptions, women police officers were no less intimidating than their male counterparts. They just did it in a touch of lipstick and a bit of discreet foundation.

Drury looked as though she'd toss me in jail without a moment's hesitation but maybe her severity was overcompensating for her blond good looks. In her line of work, that had to be a liability.

"I work as an affiliate of Interpol," I explained.

"So you say, and yet Interpol claims to know nothing about an undercover event at the Broadhurst tonight," the woman said coolly.

"But you have heard of us?" I pressed.

"We ask the questions here, Ms. McCabe," she said, "and our question to you is why, at approximately 10:35, did you penetrate the museum illegally if not planning to steal? There are no signs that there was any other unauthorized persons there, just you, and that you apparently placed a red scarf on a statue. Did you plan to play some ridiculous practical joke?"

"Absolutely not, and I didn't put that scarf on Apollo, either. That trick was probably done by the man who lured me there in the first place, a man calling himself Markland Rodgers."

"The deceased Markland Rodgers, do you mean?"

"He didn't look deceased to me." I wasn't trying to be smart, it just came out that way. "What I mean to say is, that he tricked me by claiming he was somebody he wasn't." There was no way I was implicating Rupert in any of this. That was our agency policy: call one of our members at the first sign of trouble but never, ever imply that one of them was involved.

"Prove it. The security footage has mysteriously evaporated. You don't know anything about that, do you? Listen carefully, Ms. McCabe, it is a criminal offense to trespass on government property after hours, let alone tamper with security systems and deface art. You are in serious trouble here. Make it easier for yourself by naming your accomplices and tell the truth."

Shit. Beside her at the metal table sat her assistant, a Detective Sergeant Balcom, with a bald egg-shaped head and a brooding expression. Did they hire police based on their ability to glower?

I looked from one to the other. "I wasn't responsible for accessorizing Apollo," I explained again. "That was the trick of the person calling himself Markland Rodgers, like I said. He claimed to be working at the museum and requested my help to decipher anomalies occurring, specifically in regards to objects that apparently moved at night."

"Moved like levitated?" Drury asked, eyebrows arched over her chill blue eyes. Damn if she didn't pluck her brows.

"Not levitated, no. More like shifted. Anyway, I believed that notifying the authorities at that late stage would take too much time and that a possible theft was about to take place tonight so I risked everything to make sure I was around to catch him. I was there to prevent a crime, I said, not to commit one. Do you really think I'd risk my reputation in order to decorate a statue with that ridiculous scarf? It's really not my taste, I assure you. I go in for multiple colors and stitches."

Attempts at humor were always met with the same grim expression. This was no laughing matter. Got it.

"Had we the opportunity to study the security footage, we might be able to better corroborate your statement but the museum's system has been hacked. You wouldn't know anything about that, would you?"

"I have the right to make a phone call."

"Shall I list the possible charges you have lined up against you thus far?"

asked Drury, now leaning forward like an elegant bird of prey ready to swoop in for the kill. "Trespassing with the intent to steal, hacking government systems, planting a bomb—"

"Planting a bomb!" *Planting a bomb.* I knew where they got that. When the guard shouted at me to stop in the Broadhurst, I stopped, but told him and the arresting officers that followed not to approach me in case my phone took offense and burned them.

I didn't say *explode*—I was careful on that point—but one of the officers ignored me and moved in to take my phone, search me, and cuff me, in that order. He received a second-degree burn for his efforts, leaving me to pocket my phone, and plead with them to let me follow the police to the station on my own steam. I could sit in the back seat, I said, as long as no one laid a hand on me.

"Resisting arrest," Drury continued.

"I did not resist arrest!" I protested. "I entered the squad car as instructed."

"Because of your phone," Drury said slowly, "a phone that I understand has near James Bond capabilities with weaponized features that render it a menace to society, much like yourself, Ms. McCabe."

Menace to society—me? I was too shocked to speak. So, they did know about the Agency of the Ancient Lost and Found, after all, and that fact apparently was not going to get me a get-out-of-jail-free card. It was a moment of reckoning. For an instant, I saw myself as this police person saw me and I didn't like the view. To them, I was some kind of bumbling amateur who had been granted too much freedom while wielding a dangerous weapon that had no right to exist let alone be in my possession.

I swallowed hard. "I want that call now and a lawyer."

Drury smiled a thin tight line. She thought she had me. "Of course, but first hand over your phone. Deactivate it or whatever is necessary to render it safe."

But I couldn't do that, not without forcing it to self-destruct, which was our policy should it fall into enemy hands or be away from its owner for more than three hours. The self-destruct mode would take the recording of whatever had occurred at the museum along with it. Rupert might have a copy but I wasn't sure.

There was a worse repercussion: the moment that phone left my person, I'd be subjected to a body search, which would reveal the red envelope, the contents of which I knew absolutely was for my eyes only. This whole sorry business was designed to entrap me and I was damn well going to find out who was responsible before I trotted meekly off to jail.

There came a knock at the door, which prompted Drury and Balcom to exit the square gray room.

"Take a few minutes to consider the consequences, Ms. McCabe," Madam Officer said over her shoulder before she left. "When we return, I expect to see that mobile of yours deactivated and on the table." With that, the door shut behind them.

I gazed around me. The depressing interrogation space was perfect for cornering a suspect by the lack of options—gray, devoid of decoration, punishingly utilitarian. For a moment, my imagination had no place to hide. I had no doubt that the police were having a group think on how to wrestle that phone away from me and that my holding on to it would only deepen the level of the hot water in which I sank. Damn! But there was no way I'd just give it up.

Actually, I was more afraid of giving up my phone than my freedom just then. I knew that any jail time I spent would be short, that there'd be strings being pulled on my behalf somewhere—or so I desperately hoped—but that phone was my only connection to my freedom, my life, in the meantime. I was tempted to check it right then for messages and make a quick call but knew I was being watched in the two-way mirror. I decided to keep it safely tucked into my pocket until I figured things out.

They left me alone for well over an hour. I ended up nodding off with my head cradled in my arms on the table when the door flew open. I jolted upright and blinked.

"You're free to go," Drury said tersely.

I scrambled to my feet and darted from the room, feeling every officer's eyes glued onto my back as I retrieved my carpetbag backpack at the desk. Somebody had pulled the proverbial strings sooner than I'd hoped and I was so grateful just then I swear I would have kissed that individual on the spot.

"I'll be watching you, Ms. McCabe," Drury warned me as I headed for the door.

Clutching my bag and still dazed, I ended up on the sidewalk in the chill air outside the police station at shortly after four a.m. The city was just beginning to stir, and though I needed to hail a cab, there weren't any visible.

Then a sleek black Rolls-Royce purred to the curb in front of me. As I stepped toward it, the back door opened, and I climbed into the plush leather seat that felt like a hug about my shivering person. Beside me, Rupert passed me a cup of tea from his little tea-making apparatus with a digestive biscuit tucked on the saucer's side. I accepted the cup and saucer gratefully.

"Good morning, Ms. McCabe," greeted Sloane, Rupert's butler today acting as chauffeur.

"Good morning, Sloane, Rupert," I greeted, surprised to find my voice tight and gravelly.

"Tea first, Phoebe, discussion later," said Rupert. "We will proceed to my abode wherein you will restore your physical being before we untangle recent events."

After a few fortifying sips and a bite out of the biscuit, I figured sleep wouldn't touch me again until I found out what was inside that envelope. "I'd rather talk first. Did you get me released?"

"Not exactly," Rupert said, "I merely made the phone call to set the necessary wheels in motion. Our agency does have friends in high places who follow our affairs with considerable interest. One such friend, though not involved in the operational mechanisms of policy and governance, and who was not at all pleased to be pulled out of his bed at such a tender hour, nevertheless ensured that the detectives skewering you at the station did not have the pleasure of throwing you into a holding cell."

"They wanted my phone, accused me of resisting arrest."

"Yes, they would."

"I felt so small in there, like a menace to society." My voice trembled. "If they know about the agency, surely they also know that we've apprehended multiple criminal elements across the years and that I'm hardly a menace?"

Rupert cleared his throat. "Dearest Phoebe, do not permit anyone to make you feel small under any circumstances. You know better than anyone what you are worth and the lengths to which you have gone to assure that art returns or remains in its rightful place so that it survives for the pleasure and edification of all. Besides which, no doubt in the case of the police, there is more than a touch of professional jealousy involved. You have been granted a great deal more latitude than they and how you conduct yourself is not within their jurisprudence to condemn, though in this case, I fear we came uncomfortably close." He patted my knee. "Here we are, almost home at last. We will talk after breakfast."

Despite Rupert's long-winded approach, I was grateful for every word he spoke. I did feel less diminished. "Did you get a chance to look at the security footage?" I asked as the car slid down the darkened streets of Belgravia.

"Indeed," he replied. "The perpetrator remained concealed in a black stocking hat pulled down over his face, making it impossible for me to identify. However, since I witnessed the cad applying that scarf to Apollo and affixing the envelope to his outstretched hand with sticky tape, I believe it safe to assume that the pseudo Markland fellow, whoever the devil he is, did the deed. The body type is similar. You do still have the envelope?"

"I do," I assured him. "And," I said while digging around in my bag until my fingers touched the coin and could pull it out, "this. I'm sure the two are related. The police must have found it in my hidden pocket because now it's just rolling around at the bottom of my bag."

"And had it originally hailed from the Broadhurst, they could have charged you with theft on the spot, but apparently, that is not the case or the intent."

"The intent was to send me a message. Rupert, I'm convinced that the coin and whatever's afoot at the Broadhurst are connected."

"No doubt."

The car slipped into its parking spot around the corner leaving Rupert and I to exit into his service door unseen. I was eager to pull out that envelope and get started on the contents but Rupert stayed my hand. "Breakfast first. Never attempt anything potentially upsetting unless first well-fortified."

I was not the patient sort but was so grateful to him for rescuing me that I was willing to let him set the pace. After washing and burying my face in one of his fluffy, lavender-scented towels, I sat in his breakfast room sipping tea and admiring his collection of eighteenth-century landscape paintings while the scent of bacon suffused the air. I found the wait unbearable but other than to check my phone for messages—none but from Rupert sent earlier—I resigned myself.

Rupert sat across from me apparently checking out the news on his iPad. He struck me as unusually calm while the envelope sat untouched on the table between us, a bit damp from my body but otherwise fine. Meanwhile, I was trying not to jump out of my skin.

Finally, Sloane arrived with breakfast: sausages, bacon, sautéed mushrooms and tomatoes, accompanied by my favorite poached eggs accessorized by slightly cold toast. The moment it landed before me, I dug in with enthusiasm. Several minutes passed before I came up for air.

"Rupert," I began.

"Yes, Phoebe?"

"Let's do the deed."

"I would rather wait to properly digest before proceeding."

I sat back and studied him. "Okay, now I know that you're hesitating for a reason. You know something I don't. I'm opening that envelope now."

Rupert set his cup back in its saucer. "Very well. Let us get this over with, but before you proceed" (I already had the envelope open and was removing the contents) "consider for a moment the necessity of remaining calm regardless of what you find therein."

What I found therein was a postcard of the ruins of the Temple of Apollo under moonlight in Rome, the location printed in tiny text on the front. Flipping it over, I read:

Come say hello to your boy toy in Roma. N

$$\text{❦} \quad 5 \quad \text{❦}$$

"**N**oel." The words escaped my throat like a croak. "Oh, my God!"

"Phoebe, I implore you not to panic."

"I'm not panicking!" I cried. "You knew!"

"I did not know," Rupert articulated carefully. "I suspected, a different beast entirely. Last night while you were inside the Broadhurst, word came through our network that a person who might inconclusively be identified as Noel Halloran was seen in London two days ago. Later, information followed that the same individual had recently been spied in Rome. So far, this individual has once again sunk into the woodwork."

He turned his iPad toward me showing a blurry photo obviously taken in front of a security camera. The person was tall and angular with sharp cheekbones and a sensual mouth curled into a sneer. "Taken at a banking machine."

"But why, why the game at the Broadhurst?"

"To play you, Phoebe. Halloran always loved to taunt you and this, I presume, is one of his taunts."

"And Evan?"

Rupert fixed his gaze with mine as he laid the tablet on the table. "So far, the lad is incommunicado. No one in our network has received word from him or picked up signals from his devices since last Friday night when he was apparently in Sicily. Several days have passed with no signal. As you are aware, our phones will self-destruct if separated from our persons for an extended period of time. The lad had been working on a new version, a prototype, that appeared to die when separated from its owner but did not actually extinguish itself, rather like rolling over and playing dead."

"What does that even mean?" I sobbed. "Either way, Noel has Evan and is using him to draw me to Rome and find whatever the hell his greedy bastard heart is seeking now!"

"Stay calm," Rupert implored.

"How can you say that when your own son may be in the hands of a murdering madman this very minute?"

Rupert's hand reached across the table and clutched mine. "Because, Phoebe," he said in a soft voice, "if there is one thing I have learned after years in this business, it is that panic clouds one's thinking just when one most needs every faculty to be working to precision. If, indeed, Noel does hold Evan hostage, then together we will find him and outwit this devious bastard. We have the full force of the Agency of the Ancient Lost and Found behind us who are being mobilized as we speak. We will fly to Rome this afternoon where we will convene with Nicolina, Peaches, and Zann, all of whom will help tackle this, our most perilous mission. It does Evan no service for you to fall apart before we can set in motion a working plan."

He stood up and opened his arms. And just briefly, and just because I couldn't contain myself a moment longer, I got to my feet and collapsed sobbing against his chest like an inconsolable child while he patted my back murmuring, "There, there."

I allowed myself a good cry before pulling back, blowing my nose into the hanky he offered, and straightening my shoulders. "Okay, so let's get down to business."

"One thing, dear Phoebe, and I do hate to ask because, if in this case it were true, I am most certain that you would have told me."

"Rupert, just say it, please."

"Is there a possible way that your gifts can sense where Evan is located?"

The question was posed so piteously that I nearly broke down again. "No," I whispered. "I have never been able to find living people, even ones I love. I don't know why."

"I thought that to be the case." He was clasping his hands as if praying that it wasn't true. "Never mind, we will find him using other methods."

God, I hoped so.

OUR ARRIVAL IN ROME LATE THAT AFTERNOON FLEW BY IN A DAZE. I watched the Eternal City slide by in the late-afternoon light as Seraphina, Nicolina's assistant, drove us from the airport to her employer's Trastevere villa. Nicolina, my friend the lethal countess, was waiting for us by the door and unlike her usual greeting enveloped both Rupert and me in a real full-contact hug before settling us into her salon to await the arrival of Zann and Peaches, each on transcontinental flights.

"We have eyes all over Italy," she told us. "We will discover where Evan has been hidden, do not worry."

"Did you receive the CCTV photo of the person we believe to be Noel that I forwarded?" Rupert asked.

"Yes, and we are checking now."

"Don't apprehend him, whatever you do. I'll explain later," I said.

My state of mind had smoothed into a cool self-possession by then—all business and fixed on the matter at hand. We agreed not to discuss anything until we were all together, at which point Nicolina left to arrange for our evening feast.

After taking a snack of fruit and cheese, Rupert and I went off upstairs to nap until the others arrived. We were both deep into our thoughts by then and bone-grindingly weary.

My last task before I napped was to alert Max that I was leaving Jennifer to mind the fort solo because Nicolina required my help with something in Rome. Generally, we kept the gallery and the agency businesses separate so nothing about that should prompt any undue questions. On no account did I want Max to know that we had even so much as a whiff of Noel's appearance in case he followed us to Rome, a complication we didn't need. Rupert was not the only father missing an absent son. In Max's case, he hadn't spoken to him in years.

As for how to handle the Noel affair, I'd already thought the whole matter through and only needed to run it by the team. That would happen several hours later when Seraphina roused me from my nap with the audible equivalent of a battering ram on my bedroom door. I bounded up off the bed and ran to open it.

"Penelope arrives," Seraphina told me. Seraphina refused to use nicknames. "I pick up Suzanne next."

"Okay, thanks." I headed back into my room, splashed cold water on my face, and ran downstairs to greet Peaches where she met me with a hug designed to squeeze the stuffing out of toy animals.

"You okay, woman?" my tall friend asked after restoring me to my feet. "I only have the gist of what's going on but I know enough to figure you must be beside yourself."

"I'm fine," I gasped. "It's Evan I'm worried about. Who knows what Noel will do to him?"

But it wasn't until Zann arrived, red-eyed and zoned-out, and we all sat down to a magnificent feast of pasta carbonara, Alesso di Bollito, and roasted vegetables presided over by Nicolina that we began the discussion that we had been anticipating. We were hardly a merry-looking bunch around that table since everyone but the countess had fatigue grooved into their faces.

Finally, I felt ready to lay out the plan, asking at first that Rupert bring everyone up to speed, which he did, beginning with my night in the museum and ending with the postcard. Somehow, he managed to skip right past the bit where he fell for the claims of a man who had actually disappeared years ago.

"Postcard!" Peaches exclaimed. "Isn't that how the creep used to send messages to you at the gallery when you were still together?"

"It is," I agreed, holding up the postcard of the moonlit temple ruins between my fingers, "which is how I knew this was from him. The cards were always coded the way this one is. Here he's telling me that he has Evan, yes, but also where he wants me to meet him and the approximate time."

"Meet him at the temple of Apollo on the Palatine Hill?" Zann gasped. "But you can't do that. He'll nab you, too!"

"No, he won't," I said calmly. Really, I surprised myself sometimes. "He needs me to find whatever priceless cache he has his eye on next and, for that, he knows I need to remain a free agent. He wants all of you, too, I'm betting. He considers me his lost-art sniffer dog and you're my pack, pardon the canine references. He wants us to work as a team to help him find what he's looking for."

"Bastard," Peaches swore and ripped off a piece of bread with her teeth.

"I'll kill him," Zann muttered while digging into her food. She said that a lot but this time she meant it.

"That job is for me," Seraphina growled. Seraphina definitely meant it all the time.

"Wait, please." I held up my hand. "Here's how we have to play this: Noel thinks he knows me and he's right up to a point. He certainly knew that I couldn't resist the night in the museum with the moving artifacts thing—that was pure Phoebe bait and I took it—but there's plenty about me he doesn't know, like how ruthless I've become when somebody I love is in danger, how I've learned to lie with the best of them. He's in for a shock."

A small smile graced Nicolina's lips. "You plan to trick the trickster?" she inquired.

"I plan to do exactly what he wants me to do under certain conditions. I'll set a few terms of my own when we meet on Palatine Hill. Nobody can come with me, though. That's key. Noel knows I know how this game must be played from his perspective. The moment someone makes a move on him, Evan is as good as dead. My compliance is Evan's insurance policy, and to some extent, Noel's, too."

"Shit," Peaches muttered. "Get one thing straight, woman: you're not going anywhere without me."

"You're not hearing me, Peach," I said.

"And you're not hearing me: you're not going in there alone."

Rupert cleared his throat. When he spoke, his voice had a slight tremor. "She will not be alone as we will be waiting nearby. If the position of the moon over the ruins is, indeed, an indicator, then my estimate is that the appointed meeting time is 12:25 a.m. tomorrow morning, which is when the moon reaches its full aperture and arrives at that position in the November Roman sky."

"I'll be there, as he expects me to be," I said, taking a sip of wine. "I'll find out what I'm supposed to be seeking and ensure him that I'll do whatever's necessary to find the object or objects in exchange for Evan's life. Meanwhile, we'll be working behind the scenes to discover where Noel's keeping Evan, a location which must be found before I—we—pass over the treasure, if we find it. I have no doubt that Noel doesn't plan on keeping Evan alive once he gets what he wants."

That brought a deep chill bearing down across the table, stopping everyone from chewing, swallowing, whatever. The ramifications of what I'd just said rendered me temporarily speechless, too, even a little ill. *Oh, my God! I might lose him!* I couldn't bear the thought, felt suddenly overwhelmed by the prospects of losing the man I loved to that rat-faced, double-crossing, double-bastard Noel.

Nicolina dropped her napkin upon the table and reached over to take Rupert's hand just seconds before Peaches, sitting next to me, flung her arms around my shoulders and squeezed hard. This was as close as we'd come to a group hug.

"We'll get the bastard," Zann said with vehemence. "The Agency of the Ancient Lost and Found will not be beaten by a mere mortal like Noel Halloran. The gods and angels are on our side." Zann had a kind of out-there mystical view on life.

Seraphina, who had been sitting quietly up until then, announced: "When you go tomorrow night, we fix a tracker on him. He will not escape us!"

Noel would never let a tracker be placed on his person. He knew our ways too well to let that happen but I remained silent in case my voice cracked.

"Fear not," Rupert said, getting to his feet. "My lad has a few tricks of his own and will no doubt attempt his escape long before we need to intervene. Now, please excuse me. Damnable allergies." He exited the dining room dabbing his eyes.

That left us sitting pale and tense, supper forgotten.

"Did you say there was a coin involved?" Zann asked after a few moments.

I nodded and fished the coin from my pocket, passing it over. "I believe Noel placed it on the gallery floor knowing full well that Max was away and that our security footage would be overwritten before anyone had a chance to look at it. The gallery and the agency premises are on separate systems."

"But why place it there in the first place?" Peaches asked.

"It's his form of the bread crumb method. He wanted to slowly lead me to him in a series of clues," I said, taking a sip of wine. "Cat and mouse."

She turned the coin around in her fingers. "Looks like whatever Bastardo Numero Uno is seeking this time may have to do with either Livia Drusilla or her mighty emperor husband, Augustus." Zann, being an archaeologist specializing in ancient sites, was our other Roman expert. We had hesitated to bring her onto the team because she could be a bit unpredictable, but unpredictability is fine as long as it comes through in the end, in my opinion. In this case, my opinion won.

"Any idea what treasure associated with Livia might exist?" Nicolina inquired, tonight sitting as the epitome of elegance in her deep-blue silk tunic over a pair of matching trousers. The rest of us looked as though we'd been tossed in a dryer on the tumble setting minus the fabric softener.

"I've never heard of any treasure connected to Livia," Zann replied. "She was fabulously wealthy as any empress and mother of another emperor is wealthy, of course. By all accounts, she wielded her power behind the throne of her husband and son but anything she might have possessed would have long ago passed into other hands. Roman treasure didn't survive unless in tombs."

"That we know of," I remarked. "I have a feeling that Noel is on to some kind of lead. There's something Rupert forgot to mention when he was filling you in on recent events. He was contacted by a man calling himself Markland Rodgers, who claimed to be working for the Sir Bentley Broadhurst Museum when he experienced some anomalies, specifically artifacts moving at night. He asked us to investigate, which is how I ended up in the museum last night.

As it turns out, the real man by that name disappeared under mysterious circumstances in 2017, presumably lost at sea. No body was found."

"And you think this man calling himself Markland Rodgers was responsible for planting the envelope?" Peaches asked.

"Physically, yes, and a red knitted scarf, which he wrapped around the Apollo statue's neck, too. He was wearing that same item when Rupert and I met him for lunch. The scarf was a clue, as well, not that I made the connection at first. Noel used to tease me about knitting him a plain woolly scarf someday knowing full well that I could never bear to knit with a single color, ever."

"That Markland Rodgers?" Zann straightened in her seat.

We all turned to her. "You've heard of him?" I asked.

"Well, yes, I think so. I mean, if it's the same Markland Rodgers, and seriously, how many could there be? He was a known collector of Roman coins and, yeah, I remember something about him working in a London museum somewhere, just couldn't remember which one. He up and disappeared."

"Do you think the dude you met was the same Markland Rodgers, in which case he'd be one of Noel's stooges?" That was Peaches.

"This one is definitely in cahoots with Noel but whether that was the same Markland that disappeared is another question," I said, picking up my fork again. "As usual, this feast is fabulous, Nicolina. Thank you. It will restore our bodies if not our spirits."

"Restore one, the other will follow," our hostess remarked with a sad smile.

At that moment we heard a phone ringing the familiar strains of the agency ringtone, which is kind of an alien twang. Immediately, we all set down our forks and checked our pockets, everybody wondering whether they had left their phone in one of the salons. But it wasn't ours.

Rupert stepped back into the dining room moments later holding his cell. "I have just received a call from one of our London contacts. A body identified as belonging to one Markland Rodgers has just been fished from the Thames, quite dead, and quite recently, too."

6

"Why would that rat-faced bastard kill one of his own accomplices?" Zann asked as we stood around a map of the Palatine Hill in Nicolina's lab late the next afternoon. The lab was half-workspace, half-gallery of ancient bits Nicolina had acquired over the years and therefore the perfect place for us to have our meetings since it had plenty of room to spread.

We had all slept well into the morning, awoke to devour a long multicourse lunch, and now stood plotting our evening mission. Only Rupert hadn't joined us yet as he was wrapped up in conversation with our affiliates upstairs.

"Perhaps because Markland got greedy and Noel doesn't permit overt greediness among his minions. That's his sole domain," I remarked, staring glumly down at the map. "Anyway, that's my guess. Either that or he was afraid Markland would get picked up by the police and squeal."

"Another likely possibility," said Peaches.

"So, it appears that the real Markland hadn't died years ago after all but has feigned his death so he could go offline and work with Noel," I added.

"Which means that Markland might also have been working for Alesso Baldi and his art-heisting arms ring," Nicolina remarked. "We know that Noel is still head of that operation that funds arms and drugs with stolen art and antiquities. It's still active in Europe under Noel's control."

"That is what Ev has been working on since Florence," Peaches added.

I knew that, too, and it had been a source of anxiety to me ever since.

"Okay, so what do we know about Noel's chosen rendezvous site?" I asked, tapping the map. It's not that I didn't care about the hapless Markland or Noel's arms interests but I had other concerns just then.

"The Temple of Apollo Palatinus was dedicated by Augustus to his patron god Apollo on the site of where a lightning bolt reportedly struck the interior of one of the emperor's properties," Zann began. "He vowed to give the god this honor on that spot if he was successful against Mark Antony and Cleopatra at the Battle of Actium in 31 BC. He definitely was, if you recall. Is there anyone who doesn't know the story of Antony and Cleopatra?"

Well, of course. Cleopatra, one of the most famed queens in history, and her Roman general lover, Mark Antony, launched a war against mighty Rome in order to keep Egypt and her queen sovereign. The Hollywood version closely aligned with the historical one in most details, and to this day I always saw the Egyptian queen as Elizabeth Taylor and Richard Burton as Mark Antony. However, in reality, the real Cleopatra would have been as much Greek as Egyptian since she hailed from the Ptolemaic dynasty and traced her lineage back to Alexander the Great. "So this site definitely existed during Empress Livia's time," I mused.

"Oh, absolutely," Zann continued enthusiastically while running one hand over her blond brush cut. "All the Roman bigwigs lived on the Palatine Hill when in Rome, though any self-respecting emperor had villas all over the place, too. In the case of the mighty Augustus, who was born Octavian, by the way, he designed porticoes linking his private abode to the temple, the whole thing looking down on the Circus Maximus where the chariot races took place. Kind of like having the best seat in the house for the Indianapolis 500 or Le Mans."

"Pretty elaborate construction, too, if I recall," Peaches added. "Frescoed halls, ivory doors, a portico of the Danaids with yellow marble and black marble statues, elaborate carvings, Carrara marble everywhere—wouldn't you just love to see that?"

"There was a library in the temple also," said Nicolina, "a library that once held the famous Sibylline Books that the Romans consulted during times of disaster, plus sculptures, many sculptures, described by ancient sources as coming from all over the Roman Empire."

"So, it was an architectural and artistic treasure trove," I said, "but surely nothing is left up there?"

"Only ruins," Nicolina said. "The statues and art, whatever survived, have been picked over—is that the correct term?" she asked, turning to Peaches.

"Picked over, looted, stolen, absconded with, or vandalized," Peaches suggested with a shrug. "Take your pick."

"All of the above," Zann remarked. "Some pieces did end up in museums but not many. I did a season with an archaeological team up there once and though it hasn't all been excavated—the ruins are, like, superhuge—what's left is whatever looters didn't think valuable enough or considered too big to move. There are a few broken capitals left of the temple, plus foundations, walls, and a colonnade that's been reconstructed, plus a lot of the underlying brickwork. That's it."

"And yet Noel set this as our meeting place so it must feature somehow." I stared down, struck by the sheer size of the Palatine area. "I presume that I can't just walk up to this place?"

"It is barricaded off as in an archaeological park by a fence but we can get in easily enough," Zann said. "It's too big an area to secure, really, but we have our ways, don't we?" She gazed at each of us hopefully. "In fact, I'd be happy to cut a hole in the fencing using my phone feature." She was holding said item aloft. Since she'd been admitted into the Agency of the Ancient Lost and Found, Zann took great satisfaction in using the assigned phone whenever she could. Unfortunately, so far she hadn't much opportunity since the use of these special features were closely regulated.

"No need, thanks," I said. "We want to enter as unobtrusively as possible."

"Oh, sure," Zann said, looking disappointed.

"We will use something to climb over," Nicolina offered.

"A ladder," Peaches suggested.

"A ladder, yes," the countess agreed.

"Anyway, Phoebe's not going in there without me—a deserted mausoleum, a tumble of ruins in the dark, a murdering bastard hiding out in the shadows— are you kidding me? Where Phoebe goes, I go. End of story." That was Peaches standing tall and proud (and maybe a little ferocious) in her purple leather jumpsuit. She had taken her bodyguarding job seriously ever since we bonded back in the Jamaican jungle. Naturally, she was so much more than just my bodyguard. Her engineering knowledge had often proved indispensable to the team.

I placed a hand on her arm. "Thanks, Peach—I mean it. You're the best guard a body could want but I have to go in there alone. I have no choice in this but, believe me, I won't be harmed. Noel needs me alive and well. You can't cage or wound a sniffer dog and expect her to go out and track down your latest quest. If he sees that I have company, the meeting will be over before it begins."

Peaches looked at me as though she'd use bodily force to remain by my side, if necessary, but Nicolina intervened. "We must trust Phoebe's instincts. Never do they lead her astray. We will be waiting for her beyond the fence and will leap to assist at the first sign of trouble."

"And remain in constant communication via our phones," added Rupert.

"Yes, exactly." I nodded with a sinking heart. It was one of those conundrums: I needed agency support and yet their active involvement could complicate everything. For one thing, they liked to communicate with me when I most needed to concentrate.

But it was settled: that night at 12:05 a.m., I would end up on the other side of gates of the Palatine Hill leaving me enough time to make my way to the Temple of Apollo to meet my nemesis, one of the most dangerous men in the world, by my estimation, excluding political despots.

Was I frightened? Strangely, no. I was furious; I was resolute; I was locked deep in some frozen state that I hoped would carry me through the night. Because I didn't need emotion just then, I needed resolve and, above all, to keep my imagination from wandering to what that bastard might do, or might have already done, to the man I loved.

Yes, I used that word freely now.

I spent the rest of the afternoon and early evening researching Augustus and his empress, Livia, and Roman history in general. With the additional help of Nicolina, Rupert, and Zann, I caught up on the history of the most powerful republic in the ancient world, one which had conquered more countries and cultures globally than any other civilization then or since. As a result, my awe of all things Roman intensified.

"They were a powerhouse," I remarked. "When you consider the massive structures they erected, the feats of engineering, who they conquered."

"Their legion of slaves. They'd never have all those accomplishments without their slaves," Peaches said with a grimace. "Consider slavery as the true engine behind their building feats." Nobody would ever argue with her when it came to the oppression angle.

"Do you know that when the sewers were being dug, the slaves who were forced to do the work, most of whom were captured enemy soldiers, claimed that they would rather have died in battle than be subjected to that?" Zann said. "It was a brutal civilization, too."

We had decided that the rendezvous must go as planned even if it rained or if the moon was shrouded in cloud cover but, as it turned out, that November night Rome was as clear and crisp as the best autumn eve anywhere.

I donned the leather jacket Nicolina had bought me years ago with black jeans and equally black sneakers, accessorized by my Melancholy knitted wrap used as a scarf since those tones were dark enough to blend.

While dressing, I found a gun tucked into the secret pistol holster of my jacket, no doubt put there by either Seraphina or Nicolina, neither of whom believed a woman should venture forth without a firearm. I left it in the bedside table drawer. After all, I had my superphone with which Noel had already suffered a nasty encounter long ago. Besides, I was probably safer against random fits of violence than I ever had been in my life. It was in Noel's best interest to keep me safe.

"I can't believe you're so calm about this," Zann whispered as we piled into the car for the trip to the Palatine Hill. Zann was rarely calm about anything but seemed to always run on the hyper setting.

"I'm just focused," I told her. "Speaking of which, could all of you try not to text me while I'm in there? I'll contact you if there's trouble and you have trackers on me, anyway."

Nobody said a word.

Seraphina would drive Zann, Peaches, and me while Nicolina and Rupert followed in the more luxurious car. Nicolina kept two vehicles in Rome, a little Fiat for bombing around town and a Maserati for "touring." The idea was that one car would wait for me on one side of the hill and the other on the opposite end. I was to climb in just beyond the Circus Maximus but nobody knew for sure where I might exit.

The Circus Maximus, translated from Latin into "the largest circus," was situated in the valley between the Palatine and the Aventine hills, two of the famed seven hills of Rome. At one point, it was the biggest track in the Roman Empire and served multiple uses including to honor gods, host victories, and stage feasts of all sorts but mostly served as a venue for chariot racing. Under the moonlight just then, it looked like a large uneven playing field with spotlights on the occasional tumble of stones.

Because it was such an open area with a main road running along beside it, we decided that the best entry point into the hill compound was there. We could park the car by a fringe of trees and set two of our members to watch the road while I climbed up over the stone wall to the foot of the Palatine Hill, scrambled across a grassy knoll, over the wire fence, and into the park.

Maybe it shouldn't have been as easy as it was. It's not as if Roman monuments had no security against vandals and mischief-makers but the area was too huge to lock down completely. Anyway, the ladder contraption Seraphina and Peaches constructed worked to perfection.

Once I was on the other side and within the park proper, all I had to do was watch out for roaming guards, and dogs (just guessing), stay away from spotlights illuminating the ruins, and disarm any perimeter alarms my presence might trigger. My phone would signal electronic trip wires not visible to the naked eye. In addition, Evan had made additional improvements to our super-phones by adding a personal space alarm, which would ping should anybody approach within ten feet of my circumference.

Evan. The thought of that brilliant man, head bowed over his circuitry, glasses perched on his perfect Roman nose, almost doubled me over. The last thing he had done before leaving on this mission was to pull me close and whisper sweet nothings into my ear. True, Evan's sweet nothings were often packed with instructions woven among his loving words and, with his arms encircling me, I could hardly focus on the content. I was pretty certain those murmurings had to do with the phone. I pulled myself up short, suppressed the wave of pain, and forced myself back into line. I didn't have the luxury of pain.

A text popped up on my screen seconds later. Rupert: *All going according to plan? We cannot see you from where we are stationed.*

I had been walking for several minutes and now gazed around where I stood on a cobbled path. Columns, steps, and foundations silvered by the moon all loomed around with ink-black shadows congealing in the hollows. Far off to my right over the tops of the ruins, I could just see the dome of St. Peter's glowing in the distance while all around hunkered three thousand years of Roman ruins pressing against me in majestic, impenetrable darkness. For a moment, I really craved to be alone in ancient Rome.

Sighing, I texted: *I can't see anybody from where I stand.*

Rupert: *Under the circumstances, we'll consider that a good thing. You are located on the east end near the Temple of Castor and the Tibetan Palace. Proceed toward the House of Augustus to which the Temple of Apollo is connected. Zann has sent you a map to take you there. Open it on your app.*

I switched to my map app, and immediately a simple diagram popped up where a moving red line now snaked amid the squares and boxes. I took my next step forward.

The ruins of the House of Augustus required more climbing up cobbled lanes, around hunkering foundations, past vacant haunting shells of buildings where shadows were all that remained of once mighty gods and men.

This park was not open at night so no pathway lighting was provided. Parts of the way were so dark I had to use my phone to keep from tripping on the uneven ground. When the red line on my phone indicated that I had arrived, I couldn't believe the sheer size of the ruin that rose up on my right—as big as one side of the Colosseum with a two-level brick portico rearing like a huge wall, yet nothing matched the columns in the postcard view. I hastily typed a message to that effect.

Zann replied. *Keep going. You're at Augustus's palace. The Corinthian columns and stairs that are the temple entrance on the postcard are on the other side.*

Great. More walking through the ruins. So I kept following the new red lines that had appeared on the map. I heard a crack behind me. Swinging around, I stared into the darkness. Nothing.

"Hello?" I whispered as if I expected my stalker to answer, which I didn't, really. It was probably one of Noel's minions keeping an eye on the prey. I turned and continued, knowing that I was being followed and not caring.

Any time I walked through an historical site, especially when alone, I felt things plucking on the edges of my mind like whispers beyond a locked door. Sometimes I found it frightening, like being stalked by ghosts, while at other times I hardly noticed the way we absorb the sound of the breeze in the trees. At that moment, I was hardly aware of anything.

I had other things to consider right then, like how I was going to play Noel in my first encounter with the bastard since Greece. At that time, he had dressed up as a Tarot card symbol and clearly reveled in visions of megalomania. The encounter had strengthened my conviction that he was suffering under some kind of mental breakdown.

Whatever happened tonight, I couldn't fall apart, behave hysterically, beg for Evan's life, or do anything that made me look weak. I needed to be tough, play tough. I had to convince him that I wasn't the same Phoebe he remembered, which shouldn't be too hard since that was true. I had even tasered him over the heart a few years back. The old Phoebe had been so smitten by him once that she would have never harmed a corpuscle in his body. Still, the man had such an amazing sense of self-delusion that he might still believe I only tasered him out of pique.

I turned a corner and now at last could see the three remaining columns of the Temple of Apollo glowing in the moonlight like ghostly bones lost in time. The moon was almost exactly as it had been positioned in the postcard but, strangely, there were houses on the other side of the nearby fence, something not visible in the photograph.

Why would Noel choose a meeting place so exposed? The columns were perched on a mammoth block of stone that I couldn't easily climb. Now what?

Then a sound cracked the stillness behind me. I swung around. There, shrouded in the shadows, a black figure stood deep in the recess between two chunks of foundation. A shiver strung up my spine. It was him; I could feel it in every inch of my being, a fact that delivered such a quick punch to my gut that it left me reeling.

But nothing broke my stride. In seconds, I had retraced my steps, turned the corner, and scrambled over the railing as if I hadn't a worry in the world until I stood in the shadows mere feet away from the figure.

"I knew you'd come," he said softly in that sexy voice he had once used for seduction. Stepping briefly from the shadows, he revealed himself not as the thin bony man I'd last seen in Greece but more like his old self: tall, wiry, with his thick black curly hair falling around his ears. He'd gained weight, packed on some muscle, too. God, I hated him.

"Looks like you've regained your health," I remarked, trying to keep my voice steady.

"It's returning slowly," he said. "I hope you like what you see and are secretly relieved that you didn't damage me permanently. Observe—" he spread his arms "—I'm still very much alive."

Maybe second time lucky, if I ever got the chance. "You lured me here to provide a health report? Tell me what you want."

"I want you, Phoebe, like I always have. You and I are the perfect team, remember? You're my empress, my queen, and I'm everything you crave in a man, don't deny it. You can't have forgotten all those nights we spent together."

"Would that be like the night you sealed me into a cave in Greece as a sacrifice to a long-ago goddess?"

"Oh, come on. That was just a bit of fun. I knew you'd escape. You always do, my little miracle girl. I remember every moment I've ever held you in my arms, every second you yearned for me as I did you. I still want you, Phoebe baby."

God, don't tell me he was still on that line. It was as if he was listening to his own secret playlist. But I had to remember that the man was deranged and you can't argue with deranged. "You want my abilities to find lost artifacts, you mean. What was up with that Broadhurst business and why did you kill your own accomplice?"

"Do you mean Markland? I didn't kill him, babe. He got himself tangled with someone else—double-dealing bastard. As for your other question—God I've missed your multiple questioning technique or lack of technique, since that implies certain organization skills you lack—I wanted to introduce myself back into your life with a little puzzle. You love mysteries, I know, and wouldn't be able to resist artifacts moving in a museum. Fell for it hook, line, and sinker, didn't you?"

"Let's cut to the chase, Noel: what is it you want me to find in return for Evan's freedom?"

He crossed his arms and gazed at me with his head cocked, his silhouette a darker shade of black. "I intend to win you back someday, babe. Just know that I'll never let you go. What do you see in that boy toy, anyway? You told me once that you didn't go in for those muscle-packed square-jawed GI Joe types."

"I didn't fall for a type, I fell for a person." *Shit, Phoebe, just shut up.* "And if you harm that person, any deal you want to strike with me is off before it begins."

"Whoa!" He held up his hands. "You're hardly in a bargaining position."

And then something in me flipped a switch. "Not true," I said with a hard edge to my voice. "If you want me to find something for you, I do it only on the condition that Evan is unharmed, and I mean unharmed down to the last detail. I don't want damaged goods. My boy toys have to be in perfect condition or why bother? I mean, after I overcharged you with the faulty taser app, you weren't much use to me, were you?" Would he seriously believe that line? "Show me that Evan's in good condition right now."

He was standing back in the shadows again but I could sense him questioning, calculating, at first surprised and then appraising. Finally, he laughed. "Damaged goods, seriously?"

"Seriously."

"I'll tell you one thing about your latest plaything, he doesn't give up his secrets easily."

A jolt hit my gut. "Are you trying to get him to divulge how he masterminds those superphones, is that it? Good luck with that. He's MI6 trained, remember. He'd rather die than disclose secrets. I suggest you forget that angle and keep him alive as collateral with me. That's the only condition under which I'll work for you."

His eyes narrowed. "I want your whole agency to work for me, understand?"

"Understood. Now let me talk to him."

"No."

"Yes. How else am I to know that he's still alive and will stay that way until the job is done?'

You have to admit, that did have a certain logic. Turning away, I heard him tap his phone, heard it ring followed by him saying something in quick Italian. Seconds later, he approached me holding out his phone with Evan's face on his screen. I tried to take the device but he snatched it back.

"Okay," I whispered. He held the phone out again while I kept my hands plastered to my sides. The sight before me almost broke me down on the spot. Evan had been beaten yet still appeared alert, unbent. Gagged and bound, his green-gray eyes seemed to beseech me: *Don't do as he says. Never do as he says.*

"Can he see me?" I asked.

"It's on FaceTime. He can see you."

"I'm going to get you free," I told Evan. *Hold on, hold on, my love.* Then I said to Noel. "Ungag him."

"No." And with that the screen went dark. "You know now that your boy toy is alive. That's all you're getting this time."

I straightened my shoulders. "You keep him in good condition, do you understand? No more beatings, and I want to see that he's still alive and well regularly, get it?"

"And if I don't, what then?"

"Then I stop looking for whatever it is you're after and you can just go to hell." I meant every damn word.

He threw back his head and laughed that strange ha-ha-ha of his that sounded like machine gun fire, white teeth luminous in the dark. "I really did piss you off all those years ago, didn't I? A woman scorned and all that. Maybe we'll get to discuss it in earnest over a glass of wine sometime, like as in another first date."

I bit down on the words I wanted to say. "Do we have a deal or not?"

"Yes, we have a deal, my sweet. I'll keep your boy toy alive and unharmed in exchange for your services. I have you followed 24/7 as much to keep you safe as anything else. You know that, don't you? Nothing can happen to my Phoebe."

"I'm not your Phoebe," I said.

"You are now. After you get what I need, then we'll see."

Shit. "What treasure are you after this time?" I practically spat it out.

He straightened. "Okay, then, play it that way, if you must, but I know you secretly have feelings for me, too. Anyway, you're going to seek Cleopatra's jewels for me."

That was a shock. "Cleopatra's jewels!" I exclaimed. "What does Cleopatra's jewels have to do with Livia and Augustus?"

"Ah, Phoebe, I expected you to do better research than that. I have it on good authority that Cleopatra, after losing Mark Antony to suicide following their defeat in the Battle of Actium, tried to do some bargaining of her own. See, Octavian, popularly known as Augustus, planned to have her brought to Rome and trundled down the streets in the triumphal procession of shame. A queen of her note couldn't bear that, especially after having arrived in Rome years before at Caesar's side as queen defacto in 46 and 44 BC. She'd been partnered by two powerful men, lost them both, and had just lost her kingdom, too—the mark of a desperate woman."

"I know all that, Noel."

"Of course you do, babe. Did you know also that in an act of desperation, the Egyptian queen tried to bribe Augustus by offering her jewels to his wife, Livia? The empress was known to have considerable sway over her husband. Cleopatra hoped that by sending Livia a fortune worth of her jewels and a certain magic crown, she'd intervene on the Egyptian queen's behalf and let her remain in Egypt. Bribery, in other words."

I didn't know that. "And you say you have this on some excellent ancient authority? Since when are any ancient historical accounts irrefutable 'facts'?" I put the word in air quotes. "Have you lost all your archaeologist training already?"

"That's what you're going to find out for me, isn't it? But let me just say that besides the historical references, including one from Livia herself to a certain Vestal Virgin that indicates she received such a cache of treasure from the then departed queen, rumor and innuendo have lingered. I have a scholarly source with an access to ancient texts that the modern world has never seen, my little cache of secret texts."

"What kind of ancient texts?" Could it be true?

"Someday maybe I'll show you if you're good and I keep hearing that you just keep getting better. Anyway, it's believed that Livia may have hidden the jewels as a possible insurance policy of her own but they have never been found. Can you imagine how much they'd be worth, the real jewels of Cleopatra? None have survived, that we know of. It will be the find of the century, added to which the queen reportedly included her own special diadem, which she claimed had magic properties. You're going to find them for me."

"And how do you expect me to do that?" I demanded. Really, at that moment he may as well have asked me to spin straw into gold.

He shrugged. "Who cares? Do what you do: talk to ghosts, have an illuminating moment, let the sky open up and Livia drop down with a celestial to-do list. Just find it or muscle man is toast. We'll meet at regular intervals for a progress report. You'll know the location when you receive my messages, the same way as you did this time. I know you have what it takes, Phoebe. You've always been my right-hand woman."

I turned and marched up the hill into the moonlight. Turning, I spat out the words: "I never was your 'right-hand woman,' more like your bloody art sniffer dog!"

He laughed. "And now you're my art sniffer bitch."

7

I climbed into the car at the foot of the Palatine Hill shaking with anger and buried my head in my hands to keep from screaming. Everyone picked up on my mood and didn't say a word except for Zann until Peaches nudged her quiet.

It wasn't until we were back at Nicolina's lab that I filled them in on Noel's demands. Even though I had decided not to disclose his parting shot—what was the point?—what I did tell them was bad enough except for one piece of news.

"Evan's alive," I told them, "and alert, just a bit battered..."

"Could you see any details in the background?" Peaches asked.

"No, it was blanked out like in one of those Zoom screens," I told her.

I thought that Rupert might have a cardiac arrest. At least, he gripped his chest and started hyperventilating while waving away any attempts to get him to sit. "I'm fine," he gasped.

Peaches marched off and kicked a wall, which set off an alarm and earned her an Italian tirade from Seraphina.

Once everything had quieted down again, and we had all sipped substantial amounts of Vin Santo, the sweet wine that Nicolina believed fortified the spirit and made all troubles evaporate, I took a deep breath and spoke with more quiet authority than I felt. "It's okay. We must stay cool. Evan is safe for the time being. Noel believes absolutely that I require my 'boy toy' unharmed in order to follow through with his intent."

"Which is to find Cleopatra's jewels, which probably don't even exist?" Zann exclaimed. "I mean, seriously?"

"Seriously," I told her. "He says he has it on some ancient historian's authority buried in a stash of equally ancient source material that such a cache is hidden somewhere, that it was given to Livia as a bribe by Cleopatra, and that she hid it where only she could retrieve it, presumably. As if ancient historians offer irrefutable proof. Our first task is to research everything we can on Cleopatra and Livia, especially as they relate to Cleopatra's negotiations with Augustus up to and including Cleopatra's suicide."

"By an asp," Nicolina remarked.

"Most likely poison," Rupert commented, apparently having recovered, "which was the way at the time and a great deal more of a guarantee of one's quick demise than waiting for a snake to have a go at you. The stories of a basket of figs arriving with a snake tucked inside are merely the stuff of myth. Blame Shakespeare for that image entering our collective mythology. Nevertheless, the queen of Egypt escaped the fate she feared worse than death and managed to die in the dignity she craved. To her I say bravo."

"Still, never has a woman been so maligned by history, is it not so?" Nicolina remarked. "Queen, scholar, speaker of multiple languages—"

"Herbalist," Peaches added.

"Herbalist, truly?"

"Truly," Peaches confirmed. "Yet, all we remember her for is seducing two Roman generals and clocking herself out. So, like, those dudes weren't fools. Didn't historians ever consider that here was a woman so accomplished, so powerful and beautiful, that the men had never seen anything like her? Next to those obedient house ornaments back in Rome, she must have seemed like something else. Of course they were smitten."

"They believed her a goddess, the embodiment of Isis." Zann sighed. "They really knew how to do megalomania in those days."

"Since the historians were all male, of course we're forced to view history through a patriarchal lens," I said. "But Cleopatra did all the devious, conniving things that her male counterparts did and only because she was female was it considered despicable. For men, those same actions were how you maintained power back in the day." I stretched and yawned, the wine calming me down and convincing me that I could sleep for years.

"Let us go to bed and begin our work with the larks the next morning," Nicolina suggested.

No one gave her any arguments.

❧

MOST OF THE NEXT DAY WAS SPENT IN RESEARCH, NICOLINA, ZANN, AND even Rupert pulling in favors from their historian and archaeologist friends to shed more light on both Livia and Cleopatra in her final months. It took hours of piecing together the four dynamic lives that composed this ancient picture, a story powerful enough to launch plays, movies, and countless tragic romances, a story no less incredible because it was true.

The tale of Antony and Cleopatra was legendary. He, being one of the last members of Rome's Second Triumvirate, traveled to Egypt to bring the sovereign dynasty under Roman rule since the mighty Caesar had left matters unfinished before his assassination. Instead, Antony fell for Cleopatra much the way his predecessor had before him. Antony was convinced to remain at the queen of Egypt's side in order to preserve the mighty dynasty and its queen as sovereign identities. That was bad enough to give up Rome for a woman according to the folks back home but to launch a war against his home was the ultimate travesty. And all this treachery for some foreign queen?

It could only end in tragedy. After launching a war against Rome, which included audacious acts such as dismantling Egyptian war galleys in order to drag them across the land to heave them into the Mediterranean, the pair suffered massive defeats until they had no allies or resources left. Rome, led by Caesar Augustus, Antony's former brother-in-law and now uncontested emperor of Rome, had won. All that was left was for him to march into Alexandria and claim the spoils.

In the end, we imagined Cleopatra and Mark Antony holed up in Alexandria, the epicenter for learning in the ancient world with most of their powerful friends having defected or abandoned them. Even Herod, upon whom they had heaped their hopes of persuading Augustus of leniency, bolted when the tides turned. And yes, there were records of a stream of bribes and beseeches being sent to Rome at this time, including a golden scepter, crown, and throne, plus a diadem that Cleopatra sent to Livia with her jewels claiming that it had the power to bind any man to the woman who possessed it.

Though we could find no mention of what happened to Livia's gift, the accounts stated that Augustus kept most of the queen's treasures but still denied her leniency. He wanted all of Egypt's fabulous wealth to fund his wars and building projects with the captured queen to ride in as the biggest trophy of all.

Instead of capitulating to her pleas, he demanded that if Cleopatra agreed to execute Antony, her life, at least, would be spared. But she was too smart to fall for that. Once Antony attempted suicide by falling on his sword—clumsily, as it turned out, since he died slowly—she mechanized a way to follow him to the grave on her own terms. Augustus would never claim her for that trophy ride in the end.

Most of these reports came from the historian Cassius Dio, who had recorded the proceedings in some detail based on supposedly firsthand accounts. History generally supported these statements so there was reason to believe that a fortune of Egyptian treasure did return to Rome with various emissaries. Most of that gold would have been melted down and reused as was the ancient way, but could a secret cache have escaped Augustus Octavian's grasp and been secreted away by his wife?

"Therein lies the question," Rupert began while gazing down at the tomes spread across the table. "It has been said over and over again that Livia was a model Roman wife—"

"At least on the surface," Zann remarked. She, like Nicolina, had been reading the Latin texts. "Behind the scenes, she was a superb tactician and, like most Roman women with brains, assured that her husband often made decisions that she subtly suggested."

"The honey in the ear, we say." Nicolina touched her ear with one perfectly manicured nail. "Caligula was known to have said of his great-grandmother Livia that she was 'Ulixes stolatus.'"

"Ulysses in a stola." Zann nodded enthusiastically.

"A stola?" asked Peaches.

"The men wore togas, the women long loose robes called stolas," I explained.

"Okay." Peaches nodded.

"Which meant that she was brave, ingenious, and brilliant, at the very least, but wise enough never to overshadow her powerful husband," Zann continued.

"Who appeared to be devoted to her, despite his many mistresses," I added. "I mean, considering the fact that though both Augustus and Livia had children from previous marriages, specifically by the spouses they both divorced after meeting one another, they never had offspring of their own. Any Roman male could use that as grounds for divorce let alone an emperor with succession woes, and yet Augustus appeared to be devoted to his empress until the end. Livia did the noble thing: she endured his infidelities in order to see one of her children assume the emperor's seat one day, which Tiberius did."

"They say that she murdered all the young men along the way, any that might have laid claim to the emperor's seat, that is, but there isn't much proof of that," Zann added. "It wasn't an easy time to be in the army, which the men usually were. Guys were aways getting bumped off due to one thing or another, which is how most of them died."

"Indeed," acknowledged Rupert. "Nevertheless, back to the issue at hand: if we consider that Livia accepted Cleopatra's bribe, we must also acknowledge the multiple accounts that stated this empress was, at least externally, the very opposite of the Egyptian queen. She was not ostentatious, did not adorn herself with riches, and resisted all personal excesses like jewelry and baubles. She was the epitome of what her conservative husband demanded as the vestige of a Roman wife, unpretentiously in charge of the home and hearth. He even boasted that his wife and his sister sewed his own robes. Would this woman, then, be tempted to disobey Augustus, who presumably wanted all the gold to settle his debts and to fill the Roman coffers, to the point of hiding a bounty for herself?"

"Damn right she would," Peaches stated, crossing her arms. "Think of it this way: Livia was afraid that her husband might be snared by the same powerful charisma that had already bound two Roman generals to Cleopatra's side. She wanted the queen's magic crown as a kind of insurance policy. Remember that she was superstitious enough to carry an egg in her stola once as a fertility charm, right? Imagine how enticing a man-binding crown could be?"

"Diadem," Zain corrected.

"Yeah, that," Peaches continued. "I mean, if Cleopatra did offer such an item, it was a clever tactic. Livia lived in the times of gods and magic. She would have seen Cleopatra ride into Rome at the mighty Caesar's side and then watch as the great Mark Antony gave up everything to align himself with this same queen. If Cleopatra assured Livia that this crown would guarantee her power over men, why wouldn't she want it for herself? If I were Livia, I'd want all the assurances I could get and a magic crown—diadem—would do the trick."

For a moment, we all fell silent. It was more than plausible; it made absolute sense.

"Okay," I said, looking up, "let's assume that a cache of Cleopatra's jewels including this presumably magic diadem did escape Augustus's grasp and reached Livia. Where would she have hidden it?"

"Not anywhere near the emperor, that's my thinking," Peaches said, standing proud and regal like a queen herself. "She'd hide it far away from his prying eyes, especially if he was busily melting down and disassembling all the ancient pieces that he looted so far. Didn't she have her own quarters?"

"Probably," Zann acknowledged. "Most highborn Roman ladies had their own rooms."

I buried my head in my arms. "But where was Livia's?"

"The knowledge will come to you," said Nicolina quietly.

"It must," Rupert agreed. Did I detect a note of desperation in his voice or was that totally my own?

Contrary to what so many believed, lightning bolts did not slice through the heavens to inform me where treasures lay and the ancients did not send me instructions, either. My gifts reached me through a series of subtle clues combined with an admittedly powerful intuition but it was never easy, rarely exact, and never, ever quick. Yet, I needed all of those elements if I was going to save Evan.

I unconsciously fingered the Pythia key beneath my sweater. The last of the Delphic oracles had given me this gift, not in any ordinary way, it's true, but not through magic, either. Perhaps it's all in how we define magic because real magic is far more subtle than the abracadabra fairy tales of old. Either way, the fact remained that I had no idea how to proceed on this course, no inkling of next steps, and no ancient spirit would be throwing me hints anytime soon.

As if sensing my thoughts, Peaches touched my shoulder from where she stood behind me. "Maybe you have to take a walk around the Palatine Hill or any place that Livia may have hung out in order to..." She paused, fishing for the right word. "Timewalk?" she suggested.

My team understood my methods better than anyone, knew enough to realize that it wasn't a method so much as a process, and not even a very reliable one, at that. Information could come to me from multiple angles but we could never anticipate the how or the why of it. Only one thing was constant: I needed concentration.

"To begin getting in the empress's mind or whatever, you need to timewalk."

I gazed up at her with brows arched. "Timewalk?"

"Yeah, that's kind of what you do, isn't it? You walk around picking up feelings. It's part of your process. Okay, so maybe you don't want to get into Livia's mind exactly but sort of get into the ancient Roman way." She shrugged. "It's a place to start, right?"

I smiled. "Right. Actually, I love the term 'timewalk.' There are times when I've almost felt that I'm there, walking in the shoes of another person living in another time. It's disorienting and totally frightening. I try to avoid going quite so far, to be perfectly honest. Look, how about you put together a map of Rome during the days of Livia and I'll start there," I said, turning to Zann.

Zann had become our map person. She just seemed to have an innate sense of how to piece together a map based on remaining ancient ruins and to reimagine them in the way in which they must have appeared in any given century. She cheated a lot, she'd be the first to admit, using whatever sketches, diagrams, or videos that happened to exist online and there were plenty.

"Yes." Seraphina nodded, her stern little face seemingly deep in thought. "You go for walk in these places and we follow to keep you safe."

"That will work!" Peaches exclaimed, snapping her fingers. "We'll start tomorrow right after breakfast."

That would never work. Me walking around in broad daylight with the rest of the tourists? It was as if they had never heard the part where I insisted I needed to do these things alone at first, how I worked better in deep solitude. I just nodded. At a certain stage in our lives, we learn that we can't change our friends, that the best we can do is adapt to their quirks and work around them when needed.

Later that evening, after a day of research and study followed by another bountiful supper that consisted of more carbs than my body could process at one time, Rupert went to bed early and I decided to go up only minutes later. No one argued. We were all beat.

"I thought I'd turn in, too," Peaches said, catching up with me on the stairs. Though she had to be exhausted as well, I knew that she wasn't planning on going to bed early so much as not letting me out of her sight. She even followed me to Rupert's room to say good night.

"Enter," he called when I knocked.

We stepped inside his luxurious suite, recently renovated to Nicolina's exacting standards in shades of bronze and chocolate. She considered this her manly room, though Rupert had his own definition of manly and would have preferred either jonquil or chartreuse as a color scheme.

"Just wanted to see if you're okay," I told him.

"Certainly, I'm all right, Phoebe. Why would I not be?" He was sitting in one of his silken dressing gowns working on a pair of electric-green argyle socks, the entire scene the picture of relaxation.

A still life painting that looked amazingly like it could be by a Dutch master hung above the settee, similar in age and exquisite detail to a portrait that hung in my own bedroom. I'd always meant to ask Nicolina more about those but had yet to take the opportunity. My attention swerved back to my companions.

"Sure, Rupe, what do you have to worry about?" Peaches asked while sitting in a tapestry-upholstered wing chair across from his. "Personally, I plan to sleep like a baby tonight."

Rupert fixed his gaze at her. "If you are making a reference to Evan's current predicament, Penelope—*our* current predicament—I am convinced that nothing is to be gained by either panic or distress. The best we hope to do in the interim is to take what comfort we can where we can—" he held up his knitting, the beginnings of a ribbed cuff emerging from his needles "—and give those pastimes our full attention when feasible. Besides, I have complete confidence in our Phoebe finding these jewels and releasing Evan, accordingly, that is, if he does not, in fact, escape on his own."

Peaches turned to me with a grin. "See, no pressure." She was trying to lighten the mood.

"I'll do my best, you know I will." I just hoped my best would be good enough because, right then, I wasn't so sure. "Well, we'll let you get back to your mind massage, Rupert, won't we, Peach?"

"Sure." She jumped up and followed me out. "I don't know how he holds it together or you, either, for that matter," she whispered once we were back in the hall.

"Who says I'm holding it together? I'm just trying to figure out how to help this process along."

She put a hand on my arm. "Not planning anything, are you?"

"Yes, sleep." I turned my blankest expression in her direction. "That's what I need right now. By the way, how's your new man?"

Her eyes narrowed. "Are you trying to change the subject?"

"I'm trying to get caught up with what's going on with you since we haven't talked in person for a couple of weeks."

She crossed her arms. "Matt's good, thanks. Nice guy who treats me the way I want to be treated and I do the same for him, but he's not The One. So far, I'm still looking."

"Finding the right person is worth the effort," I said, thinking of Evan and all we'd been through together. In two seconds, I'd be crying my eyes out if I wasn't careful. "Well, guess I'd better get some sleep." I turned toward the door.

"Don't try anything solo, Phoebe, I'm warning you."

"Night," I said and shut the door behind me. I couldn't afford to break down or fall apart. Or heed anybody's warning, either. Maybe I'd knit for a while, I thought, but soon realized I was too tired for even that.

I set my bug scanner on and removed all the surveillance devices Seraphina had planted because she couldn't help herself, checked my messages, turned on my intruder app, activated my timer, had a bath, and went to bed, in that order.

At two a.m. my timer woke me up and I launched the hunt for Cleopatra's jewels.

8

It only took seconds to deactivate the front door alarm plus every other trip-wire electronic device Seraphina had installed. Whether she had set up an alert for when the system had been tampered with was another matter. The best I could hope for was that I'd be long gone before anyone noticed me missing. Even if they tracked me, I might gain a few hours alone with Rome.

To most, it would seem crazy for any woman to prowl the streets of a big city alone at night, especially since I avoided all the well-lit areas in lieu of the shadows. I reminded myself that I'd never felt as protected as I did at that moment. Not only did I have a perimeter alert on a phone that could render anybody helpless with the touch of a button, I knew I was being followed by one of Noel's goons whose sole mission was to keep me safe. Add to that, the few armed combat moves I'd learned over the years and I figured I had the protection angle sewn up.

Besides, there was no way I could think and muse the way I needed with the agency shadowing me. As wonderful as they were, they couldn't resist being intrusive. Somebody always had to have running dialogue with me the moment they thought they could get away with it. But I needed concentration.

Rome will always help a history walker along. The modern city had grown up embracing its past with ancient walls built into modern concrete, decapitated capitals nudging against modern office buildings—nearly something of the past on every block. It's only a short step to antiquity anywhere in the Eternal City. One only has to turn a corner.

I intended to walk the path that Livia may have taken, past the monuments that had existed in her lifetime between the years spanning 27 BC and AD 14 when she was empress of Rome. I knew that it wasn't the same Rome that we sometimes imagine—all majestic marble monuments and stunning feats of engineering. Landmarks like the Colosseum wouldn't have been built yet and Imperial Rome was in the early days when a tangle of streets and wooden hovels still made up most of the raucous city, away from the public plazas and the homes of the mighty.

The Roman Forum had existed, though, along with plenty of temples. Emperor Augustus, Livia's husband, funded by his numerous military victories, was pouring gold into multiple building projects every year of his long reign. There must have been scaffolding everywhere, slaves dragging massive chunks of marble down the streets, dust, plaster, and noise along with spewing clouds of debris. Firsthand accounts claim that it wasn't safe for a citizen to walk outside in the daytime lest he be knocked senseless by something falling from a rising building or be run over by an ox train.

Livia would never have been out in that. As a highborn woman, she wasn't expected to venture out into the streets unless accompanied by her slaves and attendants and then only in a litter for special occasions. In Rome, a woman's place was in the home or, in the case of an empress, in her palace, villa, or temple.

Women were not even considered citizens. They belonged to their husbands or male next of kin, as much a free agent as a chicken. In fact, one Roman historian—the Romans were great recorders, letter-writers, and opinionated orators—sometimes referred to them in similar terms. The only exception were the Vestal Virgins. The Vestals were very special and elevated in the social structure of Rome. They were indoctrinated as children from highborn families, remained chaste, and then were released after thirty years with benefits and tributes. For them, life really did begin at forty.

Vesta, goddess of hearth, home, and family, was one of Livia's patron goddesses. The House of the Vestals was where her priestesses lived at the eastern end of the Roman Forum with the temple nearby. A sign of their prominence was the fact that the House of the Vestals was a three-story palace with at least fifty rooms designed around an atrium with two pools—no small compound for a site dominated by women. Since the Vestals were keepers of the sacred flame of Rome, a light which was never to be extinguished, they were seen as sacred, too.

Roman poet Ovid referred to Livia as "Vesta of chaste matrons."

Livia would have definitely visited the Vestals and the Temple of Vesta located near the Forum. As empress, it would have been her duty to do so and be benefactor to the powerful cult. She was even known to have dressed in the standard divine costume of chiton and himation based on the Greek versions during certain events, wore her hair in the manner typical of the Vestals, and covered herself with a veil, as did they.

If I had been her, I would have visited the temple under cover of nightfall and struck up a relationship with these seven powerful priestesses (sometimes there were six, sometimes seven). They held the secrets of the empire and were afforded freedoms not permitted to most women, as did Livia. Would she have hid a fortune of jewels with them?

I was striding across the Isola Tiberina bridge, choosing a convoluted route toward the Roman Forum in order to avoid the busiest and more modern sections of the city. My attention was fully on Livia and grappling with where she might have hidden Cleopatra's treasure.

Outwardly, Livia was a quiet, dignified, and obedient wife and the opposite of the sensual, exotic queen that lavished herself with gold, silks, pearls, and precious jewels. Cleopatra was undoubtedly the richest woman of the known world. Behind the scenes, however, Livia, by most historical accounts, had keen intelligence with the strategic patience of a supreme tactician. Rome loved her. To her people, she manifested all the virtues of the Roman woman —in other words, not showy or ostentatious and never hogging the limelight from the mighty male. Ostentation was reserved for public buildings and events, not people and certainly not women.

Livia desperately needed to keep her husband satisfied with her role as empress—he had plenty of mistresses to take care of his other needs—but she must have had moments of insecurity, as Peaches had suggested. What if he divorced her because she hadn't borne him a child? Wouldn't that make keeping Cleopatra's man-binding diadem even more appealing?

By now, I was so deep in my thoughts that I almost didn't clue in to the fact that I was being followed. Of course, it's not like it was a surprise. Still, it was my intuitive perimeter alert that nudged me before my phone made so much as a beep.

I looked behind. The cobbled bridge was nearly deserted but for the two men that appeared to be taking an early-morning stroll beneath the street-lights. One was big and burly and of the bouncer persuasion while the other was small, dark, and shifty-looking. They were actually chatting. Neither of them should have been roaming around Rome.

"Stop right there," I called.

The two shot me a startled look before glancing behind to check out who I was talking to.

"Yes, you two." I repeated that in Italian, just in case. "I don't care if you follow me but I don't want to see you doing it, get it? Just stay way back and preferably out of sight. I'm here to do a job and I don't want you two getting underfoot."

I swung around and carried on my way. Seriously, Noel couldn't get better help than those two? He had a gang of gunrunners and an elite band of art thieves on his payroll but he sent those two bozos to guard me? It was insulting.

At least they were obedient. After that, they remained far behind me to the point where I hardly knew they were there. By the time I slipped through the empty streets, snaked along the narrow alleyways, and was just crossing the main road toward the Forum archaeological park, I really believed that the whole situation would work out as I had planned. No one had contacted me; my phone remained silent.

Just before I entered the ruins with the forest of uplit foundations and spotlit columns, I looked back to check on the bozos. One of them waved as he and his buddy bounded across the road. Unbelievable.

But I had made it. I had asked Zann to prepare a map of ancient Rome as it would have looked in Livia's time and she had delivered. Looking at her map on my phone, I was amazed at the job she'd done. I could almost follow it as if I were back thousands of years ago.

The pathway that wove through the ruined monuments should lead me to my destination: the Temple of Vesta. Zann had patched in a virtual reality tour along with overlayed drawings of what the edifices had originally looked like according to modern artists and architects. The overall effect was amazingly realistic, leaving me a sense of what it must have been like to walk these same roads in Imperial Rome.

In those days, the massive marble buildings had been painted in parts, gold embossed in others. The overall effect must have been awe-inspiring: promenades with gold-capped colonnades lining the way, gilded statues of gods and goddesses, massive buildings and columns on either side. And though the virtual tour was portrayed in brilliant sunshine, I could easily imagine what it must have looked like at night with the torches illuminating everything and braziers lit along the way.

Livia would have traveled with her entourage, well-guarded as she made her way under the Arch of Augustus and into the enclave where the circular Temple of Vesta stood.

I lowered my phone. Nothing but a few steps and three uplit columns remained of what once would have been a glorious structure. It had been round, with two rows of concentric gilded Corinthian columns and a tall narrow doorway through which one could see the fire of Rome burning brightly. The image on my phone compared to the ruins before me was a sad and sobering reminder of how time moves on, taking the greatness of man and all his creations with it.

I lifted my phone back to the virtual world I briefly inhabited, imagining Livia disembarking from her litter and climbing the steps to meet the Vestal Virgins who guarded Rome's heart. They would have had a courteous relationship, for sure, and private, too, because no one, certainly not a man, could penetrate the temple's inner sanctum without permission. Still, would Livia entrust Cleopatra's jewels to their care? The cache would be safe enough for a time. The Vestals were keepers of many of Rome's secrets, after all.

Staring up at the moonlit ruins, my imagination over two thousand years away, I thought not. Those jewels would have been suspect, much as Cleopatra herself had been. The queen of luxury with her ready laugh, quick wit, and lively sense of discourse would have been in stark contrast to the band of chaste priestesses as much as she would have been to Livia herself.

Livia, epitome of dignity and reserve, knew better than anybody how quickly the tide could turn on one's fortunes, on her husband and herself. Hiding anything in Rome was dangerous. She'd watched enough powerful men go down either in battle or through assassination, watched daughters and wives be banished, and seen what happened to her own ex-spouse. No, if Livia chose to hide this cache, she had to do it somewhere away from Rome.

It seemed so simple, yet it hit me like a revelation: the cache was not here or anywhere nearby, but I felt, suddenly *believed*, that it did exist.

A sharp cry jerked me from my reverie.

Turning, I stared down the cobbled lane behind me, washed as it was by the spotlights and ambient light of Rome itself. Was I really seeing two bodies sprawled on the ground back there or was that just a trick of the shadows?

Flicking on my taser app, I stepped toward the shapes, my heart thumping wildly. The stark contrasts of light and dark could play tricks on you here. Maybe those were not bodies but shadows? I desperately wanted them to be shadows, but after a few steps I knew better. A chill hit my spine.

No doubt about it, those were human forms—two of them, one big and heavyset, one small and lean. Without getting too close in case of an ambush, it looked as though they'd been shot, probably with a silencer. Blood was pooling on the cobbles, both were facedown, one with a gun still in his hand.

Those were Noel's men. *Shit, shit, shit!* What the hell did this mean?

A figure stepped out from behind a pediment holding a gun, masked, and dressed in total black. "You come with me quietly," he said in Italian. "No tricks."

I pressed my taser app button and zapped the gun out of his hand. It went flying away as he clutched his wounded fingers and cursed. Two other armed figures emerged from the shadows behind him. I turned and ran.

Who the hell were those murdering bastards? I couldn't think straight then since my attention was on getting away but could I really expect to outrun three guys sprinting behind me? Probably not, and really, where could I find sanctuary in a tumble of ruins, anyway? The place was a perfect spot to stage a murder, and if the Carabinieri were going to do their rounds, I wish the hell they'd get on with it.

My only hope was to reach the road at the end of the park and try to flag someone down but even that struck me as nuts. Who was going to stop for the wild woman being chased by masked armed men? *Just keep driving, plēz.* Nope, I needed another plan and fast. I needed to find a place where I could hide, find enough shelter to duck down and zap those boys, one of whom was now almost at my heels.

I swung around and aimed my laser at his feet, blasting the earth just inches from his sneakers. He jumped back while I kept on running. Killing somebody wasn't in the books, though my laser had the power to do just that.

Higher ground, I needed higher ground, but I couldn't risk climbing over the barriers to clamber up one of those chunks of stone. The park was one big active dig site, some structures under reconstruction, the whole place a mine-field of hidden pits and holes. No way. Then, looming ahead of me across the deserted main road illuminated like an ancient multitiered birthday cake rose the Colosseum.

To me in those desperate moments, what I was about to do made perfect sense: I could break the perimeter fencing, let the alarm sound, and find a million places to hide inside. The police would swarm the ancient monument and find a bunch of armed dudes crawling around while I made my escape.

The plan sounded so simple. Besides, I knew the Colosseum—sort of. I'd taken many expert tours, seen multiple television shows. There had to be a zillion places to hide in there. I only needed one good one. The key was keeping my pursuers distracted long enough to get inside.

I bolted across the road, dodging the few cars zipping by, while sending laser bolts at the ground behind me. A chunk of asphalt exploded near one guy; it slowed him down while I dashed toward the perimeter fencing looking for a gate, which I found seconds later. Once, there had been eighty entrances to the famed fifty-thousand-person stadium. A quick beam with my laser app had the lock seared open, and by the time I'd slipped through, an alarm was pealing into the Roman night. Good.

Turning, I saw my three pursuers hesitate. They were maybe six yards behind me now but apparently not keen on entering the Colosseum with the cops on the way. One of them yelled an order that sent the other two forward. Still three. Damn!

I fired at one guy, hitting his foot. A scream of pain ripped out, sending my pursuers into momentary chaos. I took a few precious moments to try searing the gate closed, which only half-worked. The scrap of fused metal might hold them back for a moment but not much longer.

As I dashed for the massive ruin, one thing occurred to me: nobody shot back. They wanted me alive. Attempted kidnapping, then, but they had to catch me first. That task just got a lot harder as sirens were already zooming our way.

I bolted under one of the arched openings and into the mighty Colosseum.

❧ 9 ❧

T he circular corridor was dark, lit only from the exterior spotlights beaming through open archways that lined the exterior. I had to put as much distance as possible between me and my pursuers before taking my first turn. I didn't want them knowing whether I went up or down, left or right.

At first all I did was run down the wide passageway, random thoughts flying through my head. The Colosseum fell into disrepair around the fall of Rome and, after earthquakes and time, nearly collapsed in on itself as people looted anything of value. The steps of the Vatican's St. Peter's were made from materials stripped from this enormous stadium.

Why was I thinking of this stuff? I needed to find a place to hide and fast!

A cry somewhere behind me was my alert that the bad guys had arrived, hopefully only two since I'd wounded number three. Due to the building's circular shape, so far they couldn't see me, but I needed to keep it that way.

Now they were shouting at one another. "You go that way, I go this way," one called.

The police sirens grew much louder, their lights flashing beyond the arches. Shit! I needed to find someplace fast!

Finally, I spied a barricaded stairway. I flicked on my infrared light, leapt over the cording, and clambered down the stairs as fast as my legs could carry me. I was entering the Hypogeum, that amazing bottom level once hidden beneath a wooden floor where secret trapdoors, circular winches, and an early form of elevator was used to lift tigers, lions, and slaves into the arena to be torn apart by gladiators. The Romans took their blood sport seriously and the Hypogeum was key to the spectacle.

Enough had been reconstructed to give a taste of what it must have been like but all I was interested in right then was diving into one of those stone cells. I needed to hide until the police rounded up my pursuers. To that end, I darted into a dank cubicle, doused my light, and sat shivering in the dark. A thousand years ago some poor creature sat where I sat, awaiting its gory death to entertain the multitude.

Feet pounded on the modern wood floor above. Men were shouting, my phone was buzzing. I muted one and prayed that the other would carry on up rather than down.

But somebody was heading my way. I could hear one set of footsteps on the concrete—no, wait—two sets of footsteps, the second many paces behind the first. It sounded as though one was chasing the other but, unlike the police, no one was calling out for somebody to stop. Weird. I sensed that one was definitely in pursuit.

A bullet pinged against stone. Somebody was shooting.

Damn. I was too vulnerable. All it took was for somebody to check these compartments and I'd be caught. I had to move. Standing up, I poked my head outside the door and saw a light moving down in the bowels to my right. I headed left, launching across an elevated walkway designed for visitors to look down upon the cages below. An estimated four hundred thousand people and one million animals were killed in the arena's four-hundred-year history and I damn well didn't want to be one of them.

Now I was bounding up a ramp, the original of which probably delivered chariots and elephants to the arena floor, but when it ended at more stairs, I took them two at a time. I was heading for the topmost level, the seating area reserved for slaves and women. I could just imagine what Peaches would say about that. Hell, Peaches. She'd be so furious once she discovered what I'd done, but for the moment, I had to remain free and alive so she could have the satisfaction of telling me off.

My phone, still on night vision, kept buzzing in my hand. I really should answer it but who had the time? When I finally reached the top level, a gate barricaded my way, one that had to be zapped open, giving time for those footsteps to gain ground behind me.

Once through the gate, I scrambled down the corridor, far less grand than the lower levels. Bursting out into open sky, the lights of Rome spread all around and nothing but a railing overlooking the stadium below, I realized that I could hear my pursuer behind me and he was closer than I expected.

"Stop!" a man called in Italian. "Or I shoot, Phoebe McCabe!"

I didn't believe him. Whoever that bastard was, he wanted me alive so I kept on running right up until I reached a dead end. A huge section of the stadium had broken away centuries before, leaving nothing but an iron railing between me and the drop below. Desperately, I scanned around for an escape hatch, finding none. Shit! Trapped, I flicked my phone on stun and slowly turned to meet my enemy.

The man stood legs apart, holding his pistol. "You drop phone." He could speak English.

"Go to hell."

He grunted, his mask awash with ambient light. He was of medium height and strongly built, the same one who had ordered his companions to follow me into the building.

"The Carabinieri are all over this place. They'll be here in minutes," I told him.

"They chase my colleague below. They think only one. You and I, they do not know about. You drop phone or I shoot." He sounded tough enough, this one, all grit and nails.

"Oh, yeah, bozo, what about the shot I heard down in the Hypogeum? That wasn't the police down there. And I'm not dropping anything."

Bozo looked confused. "No one here but us, he said. Drop phone!" He was getting angry.

"No. Drop the pistol or I'll toast you to a crisp. What do you want, anyway?"

"You."

"Should I be flattered?"

In a flash, he lunged toward me, knocking the phone out of my hand. I kicked out but he grabbed my leg and flung me to the ground before I could do anything clever. Seconds later, I was hauled back to my feet, arm twisted behind my back, and the cold butt of a gun pressed into my skull.

"Move!" he ordered, avoiding my flashing phone on the ground as if it was a ticking bomb. Which it would be if I didn't pick it up soon.

And I moved but only because he was pushing me forward.

"Where do you think you're taking me?" I asked. "You won't get far and why did you kill those other guys? Who do you work for?"

"He's my Brutus, aren't you, Alessandro?" said a voice to our left.

Even I was startled at the sound and my captor certainly was, yanking me to a halt, twisting my arm for effect.

"And forgive Phoebe's multiple-question style. It's one of her adorable little quirks," the voice added.

The safety catch on the pistol released with a click in my ear. "I shoot her if you take another step, Halloran."

"No, you won't," Noel said, stepping from the shadows. I recognized his voice immediately, of course, but why the hell was he even here? "You need her alive as much as I do."

"Who is this guy?" I demanded, glaring at Noel as he stepped closer, his gun aimed at Alessandro.

"He's my Brutus, or one of them," he replied, never taking his eyes from the other man's face. "The Brutus who betrayed me, hence the reference to Caesar's assassin and once-friend. This guy is a turncoat and he and his pals have the unmitigated gall to think they'll take over my organization. They want to kidnap you so you could lead him to Cleopatra's jewels before me."

Oh, hell. Nothing's more dangerous than a crook betraying another crook. "That's not happening. I don't work for nothing," I said. "Maybe if he agrees to get Evan Barrows to safety, I'll consider working for him instead."

Without warning, Alexandro yanked me to the right until I was hanging over the railing, twisting my body enough that one flip could send me over the edge. I blinked down at the broken shadows that made up all that remained of the brutal arena. Shit.

I had no intention of ending up down there. The bastard was strong, but holding a gun on one person while shoving another over a railing left him vulnerable.

"You don't bargain with me!" he sneered in my ear. "Halloran, you back off or she dies."

"Easy there, Sandro. Don't harm our golden girl," I heard Noel say. "Trust me, you don't want her. She's a pain in the ass. Let her go."

As if to prove his point, I leveled a back kick at Alessandro, felt my heel hit his knee, heard his cry of pain. Instantly, he released his grip on my arm long enough for me to push away from the railing. I turned just in time to see Noel shoot him in the head. Alessandro collapsed in a heap to the floor, blood pooling below him.

"Damn it, Noel! Did you have to kill him? Why not just wound the bastard and let the cops handle it?"

Noel was wiping down his gun despite the fact that he wore gloves. "So they can interrogate him and find out all about the operation? Are we really having this discussion again, Phoebe? Come on, we've got to get out of here."

Shouts echoed through the ancient stone. Many footsteps thundered on the stairs heading toward us. Noel grabbed my hand and tried to drag me down the corridor.

"My phone!" I cried, tugging in the opposite direction.

"Leave the thing!"

I twisted out of his grip. "No chance!"

Noel started cursing. "You just broke into the Colosseum; the cops are heading our way; and you just shot somebody in the head. What is it about 'let's get the hell out of here' that you don't understand?"

"*I* just shot somebody in the head?" I asked while reaching for my phone.

"Yeah, you did. Don't think I'm going to hang around here and get nailed for murder, do you?" He dropped his gun to the floor.

I was so outraged I almost zapped him with my phone on the spot only my battery was dead and somebody else took that pleasure from me. An electric-green laser bolt hit Noel in the foot. He cried out and swore viciously.

"Stop right there, dickhead, before I sever a limb."

"Peaches?" I gasped.

Noel swung around to see what I saw: a tall Amazonian standing in her black catsuit, phone held in line with his chest.

"Peachy baby, is that you?" he asked with a laugh. "Long time no see."

"Yeah, it's me, bastard boy, and I'm about to do something I've been dreaming of for years."

"Peaches, no! If you kill him, we'll never discover where he's holding Evan!" I called out.

"Yeah, Peach. Better keep me intact or her boy toy dies," Noel said, holding up his hands.

"I don't plan to kill you, Noel, though I'd love nothing better. No, I'm going to torture you until you tell us where you've hidden Evan." She took a step forward and zapped her laser at his feet followed by a quick blast to his arm.

He leapt away cursing, gripping his wounded parts. "Ouch, bloody ouch! Stop or I swear he dies!"

She must have her app set on the lowest level, enough to leave bruises without causing permanent damage. This could be entertaining.

She zapped him again, this time on the left leg. "I'm heading farther up next time, Noel, though I doubt you have anything of interest worth zapping there. Now, tell me where you've taken Evan."

He gripped his thigh and screamed, "Stop it, bitch! I swear I'll make Barrows pay for this and I'll never tell you where the hell he is even if you tenderize me to within an inch of my life."

"That's enough!" I ordered. "No more, Peach. We don't have time, and you, Noel, if you hurt so much as a skin cell on Evan's person, Cleopatra's jewels will stay lost forever. I've learned something tonight and if you want to find out what it is, you'll keep to your side of our bargain."

"Sure, I will, babe. Just call off your dog," he said, looking hopeful even with his face twisted in pain.

By now the police had arrived, calling from the far end of the corridor in two languages for us to freeze. Noel was spinning around looking for an escape hatch while Peaches lunged past him—tasering him on the knee in passing—to grab my hand. "Run!"

So we ran. Though I had no idea where we were running to since we were heading back the way I had come, back through the arched stone dead-end passageway. After about twenty yards, the wall to our left fell away onto another length of iron railing with the shadowy arena gaping below.

"Climb over!" she hissed.

Climb over the railing? But I didn't hesitate even though internally I was screaming in protest since now we were crouch-scrambling on a narrow ledge just inches away from toppling to our doom.

The cops were still calling, their shouts echoing around the ruins, flash-lights skimming the walls, while we scrambled along balancing on nothing but a few inches of crumbling brick. Soon, we reached a section of original wall tall enough to shield us from view. There we huddled in the shadows, one hand grasping the wall, the other resting on the ledge, both of us trying not to look down.

It became a waiting game. The Carabinieri were fanning through the ancient stones. There had to be at least a dozen of them, and whether they caught Noel or not, we couldn't tell. I hoped not because if he was in captivity, Evan was in jeopardy. I doubted the bastard would talk unless the Italian police were into torture, which I doubted.

The best we could hope for was to escape ourselves. Minutes turned into hours. I thought our bodies would seize into statues. A chill breeze hit the side of the Colosseum, cold enough to harden our muscles if not our wills and leave our teeth chattering.

When finally the stadium had slipped back down into stillness, only then did we risk shuffling back the way we had come and climb back over the railing on stiffened legs. By then, Peaches had been in contact with our team, who were waiting for us on the east side of the building.

All we had to do was get out undetected. She led me through tangled corridors and twisty back halls where models of the Colosseum construction sat behind glass.

"How do you know your way around this place?" I whispered, not that she was talking to me or anything. I got the sense that she was so annoyed with me that if I survived the night her fury might do me in, anyway.

"Because I did a thesis on the Colosseum during my engineering training," she told me between her teeth. "I've seen every possible diagram of this place and proposed a few of my own."

"Wow, what a stroke of luck that you came to my rescue when you did." Probably the wrong choice of pacifier.

"I suggest you stop talking, Phoeb, because I'm mad enough right now to feed you to a lion, if I could find one."

I kept quiet after that.

⚜ 10 ⚜

A t least they let me go to bed and even to put a good breakfast under my belt the next morning before I faced the agency firing squad. I was on my second cup of Nicolina's strong coffee when it began and was just about to pour a third when I figured I'd had enough. In the midst of the angry tirade, throughout which I'd thought I'd launched an adequate defense, I realized that no one was listening.

"Okay, okay," I said, swinging around from the buffet table. "I get it: you don't want me bolting off on my own, but I keep telling you that I need solitude and uninterrupted musing at the beginning of a case."

"Then we follow you like we did on Palatine Hill," Seraphina said with something close to a snarl.

"And stay in contact with you so we know you're safe," Zann added.

"No," I said. "That's the problem: I don't want you staying in contact with me because that interrupts my brain flow."

"Did being chased by a bunch of überkidnappers interrupt your brain flow?" Peaches asked, her tone deceptively mild.

I took a deep breath. "The point is that you're too intrusive: Rupert likes to text me asking where I am even though he can see my position on the tracker map; Peaches stays so close that I can practically hear her breathe; and Zann—" I took another breath "—Zann likes to send me videos and music clips—"

"Only if they're relevant and I only sent a music clip once," she protested, "and only because 'The Saints Go Marching In' was such a perfect accompaniment to your tour of that cathedral."

"I wasn't *touring*!" I said sharply, probably too sharply. "I was attempting to reach deep into myself to touch the past and timewalk, as Peaches calls it, and I didn't need footsteps, chatter, and musical accompaniment to get there!"

Nicolina sat with her hands folded on the table, taking in every word while Rupert stirred his tea with a touch more energy than necessary, his spoon clinking on the porcelain. Zann and Seraphina had their arms folded over their chests, glowering in my direction. It was a mostly impenetrable wall of disapproval.

"Okay," Peaches said slowly, lifting her head from her plate where she had been dissecting a cantaloupe into little chunks with a paring knife. "We get it: you don't want us to communicate with you when you're doing one of your timewalks."

"Love that expression. That's what I'm calling it now."

She stared at me. Hard. I counted ten seconds. "So, while you are *time-walking*, you'd much rather have Halloran's dudes tramp after you with maybe a mix of random hoods along for the ride—gotcha. But for the record, if I hadn't bypassed all your attempts to sneak away without me, where do you think you'd be right now? Let me guess: in police custody? Nabbed by one of Noel's rogue hoods? Dragged off somewhere by bastardo numero uno himself? *Dead?*"

"Granted, you appearing last night was very helpful," I began.

"Helpful? *Helpful?*" Peaches was on her feet leaning over the table toward me wiggling that knife. "I saved your ass, admit it!"

"Okay, you probably did." I really believed that I'd had it all under control but why quibble? "I was enormously relieved to see you."

Nicolina stood. When Nicolina stood, everybody paused. "I suggest a compromise," she said. "From here on, Phoebe does not go anywhere without Peaches. Nobody else makes contact—no musical accompaniment, no texting. Only Peaches. If there is trouble, Peaches signals us and we move in as necessary." Her regal gaze surveyed the room. "Agreed?"

Everybody assented except Peaches. She was too busy drilling me with a glare so fierce I swear it could have chipped stone. There was only one way for me to smooth things over.

"Okay," I blurted out, "I'm sorry, Peaches, okay?"

"Sorry for what, that you lied to me?" she demanded.

"Not lied, exactly, more like dissembled, but yes, sorry for that. Am I forgiven? Can we just move on because, as I said, we now know that Cleopatra's jewels do exist, that Livia hid them somewhere, that they are not in Rome but somewhere else."

"And," Rupert added, setting down his spoon, "that Noel has a breakaway band of Brutuses—or would that be Brutii?—after the treasure for themselves, an unfortunate and completely confounding factor bound to throw another hurdle into an already snaggy and grievous situation."

"There," I said, spreading my hands and grinning. "Couldn't have said it better myself, especially in so few words. Can we just get on with figuring out where Livia may have hidden the jewels now?"

It was not a tribute to my persuasive powers that they finally relented but more to the fact that we were running out of time. Every minute that ticked away took us farther away from Evan. We had no idea what condition he was in, really. The pictures that say a thousand words also lie just as richly.

Back down to the lab we trooped to resume our research and to figure out where beyond Rome an empress might hide a stash of riches. Added to that, we were also focused on finding where Noel might be holding Evan. Odd as it seemed, finding Cleopatra's gold seemed less impossible than finding Evan.

"Don't you get an inkling of where he is, like as in a sixth sense or something?" Zann asked me.

Nicolina's luxe museum-cum-restoration-lab had been commandeered as our command central. Computers sat open on maps and Google Earth, various facsimiles of ancient charts sat spread over the light tables, and one counter held nothing but books. I had assigned myself to the desk opposite Zann where I spent hours scanning translated tomes while she raked the Latin equivalent.

Looking up from reading Ovid, I made a face. "I know it seems that I should be able to divine where he is," I began, "but for reasons I can't explain, my finder gifts don't extend to living people. I've tried and tried but I can't see Evan in my mind's eye except in my memory, and have no clue where to find him." Pausing for a moment, I added: "I thought maybe that he was shielding his mind from me, maybe trying to protect me against something, but now I really don't think that's it. I've never been able to find living people. Even when a kid and playing hide-and-seek, I never had any special advantage." I shook my head. "I can only search the past. It's so frustrating."

"Ever played pin the tail on the donkey?" asked Zann.

I stared at her. "Sure, as a child."

"So how good were you at finding the donkey butt?"

"I don't remember. Donkey butts haven't featured in my memory for a long time."

"What about dowsing for water?"

"I tried it once and found an underground stream but anyone can do that."

"Not everyone." Zann leapt to her feet. "So, maybe we're going about it the wrong way. Maybe we need a different approach."

"What kind of approach?" I asked.

"The pin-the-tail-on-the-donkey method," she responded, marching me over to the map table. She tapped her finger on Italy, a detailed map Nicolina had placed below the glass for our reference. "We'll use a kind of divining rod approach. Close your eyes," she ordered.

Now, Zann was our most unpredictable agency member. A true divergent thinker, nobody quite knew what she would come up with next or what she would do next, for that matter. I was always the one willing to give her ideas a try. That's how she made it onto the team when the others had protested. I was her guarantor, in a manner of speaking.

"Eyes closed," I announced, squeezing my lids shut.

"Turn around."

I turned around.

"Again."

I turned again. Next, I felt Zann guiding me back toward the table. "Hold out your hand and place your index finger down somewhere below."

I did as I was told and when I opened my eyes again I found everyone gathered around staring at my finger planted roughly on the lower shin of Italy's boot.

"That's not a method so much as a stab in the dark," Peaches commented.

"It may seem random," Zann informed her, "but even random acts may have significance if the person doing the randomizing is gifted."

"What I mean is, surely you don't think Evan is hidden in—" she lifted my finger "—in Salerno?"

"Why not?" Nicolina inquired.

Rupert leaned forward. "The last I heard, Evan's devices were signaling from Sicily and a day later from Naples, before going dark in the most unaccountable manner."

"Naples is close to Salerno," Nicolina reminded us.

I was staring at Zann. "Did Livia or Augustus have a vacation villa away from Rome?"

She nodded. "They had a place known as the Villa of Livia at Prima Porta, maybe seven miles north of here, which was part of Livia's dowry. But, as emperor, Augustus probably had vacation homes all over. The fact that no one's recorded others doesn't mean that they didn't exist."

"Or that Livia didn't have a place of her own," I said, turning to everyone in a sweeping gaze. "Livia was one of the few Roman women who could own property in her own name. You can believe that she influenced her husband to ensure that happened during his lifetime. What if she had a little bolt-hole where she could retreat while the emperor was off waging his wars?" I rubbed my hands over my face. "What do we know about Livia's properties?"

"She lived to be eighty-six so she had plenty of time to accumulate bolt-holes," Peaches remarked. "If she was afraid of hubby finding something significant, wouldn't it make more sense to hide a treasure where he never visited?"

"Yes," Nicolina agreed. "The emperor was a powerful man and any place he lived would be filled with his loyal slaves. Livia required a place of her own."

A wave of shivering overtook me. I closed my eyes, suddenly beset with images of flowers and birds washing across my eyelids. It was dark in there. I seemed to be peering into someplace crumbling and smothered in shadows. *Smothered.*

"She hid it someplace dark," I whispered, backing away, "in a room, a room that has remained hidden for centuries." I paused, gazing stricken down the halls of time. "There are bodies, writhing bodies, all around, above and below, people dying horribly. I can hear screaming, a girl crying."

"Like from what, a fire?" I heard someone say.

"Not fire," I mumbled, "something much worse."

"A volcanic eruption." That was Nicolina's voice. "Phoebe, do not go there. You are not prepared."

I wanted to escape this place but had no idea which way to go, where to turn. People were screaming, *I was screaming.* Somebody began shaking me. "Phoebe, Phoebe, come back!"

But it wasn't so simple. It took minutes, maybe twenty or more, before I could pull myself up from the past, gasping for air as if trapped inches away from a hideous death. I'd never experienced anything like that before and never wanted to ever again.

When I came to, I was huddled in a corner with my hands covering my head. They were all crouching around me, Rupert urging me to sip a mug of tea.

"What just happened?" I gasped.

"You had an event," Zann said excitedly. "Seriously, a bona fide past-witness event! It was amazing! Tell us every little detail."

"It was horrible," I whispered.

Peaches's arm was around my shoulders. "Try to get past it, pull yourself away." She glared at Zann. "Back off." And to me she said: "You're here now, safe in AD 2022."

Turning to her, I said: "Livia buried Cleopatra's gold somewhere that is now deep under a mountain of ash."

"Shit, Pompeii?"

"Yes, Pompeii," I said. "I'm sure it was Pompeii."

"Your finger did touch Pompeii. Livia could have had a place in Pompeii," Zann said excitedly, "but how could we ever find that? Livia died in AD 29 and Mount Vesuvius obliterated the city in AD 79. That means that somebody else must have owned that villa for fifty years following her death."

"Maybe a trusted friend," Nicolina commented.

"There's still the little problem of a mountain of ash and hardened pumice heaped all over the ruins. It's still only partially excavated. Like getting through that is no piece of cake even when Phoebe locates the exact spot." Zann again.

And what would I need to do to find the exact spot—die a thousand deaths? I didn't think I could do it, didn't want to do it.

With Rupert on one side and Peaches on the other, they half lifted, half dragged me into a chair. Lots of strong tea followed. Several minutes passed during which my world settled into current reality with no more shifting images, no more burning in my throat and nose, no more fumes and smoke. The trauma, however, lingered.

I blinked. "I never want to go back there."

But, of course, I had no choice. I knew that. Evan's life depended on it.

My friends were silent, busying themselves with maps and computer screens in an effort to give me space. Mostly, I just stared unfocused at the tiled floor. Out of my peripheral vision, I was aware of Zann repeatedly trying to lurch out of her chair, no doubt to grill me further on my experiences, and of Peaches pushing her back into her seat every single time. That made me smile.

"Ahem."

I turned. Rupert had been sitting beside me yet I had failed to notice. "Dearest Phoebe, it behooves me to mention something now that you are, er, somewhat recovered. A matter of import, as it turns out, and it recently arrived in the mail. Actually, not the mail exactly but discovered by Seraphina in Nicolina's brass postbox fixed to her door. The camera had been covered and—"

"What?" I asked.

He passed me a postcard. "This came this morning, a few moments ago, in fact."

My stomach clenched. "From Noel?"

"Apparently. The wily cutthroat must have somehow escaped police custody and made his getaway, he being a devious character and known to be an artful dodger of sorts."

He continued speaking but I wasn't listening because I was too busy staring down at the streets of Pompeii, the sun beaming low in the west to gild the ancient stones. Flipping the card over, I read:

See you later this afternoon. N

Jumping to my feet, I cried: "He knew! The bastard knew the whole time that Livia buried her stash at Pompeii! He was just playing me!"

"Perhaps he was testing you," said Rupert quietly, looking up. "More worrying is the fact that somehow he may have deduced that you have successfully located the treasure's location this very morning, which means—" he took a deep breath "—that our data explorations are not secure."

He got to his feet and projected his voice into the lab. "From this point forth we must assume that our network has been infiltrated sufficiently for an outside source to determine our search paths."

"Our cookies?" Seraphina demanded. "Impossible! No one sees my cookies! I shield my cookies always!"

"The digital Cookie Monster," Peaches muttered.

"My network is tight, so tight that nobody hacks in!" Seraphina continued.

But we all knew that few networks are that iron-tight. Evan always shored ours up on a continual basis, technical genius that he was. He surveyed our electronic guard posts daily looking for weak spots, areas of vulnerability. He'd never have let this happen, not in our internal network, not on his watch.

Evan.

I collapsed into tears.

❧ 11 ❧

We drove down Italy's shin, arriving in modern Pompeii later that afternoon and booking into a little hotel within walking distance of the gates of the ancient city. Somehow Nicolina had arranged for us to take over the hotel's top floor with its three master suites and four single bedrooms, some of which would remain unoccupied, in order for Seraphina and Peaches to install electronic trip wires and a variety of other perimeter alerts.

Strangely, I didn't seem to care what was going on around me. I appeared to be in some kind of emotional lockdown.

"I believe you are suffering from a mild form of post-traumatic stress," Rupert told me. "Apparently, whatever you saw during your episode appears to have been so disturbing that it is as though you suffered the trauma yourself."

I gazed across to where he sat in the chair opposite mine. "Luckily, I pulled back in time before...she actually died, and I was a witness, not a player." Pausing for a few seconds, I added: "Though I felt the suffering as if it were my own."

"Because you are an empath," Nicolina said quietly.

Suddenly, a well of emotion surged to the surface and I desperately needed to talk. "There was this intense struggle to breathe and I could feel her panic, the horrible, hideous panic, but not her death, though that was sure to follow. What I experienced was bad enough."

"Whose death?" Zann asked.

"I have no idea—definitely a woman. She came to retrieve the jewels, thinking she'd escape with the booty, but she was worrying about somebody else, too—a girl, I think. I could sense her thoughts, her fear."

"Are you certain it was a she?" Peaches asked, sitting on the end of the bed.

"She," I confirmed. "A single terrified woman maybe only minutes from death."

"Did you have any sense of how she obtained the jewels?" Nicolina asked.

"No," I whispered. "I didn't remain there long enough."

I was instructed to rest until the estimated meeting time, which only gave me less than an hour. Our plan was for the entire team to enter the gates of Pompeii but that only Peaches would remain near me during my meeting. We assumed that Noel had chosen a public place as extra security against his Brutus, who would no doubt be present, too. Somewhere.

"Imagine him calling this turncoat 'Brutus,'" Rupert mused.

"He was always a Shakespeare fan and used to quote sonnets to me," I said.

"That's because the bastard couldn't come up with anything original," Peaches remarked. With her arms crossed, she glared out the window toward the balcony as if expecting said bastard to appear at any moment.

"There's no evidence that Caesar ever said, 'And you, Brutus?' when that gang of senate thugs murdered him," Zann remarked.

"Yeah, so what does that fact have to do with anything?" Peaches growled. "But back to meeting Phoebe in a public place—what's with that?"

"Evidently, the wily cutthroat believes himself safe against Interpol and every other potential threat as long as Evan remains in captivity." Rupert had prepared himself for the afternoon by dressing in his version of a British tourist, circa 1952. No one had the heart to tell him that the straw hat, natty linen jacket, and tonal ascot that matched his yellow socks was not what the typical tourist wore in this century. Sartorial splendor ruled.

"And he's probably right," I said with a sigh. "There'll be so many people milling around no one will pay much attention to us and I should be able to get what I want out of Noel without attracting too much attention."

"What do you want out of him?" Zann asked quickly.

"Proof that Evan's fine, for a start; answers as to why he failed to mention that he knew Cleopatra's jewels were buried in Pompeii all along. Why waste my time?"

"I'll be nearby," Peaches stood and took a step toward me.

"I know," I said, looking up and smiling at her. "Just don't kill him."

"I won't, not yet, anyway."

And so we left our hotel-cum-fortress and strode down the streets of the modern city of Pompeii as if playing tourist was all we had in mind. We'd all dressed in relaxed touring gear, though some of our members stood out more than others. Nicolina no doubt believed a cashmere leisure suit perfect for a comfortably cool November day while Peaches only seemed to wear leather when on the job. Zann and I were the only two that could do tourist properly, though she was perhaps a little too attached to her fanny pack. I preferred leggings, a sweater over a T-shirt, and my jacket as in the layered look. Personally, I thought I was rocking it.

I'd been to Pompeii many times before and the ruined city always moved me while the modern version disappointed me in equal parts. Strange how I kept expecting the modern community that grew up around the ruins to have the same magnificent gravitas as its predecessor but of course it couldn't.

There were people milling everywhere, most of them exiting the gates after what I could only assume was a fascinating tour through the ancient town. Only one hour until closing.

"I suspect Halloran will approach you rather than you resorting to the necessity of seeking him out, Phoebe," Rupert said after he'd purchased our entry tickets, dusted a fleck of something from his jacket, and passed us each the accompanying map. "We shall unobtrusively linger about as if admiring the ruins while remaining at a suitable distance behind you at all times."

"If anyone comes too close, we attack," Seraphina said. "I zap." She held up her phone, prompting me to send Nicolina a pleading look.

"We will not zap," Nicolina assured me. Turning to her assistant, she added in Italian something to the effect of *Do nothing until I give the signal.*

"Don't come too close. Noel may not approach if he sees I've brought a crowd," I warned.

"We will stay behind but Peaches remains with you," said Nicolina.

"Of course."

That settled, we proceeded into one of the most intact cities of the ancient world, preserved in pumice along with Herculaneum since AD 79. Most visitors were making their way toward the exit but Peaches and I headed against the flow.

"I remember that street shown on the postcard," I told her as we ambled along. "It's noted for those circular stepping stones rising up from the road which prevented citizens from stepping into horsey doo and other muck. And then there's the remains of that gate or whatever that arch was. I think it's just up ahead, around that corner, and down the next street. Anyway, that's what I'm guessing from the map."

Which was the route we took.

"Okay." Peaches was constantly checking behind our backs as well as her phone for messages from the team. "Think they've successfully melted into the stonework but I don't know about that couple following us."

I turned in time to see a short blonde woman in jeans, cropped white linen jacket, and sunglasses lift her iPad aloft to photograph a building. Beside her, a tall good-looking man appeared to be discussing the details in his jeans, sweater, fedora. "They look like well-heeled tourists but they're not. Keep walking."

We turned a corner that took us to a cobbled lane wedged between the reconstructed walls of the ancient town. "This street is where they used to sell bread and other goods," I said, "kind of the vendors' lane, and look, there's the chariot tracks and the gate. This is the road. Where are our followers now?"

Both of us turned to look. The street was deserted.

"Don't know whether that's a good or a bad thing," Peaches whispered. "Let's keep walking."

So we walked but our pace was more of a stroll now. I kept expecting Noel to appear, for once *wanted* him to show up so I could get this latest episode over with and make him prove to me that Evan was alive and well. I was itching to see Evan again.

"So, where is the bastard?" Peaches asked, scanning the now empty sunset-washed street.

"My question exactly. Where the hell is he? I'm here at the appointed spot or is this another of his little games?"

"Maybe he won't approach as long as I'm with you."

"Maybe."

We continued to scan the empty road, unsettled by the stillness and the lack of tourists, the lack of Noel. I tried to fill up my anxiety with chatter. "They used to regularly flush the streets in order to rid it of waste and stuff, which is another reason for the stepping stones." I narrowed my eyes. "So am I seeing things or did a shadow move beside that arch up ahead?"

Peaches turned. "I didn't see anything. I'll check it out. You stay put. Stand right in the middle of the street—right there—" she pointed "—and I'll be back in a sec."

I took out my phone, flicking it onto my stun app while also engaging the perimeter alert. Shielding my eyes against the glare, I watched Peaches slip against the wall and duck out of sight.

Seconds turned to minutes. I watched the long shadows stretch across the street as the sun sank lower in the sky, wondering whether those long ago

Pompeians watched the same shadows while waiting, maybe for their horse to be shod or something.

But soon I grew uneasy. "Peaches?" I called. No answer. Nothing lay in my view but a deserted street. I was just about to follow her toward the gate when my parameter alert pinged at the same time a voice echoed inside the building to my right.

"Phoebe McCabe, I have something you want," said a husky Italian-accented woman's voice.

It was the blonde tourist striding from the shell of the ancient building, alone and smiling.

"Who the hell are you?" I demanded, holding up my flashing phone.

"Your friend, or so I hope we will become," she said. "Put down your phone if you want to see your boyfriend alive. Do not worry. Your friend is unharmed and waiting up ahead, and your team—you call them your team, yes?—they are all fine, too, just delayed."

"What do you want?" I was alarmed, of course, but at least this one wasn't holding a gun on me.

She stepped closer, all smooth tan and white teeth. By the lines around her mouth, I estimated her to be maybe in her early fifties. "To negotiate, no more. You have something I want or can obtain, and I have something you want." She held up her iPad showing a live feed of Evan lying on a narrow bed with a compress or something on his forehead.

"He was hurt but I have had a doctor take care of him. He is resting now and will be fine."

I stifled a cry and made to grab the tablet. She pulled it back. "First, disarm your phone."

As soon as I did that and shoved it into my pocket, she passed me the tablet. I stood gazing down at the man I loved, wanting to speak to him so badly my heart ached. "What did you do to him?" I demanded.

"Nothing. Halloran beat him but we rescued him and now keep him safe."

"Take me to him!" I demanded.

"First we talk."

"Why can't he open his eyes?" By that time I just wanted to scream.

"Because he is resting," she said softly. "He will be fine. It is not my intent to hurt him or you, Phoebe. I want only to talk, you and me, woman to woman. If you come with me now, we will go to a private place to parley and then I will release you, unharmed. This I promise."

"And Evan?"

"He must remain in my care until he is well enough to travel. Noel had him beaten while he was unconscious—the coward. I keep him for now but he will not be harmed further. You see, he is very comfortable."

"Why should I believe you?" I looked over at her, all smiles, her hair pulled back into a roll at the base of her neck.

She gently took the tablet from my hands. "Because I am not like the others, the idiot men. I do not like violence for violence's sake and prefer to do things my own way just as do you, but I am not stupid, either. You will come with me because if you do not I must take other measures. I am sorry but this is how it must be."

Tapping the tablet, she turned the screen toward me so I could see the guy sitting on a stool beside a barred door, one hand holding a gun. "He waits outside the room where I hold Evan."

"You would have him shot?" I demanded, suddenly wanting to singe her tanned limbs until she looked like a barbecued potato.

"Only in the foot at first, later in the knee, and maybe move upward from there, though that would be a shame. Please do not make me do this. Come with me quietly. Order your friends to back away. Text them now, then drop the phone to the ground and follow me."

She walked a few paces away. I stood frozen to the spot, twisting with indecision, burning with fury.

She turned. "Come, Phoebe. I don't expect you to trust me yet, but if you are as gifted as they say, then you know that I speak the truth. I will not hurt you or Evan if you come with me. All of your questions will be answered truthfully and you will be delivered back to your hotel tonight once we reach an agreement."

"What about Evan?" I needed to go to him so badly it was like a physical pain in my gut.

"I hold Evan until the deal is completed, I said."

"Deal?"

"We will strike a deal, yes."

Without deliberating further, I pulled out my phone and tapped out a group message telling everyone to stay away when they saw me exiting the gates, that I was working to find Evan, and they must not interfere. They were not to follow me, either.

"They'll track you," I told her as I placed my phone on the cobbles.

"They will try. Quick now before the gates close."

12

Together we strode out of the gates of Pompeii as though we were friends discussing life. I held up my hands for Rupert, Zann, and Nicolina to stay back while glaring at Seraphina not to use whatever weapon she seemed be holding under her jacket.

"I see that you prefer flats. I do not like high heels, either," the woman was saying. "Give me low heels any day so I can run, jump, move. A woman should not be imprisoned."

"Neither should a man," I told her.

She laughed. "I refer to being imprisoned by society's concept of female sexuality but I agree."

I turned to see Peaches running up to the gate holding both my phone and hers. I shook my head. *Stay back!* I mouthed. She remained riveted to the spot, eyes screaming fury.

"I don't even know your name," I said as she led me toward a silver Ferrari idling across the road.

"My name is Sofonisba but everyone calls me Sonny."

"Sofonisba as in Auguissola, the famous painter?"

"Exactly. You might say that my parents were art lovers, especially my father."

I climbed into the back seat beside another good-looking, well-dressed man, who grinned and saluted me. Sonny climbed into the front beside the driver, the companion I'd seen earlier. The car was heavily scented with the olfactory punch of men's cologne and perfume, the expensive multi-nuanced kind. I watched my friends running up to the sidewalk behind me as the car pulled away, my heart aching and every inch of me bouncing back and forth between fear and anger.

"So are you part of Noel's 'Brutus' crew?" I asked as we negotiated the streets, twisting and turning toward the bay. Ahead the sun was sinking into the horizon, turning everything gold-tinged deep fiery orange.

"Does he speak in those terms? But of course he does. Fool! He sees everything in fairy tales and literary references because once upon a time he actually read a book or two. But he is more my Brutus than I am his if he uses the term to mean that I betrayed him. I only claim what is mine. Isn't that right, boys?"

The boys laughed and nodded, the one beside me saying in Italian something to the effect that Noel would get exactly what he deserved.

"Where is Noel, anyway?" I asked, sensing that the men were primed to agree with anything Sonny said.

"In jail where he belongs, only I would prefer him dead," she replied. She flipped up her sunglasses and turned around to me with a brilliant smile. Coral lips, thickly mascaraed lashes.

"The police picked him up that night at the Colosseum?"

"Yes, but how long they will hold him is another matter. No doubt he will have some story and grease the palm of someone high up in the government to secure his release. The old-boys network is very alive in Italy as in anywhere and money always talks loudest. Unfortunately, Noel has many connections."

"But he's an international art thief wanted by Interpol."

"Who has a new identity and tidy alibis for all the crimes he is accused of."

"But he killed a man that night," I said through my teeth as I leaned forward. "Shot him in the head."

Sonny lowered her sunglasses and faced the front again. "My brother, Alessandro. That is who he shot."

"Oh." I sat back in my seat. What do you say to the sister of the dead man who tried to kill you? "I'm sorry for your loss. Were you and Alessandro working together?" Okay, so not the most sensitive question for the moment.

She waved her hand for me to stop talking.

"We speak more later," the driver said. "For now, enjoy the ride."

Yes, enjoy my kidnapping ride, but I kept quiet after that, listening to Sonny sobbing softly as the car pulled into a gated marina. Confusing. So, Sonny and Alessandro had been working against or with Noel? And could Noel seriously escape the police so easily? And where the hell were they taking me?

As we moved from the car to a speedboat, I couldn't wait to get my answers, though I had so many by that time that I hardly knew where to begin. "How did you know where Noel was keeping Evan?" I asked, pitching my voice over the engine as the boat zipped across the waves. We were in the Bay of Naples and for once the beauty around me didn't absorb my attention.

Sonny appeared to have recovered as she leaned back against the leather seats, apparently savoring the view. Laugh lines and creases grooved around her mouth and the corners of her eyes. "Because he told me," she laughed. "He told me everything, thinks that I am smitten with him like all women, like you were. Noel is a narcissist, yes?"

I couldn't agree more. "Totally. So you sent me the Pompeii postcard this morning, not him?"

"Yes. I knew that he sends you messages through the postcards. I also know that Livia had a villa in Pompeii but he did not know that until I told him. My mistake. Still, I did not tell him everything. His vanity marks him an easy man to fool."

"But how did you know that I knew about Pompeii?"

"We were able to hack into one of your computers."

"That was you? But our system is practically unhackable!" I exclaimed.

"So you think. Ah, here we are."

I racked my brain thinking of how they could have broken Evan's firewalls, but finally decided that without Evan to monitor our technical defenses, we were all vulnerable.

Attempts at conversation ceased as we pulled up to a large yacht moored in the bay, one of many luxury craft rocking at anchor there. I turned to glimpse Mount Vesuvius far in the distance, thinking of it as a symbol of brooding danger and impending death.

Seconds later, I ignored the hand a uniformed man offered and climbed up the steel ladder unassisted. By now I was more intrigued than worried. I needed to know more about this woman who had apparently foiled Noel and to get Evan back any way necessary.

Inside, the yacht was as magnificently appointed as I would have expected but I was less interested in the sweeping views, glossy marble surfaces, and deep leather everything else than I was about the art. There were paintings on every single wall, including one by Sofonisba Auguissola, a painting of her sisters playing a board game in a garden, a favorite subject in her early years. I recognized the other art pieces but not that particular one. It was a completely new painting to me, though the artist was unmistakable. "Is that—?"

"It was a twenty-first birthday present from my father and one I cannot bear to part with, though I know it is worth millions. That one is a copy, of course. The original is safe elsewhere."

"I've never even seen this piece before," I marveled. "It's fabulous!" I swung around. "But the original belongs in a gallery." The other reproductions were equally stunning. I recognized the Botticelli portrait on one wall was safe in the Uffizi because I had more or less put it there two years earlier. Now I was beginning to understand. "Is this your father's trophy wall?"

Sonny laughed. "In a way, yes. He either owned or coveted the original of every one of these pieces."

She had taken a seat at a table, a sinuous current of white marble flowing in and around padded chairs down the length of the cabin. For the first time, I noticed that a lavish buffet had been set out with silver serving trays warming over burners, oysters and other seafood heaped onto crushed ice, cheeses and finger foods. "Come join me," she said. "We will talk over a meal, the best way to strike a deal, no?"

I stepped toward the table. "Your father gave you a painting by your name-sake Auguissola for your birthday; you want to discuss me finding Cleopatra's jewels in exchange for Evan's freedom; you usurped Noel's plan; and one of those paintings over there I helped repatriate. I'm beginning to get the picture —no pun intended. You are Alesso Baldi's daughter, the late arms dealer who's career I helped end in Florence."

"Ah," she said with a sad smile. "So you make the connection. Yes, I am Sofonisba Baldi, but I am sure when you met him, my father did not mention that he had a daughter."

"We didn't exactly discuss family life. When I saw him, it was under circumstances not unlike these. I was being held hostage while your father sought a priceless Renaissance masterpiece through my efforts—the original of that one there. Little did I know at the time that Noel was working in the background or that he would step into your father's shoes after his death."

"But that was not the last time you saw my father. You last saw him on that Florentine roof, yes?" Her tone was questing, sharp but not bitterly so. "You had that Botticelli and Papa wanted you to give it to him."

"Yes. That's where he fell to his death. I'm not responsible for that, by the way, but if I had been, I wouldn't apologize since he was trying to kill me at the time."

Sonny nodded. She had lit a cigarette and sat gazing into space. "Yes, and he would have done, too, had he caught you. My brother held you responsible, of course, but I knew you were not to blame." She gazed out the windows.

"Your brother tried to kill me, too. It's safe to say that I don't feel all warm and cuddly about the Baldi family."

That provoked another sad smile. "I am certain that is true but you are now meeting the new leader of the Baldi family. My father was the agent of his own demise, an obsessive man who wanted more and more, a greedy man like the emperors he aspired to, always after the next conquest." She sighed, blowing a plume of smoke toward the bay. "I think sometimes that all this power and money makes these men crazy."

"I recall his Roman legion playacting."

"All these greedy men!" She lifted one hand to the sky in disgust. "My brother also, though he did not possess the skills to run the organization and Papa knew this. He refused to appoint Alessandro as his successor. He gave that honor to Noel Halloran and that decision has torn this family apart ever since. Now it has also cost my brother's life."

"Because your brother resented Noel and was determined to run the organization himself? Is that why he and his goons chased me into the Colosseum, because he planned to beat Noel at the game?"

"Yes."

"Where are you in all that?"

"Nowhere," she said definitively, turning a frank, steady gaze toward me. "I did not agree with that approach but, of course, Sandro never listened to me. He said I was too soft. He thought me good only for getting information out of Noel, for playing on the man's many weaknesses with sexual favors, which I did, though it turned my stomach." She shrugged. "All the time I study, I watch, gather information. I played the good girl all my life while waiting for my moment to take command."

"Much like Livia," I said, stepping toward her, "only the empress never openly ruled Rome."

If possible, her smile widened, a smile that dazzled. "There are many ways that we women survive surrounded by powerful men, am I right? Sometimes, we simply allow them to self-destruct." She picked up one of the shells that fanned over the mountain of crushed ice and slid an oyster into her mouth. I watched her swallow, taking her time to savor every second. "Oh, delicious. Try one."

"So you bided your time," I said, dropping into one of the plump leather chairs.

"So I waited for my opportunity because I knew my brother and Noel would likely kill one another before this is done." The word *kill* came with a throat-slitting action. "Now the waiting is over. One is gone and the other I will watch be swallowed by his mistakes. Noel still has his supporters, true, but I will win them over to my side with the necessary incentives. Besides, Noel has lost his—what do you say—his marbles?" She dropped her empty shell onto a plate and tapped the table with one long red nail.

I nodded, waving the smoke away. "Do you mind?"

"I apologize. You do not smoke." She ground the cigarette out in an empty shell. "There."

"Thank you. How many minions remain in Noel's camp?" I asked. Though I didn't want to like her, I did.

"Only the ones who will not work for women even if the woman treats them better than the man. Such stupidity, these men and their machismo."

"And how do you plan to win those knuckleheads over?"

She rubbed her fingers together. "The old-fashioned way: I will offer them more money, and if they do not take it—" she shrugged "—then I dream up their severance package. Enough talk for now. Eat and then we will talk more business after."

I chose a chilled oyster sprinkled with herbs nestled in a shell. In a moment I had popped it into my mouth, savoring the complex mix of flavors that excited my tongue as it slithered down my throat. The unexpected can be such a thrill. "Why couldn't you claim the organization outright? Didn't you have as much right to it as Alessandro and certainly more than Noel, your father's antiquated rules of succession notwithstanding?"

"Ah, but the antiquated rules of succession are always standing. I am a woman," she said, turning her mascaraed eyes toward me. "I belong nowhere but as a beloved daughter, sister, and wife according to the old school. My men believed that important positions must always go to a man."

"Has nothing changed in thousands of years?"

"Not for my father, who idolized Roman emperors. I spent my life trying to prove my worth but still I was overlooked, even after Papa decided that Alessandro did not have the temperament—too impulsive, too immature, too totally unsuitable. But I had the necessary abilities plus I study history and speak many languages, making me even more valuable." She tapped her skull. "And yet Papa still refused to consider me."

"He really did follow the ancient Roman rule book, didn't he? I remember how he gave his minions titles straight out of a circa 50 BC theme park."

"Sad, isn't it?" Sonny said. "The games these men play. I loved my father and my brother, too, but it is time that women rule the world." She held my gaze.

"So rather than a man coercing me into stealing precious objects on his behalf, a woman taking the reins somehow makes it all better?" I devoured another oyster.

Sonny laughed her fully throaty chuckle. "Not quite, Phoebe. The difference is that I will deal fairly without unnecessary brutality. Besides, nothing you do will stop corruption no matter how high a horse you ride. I suggest a way to make things better for both our positions."

I stared at her in disbelief. "You suggest that your style of corruption will somehow improve my goal to return art and antiquities to their rightful owners or to museums and galleries?'

"I do. The key to successful negotiation is to ensure that both parties walk away with something they want. In this case I want Cleopatra's jewels and so do you but you also want Evan. This lays the foundation for a long-term arrangement."

My next oyster paused halfway to my lips. "God, don't tell me that you plan on holding Evan indefinitely?"

"No, of course not!" She flipped open one of the silver serving dishes and scooped out a bit of what looked to be fresh hand-rolled tortellini onto a plate, adding a little mixed salad, and roasted vegetables from another charger before extending the plate to me. I took it. "He is not so easy to hold, though I am certain you have no trouble. No, I plan to strike a deal with you, one I think you may find quite interesting. Now eat. Then we talk further."

So I ate, the food delicious, my mind churning with every bite while the sun disappeared behind the horizon and the twinkling lights of the coastal towns sparkled in the distance. Sonny was not my typical adversary. For one thing, she was sane or, at least, not delusional but no less dangerous. She still held the man I loved captive and what she wanted ran contrary to everything I believed in.

We were just finishing up our fresh fruit dessert when the driver of the car popped his head into the cabin and asked a question I didn't catch. I had seen him and several other men striding by on the deck outside but nobody but the occasional white uniformed server had entered. Sonny waved him away.

"Your husband?" I asked.

"Luca? No, I don't have a husband or need one. Luca is what you might call a boyfriend. Though not as interesting as yours, he's certainly useful and enjoyable in other ways." She gazed at me slyly. "Your Evan is very handsome and smart, too, a worthy partner. Had I such a man maybe I would reconsider."

I stared at her.

"Oh," she laughed, flapping her hand. "Do not worry. I will not steal him from you. I believe in honor among women. Hands off another's man."

"Unless you kidnap him and lock him up in a room somewhere, at which point I presume it's all hands on," I remarked.

That prompted another whoop of laughter. "I didn't kidnap him, Phoebe, I rescued him. If you only saw where Noel had been keeping him and under what conditions, you would thank me. Noel hates your Evan and would use any excuse to see him die a horrible death. Often he would tell me of the ways he planned to end his life. Castration while you watch was mentioned. But first, he said, he would win back your heart."

"He really believes that I would love a man who tortured another to death?"

"Noel is loco." Her index finger stirred the air next to her head. "I think when you tasered him, it scrambled the circuits in his brain."

"Maybe. So, where are you keeping Evan?" I gazed around the cabin, hoping against hope that he might be somewhere nearby.

"Not here," she told me. "I am not so foolish. I have him secured where neither you nor your team would ever find him. There he stays for me to admire on my monitors until our deal is complete."

I took a deep breath and closed my eyes. "Let me see him again."

"Soon."

"You want me to find Cleopatra's jewels."

"Yes. My father talked often about the marvelous Phoebe McCabe and how she had this uncanny ability to locate ancient treasures. Noel, also, spoke of you often, though in a much different way. When a man speaks of another woman when he's in your bed, you pay attention. In my case, I encouraged this talk because I wanted to learn everything I could about my new partner-to-be."

"I'm never going to be your partner," I told her.

"You haven't heard my deal."

"I doubt anything will make me change my mind."

"We will see, but let us begin by establishing trust between us, Phoebe. This is the first part of my proposal: you will enter Pompeii tonight and locate Livia's villa."

"What's the second part?"

"That I tell you later. First the jewels."

"Just like that. How do you know the cache even exists?"

"Through research, of course. One thing I have in common with my father is a passionate interest in Roman history, all history. He amassed a library of original scrolls, letters, and documents from ancient sources, most stolen, of course. He could not read them. That he left to me. I have degrees in art and history, speak many languages, and read both ancient Greek and Latin. It is through a private letter by Livia to Carola Publius, a Vestal Virgin during the reign of Augustus, that I first learned of the plot that would span generations. The Vestals were entrusted with Cleopatra's jewels for a purpose. They wanted to see a woman someday rule Rome."

That stunned me. "Rule Rome how?"

"They believed that Cleopatra's jewels would ensure the training and preparation for a select young girl to become the wife of a powerful man who would one day become emperor. They trained her to rule behind the scenes much like Livia had. She was to be the power behind the throne. To that end, the Vestals kept the jewels in trust and worked behind the scenes to ensure their plan. The Empress Livia was the orchestrator of it all. It was she who gave the villa in Pompeii to the Vestals."

"Isn't that unusual, leaving valuable property to another group rather than to your own family?" I asked, intrigued despite myself.

"Yes and no. When you were Livia, you made things happen, and as this gift of property was to the Vestals and she their benefactor, it was acceptable. The Vestal Virgins held more property and power than any other group of females in Roman society."

"So the Vestals owned a villa in Pompeii where they nurtured this young woman?"

"Yes. Letters passed secretly from Livia to the Vestals until Livia's death and, true to their word, the priestesses carried on the trust in the years afterward. By AD 70, the villa was in possession of a retired Vestal named Flora, who was the guardian of a girl they groomed to become the wife of the Emperor Titus."

My brain scrambled through bits of Roman history. "But didn't Titus have a wife?"

"Not at this time. He would later marry Arrecina Tertulla and if there was another candidate in the wings, she could easily be disposed of. This was the age of expedient executions, after all, and there was always divorce. Regardless, they believed they had the power to make Titus fall in love with their chosen one."

I stared, baffled. "Livia trusted a fortune in jewels to the Vestals to put another woman in power after her death? Surely they didn't believe it could be so easy?"

"Faith is a powerful thing," she said softly. "Once we forge it, nothing less than a cataclysmic disaster can shake its foundations. Yes, Livia wanted to see another woman—a trained, educated, shrewd woman—take the reins in Rome much as she had with Augustus. She believed that Cleopatra's jewels contained that power."

"The diadem, you mean." I said it with conviction. Did she really think she could hide that piece of critical information from me?

Sonny's expression hardened ever so slightly. "The last keeper of this mission was named Flora," she said hurriedly. "Now, tell me, Phoebe, have you sensed Flora with your second sight?"

I met the eyes watching me with a calm, searching intensity.

"You think you know a lot about me, don't you?"

"I know that your gifts are strengthening. Am I right?"

"Perhaps. I have felt things, it's true." Why not tell her since she apparently knew so much already? "There was a woman trying to retrieve something as Mount Vesuvius blew. I briefly felt her fear. It was horrible."

"It would be." Sonny reached across the table to grip my hand. It took me so much by surprise that all I could do was stare down at her long nails. "You have the true gift, Phoebe, and share the same passion for history as I do. Please understand, I want to know this woman and to touch the same jewels that Cleopatra and Livia held in their hands. Do you understand this? It is not all about the lust for riches. I have that also, I cannot deny it, but I want to know those that came before me even more. I want to connect with the past. If we work together, you will have access to a history you never knew existed. I would open the doors and you would enter and find the souls that once lived there."

I swallowed and tugged back my hand. "Let me see Evan again. Now."

Without further ado, she retrieved her tablet from the chair beside her and tapped the screen. Propping up the stand, she turned the iPad around. "There is nothing much to see but a sleeping man. I will watch you watch him."

I pulled the tablet toward me to gaze at Evan, who did appear to be sleeping. His head had changed position from the last time I'd seen him but I could tell he was breathing steadily. Both arms lay on the blankets and it looked as though a splint had been applied to his right index finger. The gray stone wall behind him was bare, with no distinguishing features. "What are his injuries?"

"He'd been drugged and beaten, which has left him bruised but with no apparent lasting damages other than a broken finger and a cracked rib. The worst damage was through the drugs."

"Can he hear me?" I asked.

"Perhaps. Press the microphone icon and try."

My finger pressed the icon. "Evan, Evan, can you hear me?"

A light movement of his head and briefly his eyes fluttered open. "Phoebe?" he murmured.

"Evan!" I thought I might do something idiotic and cry.

"Are you safe?" he whispered.

Just like him to think more about me than himself. "I am fine," I told him, studying the two-day-old beard, the grooves beneath those beloved bruised eyes, and wanting to touch him with so much need. "How do you feel?"

"Tired." He could not see me, I realized, and could only hear my voice. "Don't give in to their...demands. What...happened to Halloran?"

"In jail but we don't know for how long."

"Where...are you?"

I glanced at Sonny. "On a yacht in the Bay of Naples, special guest of one Sofonisba Baldi, Alesso Baldi's daughter."

Evan appeared to have fallen under again. "Damn! What have you given him that makes him so tired?" I demanded.

"Painkillers," she said. "You have seen enough."

I touched the screen with my fingertips. "I'll do what I have to do to get you back. Trust me to know what that will take," I said quietly, trying to sink myself body and soul into the screen to feel his arms around me. "Anyway, stop telling me what to do. You know that never works. I love you, that's all you need to know."

Sonny retrieved the tablet, leaving me aching with words left unsaid. "That's enough," she said before flicking the screen off. "This is all very touching and I do love romance but I have done as you asked. Now it is time for you to do your part. I will tell you the second half of my deal: if you find Cleopatra's jewels for me, not only will Evan walk away a free man but I will give you half of whatever you find."

I stared, stunned. "You're offering me half of whatever *I* find?"

Sonny flicked her hand impatiently. "You are not listening: you will have half of that cache for your museums and art galleries. I only want the diadem and a few choice pieces. I do this as a gesture of trust and to prove to you the value of an extended partnership. If you work with me, you will retrieve more treasures than you ever could find without me."

"Because you're operating illegally," I pointed out.

"Is it not better to have some priceless lost antiquities than none at all? You will not find them without me, Phoebe. I know of treasures you don't even realize exist. Think about it. Either way, tonight, you will enter Pompeii and find me Cleopatra's jewels. Flora is waiting to show you the way."

$$\maltese \quad 13 \quad \maltese$$

They dropped me off outside our hotel at approximately ten p.m., leaving me less than an hour to get ready for the night's operation. Peaches had been pacing outside when she bounded up to me.

"Phoebe!" she called, throwing her arms around my shoulders. "Thank God you're all right! Who the hell are those bastards? What's going on?"

I told her, told them all in more detail later in the hotel room, explaining the torturous family dynamics of the family Baldi, and where that put us on our quest to find Evan.

"Did you get a sense of where they were holding the lad?" Rupert asked.

"No," I told him, "only that he was being much better treated than when he was held hostage by Noel. Sonny told me that the bastard had kept him drugged and bound in some abandoned basement in Naples. Once she mobilized her takeover plan, she claimed that it was relatively easy to break Evan free and take him to this new location. He was in rough shape, though, she said, unconscious at that point. He was still groggy."

"So Sonofabitchi Baldi acted on her takeover plan following her brother's death and Noel's incarceration?" Peaches asked.

"That's it in a nutshell." I then explained how Noel ended up on the senior Baldi's succession plan against both siblings.

"Because a woman could not inherit the dynasty," Nicolina said.

"Straight out of the history of the Roman empire," Rupert remarked.

"Straight out of the history of mankind, which has always neglected women's leadership. It is very much like my own family," Nicolina remarked. "Your English term *man*kind says it all."

"Only in your case, dear Nicolina," Rupert began, "you convinced your brother otherwise and regained your share of your inheritance, whereas, if my memory serves me correctly, the emperors and empresses of yore preferred poisoning their siblings in order to settle matters of inheritance."

Nicolina smiled. "I might have shot my brother if he had not come to his senses. Even Cleopatra saw to her siblings' demise."

"But only to keep them from killing her first," I commented. "Anyway, Sonny, as she insists I call her, prefers attrition by natural selection: let the strongest survive, in other words. Though Noel has not yet been removed permanently from the picture, when he shot Alessandro Baldi and ended up in jail, he essentially opened the path for Sonny's takeover."

"On that point," said Rupert, clearing his throat, "I have made a few discreet phone calls to my Interpol sources but they assure me that they have no man fitting Noel's description in Italian custody."

"But he looks exactly like his old self and was caught red-handed in the Colosseum with a dead man," I protested.

"Yes, but I could not very well disclose our knowledge of those events, and apparently the man in custody did not waver from his statement that three armed men and one woman chased him into the Colosseum to rob him and that one hapless male victim was killed after an argument erupted among his companion thieves as to who would claim the Rolex watch from Noel's wrist."

"Attempted robbery, seriously?" Zann asked.

"Seriously enough," said Rupert. "Halloran now operates under the name Peter Buck, a British financial adviser and investor, and the dead man's identification named him as a poor refugee from Sarajevo. Evidently, those were the aliases the Baldi cutthroats used for the night's adventures."

"I don't believe it," Peaches said, shaking her head. "These bastards can cover their tracks better than a nest of pit vipers in the jungle and have the gall to muddy the reputation of refugees everywhere."

"Can you pull any strings to keep Noel in jail?" I asked Rupert.

Rupert sighed. "Sadly, no. Being no longer among Interpol's inner ranks, I have little influence. That has become Evan's sole domain within our agency and I regret to say that most of my old contacts have now retired."

"What about Agent Sam Walker, my old contact in London?"

"Now promoted and no longer at the end of a phone."

"So, one way other, we still end up in the same place," I said. "Sonny has taken over from Noel and plays a different game, or should I say, the same game with a different approach. We are working for her now."

"Shit, no!" was Peaches's initial response. "We're not going to work hand in hand with a wolf in ewe's clothing! Are you seriously planning to go in there tonight with her and those henchmen?"

"Yes," I said, "and I need all of you with me. That's the plan: we work as a team, me to locate Livia's villa through Flora and they to excavate where necessary to reach the hoard."

"No," Zann protested. "That's archaeological sacrilege! What if they destroy valuable historical artifacts getting to the hidden stash?"

"Good point, but maybe with our tools—X-rays and ground-penetrating radar apps—we can locate the treasure with a minimum of disturbance of the surrounding area," I said. I knew better than that, of course, but I clung to wishful thinking.

"That's nuts!" complained Zann. "Of course there will be damages and something will inevitably be destroyed."

"Something will inevitably be destroyed if we do not cooperate," said Rupert, sitting with his hands clasped on the room's only table. "Evan, to be exact, our team member and—" his voice hitched "—my son. We have little choice in this matter but to proceed on Sofonisba's terms. Is it so very different from Noel's initial demands?"

"Yes," I said quietly. "I believe Sonny partly tells the truth, Noel only lies."

"An honest thief?" Peaches demanded.

I took a deep breath. "When she said that Evan would be released if we comply with her terms, I believed her. Noel wanted him killed one way or the other. She claims to want my cooperation long-term, whatever that means." I looked up and met their gazes one by one. "Please, trust me in this. Tonight we do what must be done in order to free Evan. After that, we can worry about the consequences. None of our options are great, either way."

"You know I'll follow you to the moon and back, woman, but just for the record, I protest to everything we're going to do tonight," Peaches said, standing ramrod straight in the center of the room.

"Me, too," said Zann.

"I also," said Seraphina, thumbing her chest.

Nicolina continued to sit in one of the chairs, gazing serenely at some unfocused point on the opposite wall. "We do what we must to save those we care about because, in the end, we must always put the living before the dead. I am with Phoebe."

"Amen," whispered Rupert.

That silenced everyone. I shot her a grateful look.

"So what's the plan?" Peaches asked with a gusty sigh.

"We enter Pompeii at eleven p.m. Sonny has arranged something with the security guards—a substantial donation to their retirement fund, she calls it. We enter at the east end of the complex, which is hidden from the road, using an access gate known only to employees, after which I am to roam around the town until I can feel Flora."

"Do you expect it to be that easy?" Zann asked.

"Of course not. I don't expect anything to be easy. For one thing, I can't guarantee that I'll have an event. They seem to come randomly or, at least, I can't figure out the process yet. Still, I'll put one foot after the other to move myself forward as must all of you." I stood up. "Let's get ready."

It was agreed that Rupert would remain behind to coordinate our work though his laptop. The rest of us galvanized as a team, reviewing whatever apps and associated tools we had to work with. Evan had always been our leader in this area. Without him, it was excruciatingly difficult in more ways than one.

"Are you seriously wearing that tonight?" Peaches asked as we readied for the night's events.

I gazed down at my black leggings and black tank top with the black jacket over all. "What's wrong with this?"

"You need leather pants," she pointed out.

"I do not need leather pants," I laughed. "I need a miracle."

One of the riskiest parts of the whole night's enterprise was having my team work cooperatively with Sonny's. We were to meet outside the designated area near the Porta Vesuvio and then proceed deeper into the ancient town to work out next steps. Her people were to guard the facility against interference as well as to provide whatever grunt work would be necessary once Livia's villa was located. We were assured that we would be sheltered behind the buildings and high walls, meaning that all of our efforts inside Pompeii were secure. I didn't believe any of that but I was committed to going forward.

"I don't like this," Peaches whispered as we officially met the six worker bees Sonny had brought, including men with shovels and axes.

"Neither do I," I responded, "but let's just get through it."

Sonny was as cheerful as if we were two families co-planning an outing. "Where do you think we should start?" she asked, shining her flashlight down upon a reproduction of an ancient map of Pompeii circa AD 60. She seemed excited yet distracted. "Hey, Luca, you stay with me. The others fan out with

Phoebe's crew," she added in Italian. Luca seemed bent on charming Nicolina, who stood regarding him skeptically, but he tore himself away and returned to Sonny's side.

"I have no idea where to start," I said, gazing down at the map, keeping one eye on my team. I desperately needed everybody to get along and avoid any fits of temper the evening might provoke. Seraphina looked to be spoiling for a fight and, for once, Peaches would probably take her side. "Where did you get this map?"

"It was in my father's collection, now in my collection. I told you I have many original resources." Tonight Sonny was dressed in black stretch leggings and a black hoodie blending in with the evening's noir color scheme. Every strand of her blond hair had been tucked under a kind of black skull cap yet her makeup appeared to be applied as if she was attending a party.

"You see how all the villas are marked." She tapped the photocopy with one long nail. "Only they do not tell you who owned what or lived where except for a few cases where I have written in the modern names for them—Villa of Mysteries, Casa di Marco Lucrezio. This is typical because in those days everyone knew where everyone lived."

"In that case, it's probably best if I just walk and see if I can feel anything," I said.

She looked at me. "Is that how it works?"

"Sometimes."

"Only sometimes?"

"Only sometimes." I studied the map. "We know a villa wouldn't likely be on the Street of Tombs, or at the gladiator barracks, or the theater, but what are these big unlabeled rectangles here and here on the—" I shone my phone light onto the map "—Via Slabiana?"

"Possibly villas yet to be fully excavated. It could be any one of those."

"Then I'll start there."

"I will follow you."

"So will I," Peaches said, stepping forward.

Sonny looked way up at Peaches, taking in the warrior stance, the grim expression. She turned to me. "You have your own gladiator?"

"Her real gladiator is in captivity, thanks to you," said Peaches between her teeth.

Sonny returned her gaze to Peaches. "I consider Evan to be more my guest than my captive. Now he eats well, much better than when Halloran held him. It is not necessary for you to come with us. Phoebe is well-protected."

"By whom—you, the one who kidnapped her?"

"I did not kidnap her. I asked her for lunch and we talked."

"I'm coming. You don't know what's necessary to protect Phoebe. I do," Peaches said. She stood with her hands on hips glaring at Sonny as if she were a rabid dog.

Sonny just kept gazing up. "And your name is?"

"Peaches and she's my bodyguard as well as an engineer with a keen interest in ancient architecture. She comes, too," I said.

"Fine." Sonny threw up her hands and marched down the street. "Coming?" she called to us over her shoulder.

Peaches bounded up to her in two long strides and pointed to her heels. "You walk back there. Phoebe goes first, unless you say that you're now the new superpower of lost things, in which case you don't need to coerce us, after all."

"Okay, okay," the woman laughed. "I walk behind. Where do you walk?"

"Behind you to make sure nobody tries anything funny." She shot a quick look over to the line of people studying us from the middle of the ancient street—our team on one side, Sonny's on the other. "Then, if Phoebe senses something, I'll call my people, who will call your people and then they can all bring along the heavy equipment."

"All right, all right. Look, I am walking behind Phoebe, see?" Sonny rolled her eyes as she passed me. Seconds later, Peaches was striding behind her and we all took off down the cobbled street.

Being in an ancient partially reconstructed city after dark was a strange sensation, especially once we'd turned the corner and the modern city lights were shielded from view. There were still spotlights and uplighting at regular intervals, which led me to believe that there were occasional special event nights or that the guards patrolled the full property under normal circumstances.

The lights made it challenging to imagine the streets after dark in ancient times, though I mentally swapped the electricity for braziers and torches, which helped. There might be parties and dinners held at the villas of the wealthy while the common folk plied the bars or worked the streets. Pompeii had been a vacation town and was likely active well into the wee hours of the morning, much like today.

As soon as I strode those streets, I expected something to stir within me but instead my brain was fixed on more pedestrian matters—the soft slap of Sonny's and Peaches's shoes on the cobbles, the whispered voices of the team echoing down the lanes, the faraway sound of a honking horn.

What would Flora have been thinking on the night that Vesuvius erupted?

It happened in the evening but no one knows exactly at what time. The reports vary.

Flora, a trusted retired Vestal Virgin tasked with a critical mission which she may have even considered in some way sacred, lived here hoping to fulfill her task. I turned a corner and continued walking. *Flora, speak to me.*

"Getting anything yet?" Sonny asked.

"No," I said crossly, "and I won't either if you interrupt me."

"Okay, okay. I keep quiet."

But that made no difference. I was distracted and the only sounds that penetrated my mind were footsteps and modern noises. Flora, if that's who I had sensed the day before, remained locked in time.

And then Sonny's phone rang.

"Well, damn!" Peaches cried. "Couldn't you have put that thing on mute?"

"No, I could not!" snapped Sonny. "I am running a delicate operation here and must stay in contact with my team."

"You could still mute the ringtone!"

But Sonny wasn't listening. With her phone pressed to her ear, she turned her back and stepped onto the nearest curb where she spoke in rapid Italian.

I caught Peaches's eye and shook my head. "This isn't going to work," I whispered.

"You're telling me. Joining forces with Sonofabitchi Baldi was the worst possible idea."

"That's not what I meant," I remarked.

"I know what you meant. Ditto for what you meant." She added air dittos for effect.

Before we had a chance to comment further, Sonny had returned. "We have a problem. Noel has been released from prison in Rome."

"Hell," I said.

"Do not worry. I will take care of him. Now let's get back to finding Flora before he figures out where we've gone."

I shook my head. "That's not happening, not tonight, anyway. Tonight's efforts are over. We try again tomorrow and this time we do it my way."

14

"Now what?" Peaches asked when we had returned to the hotel. She hadn't stopped pacing since we had arrived. Seraphina just sat glowering at me, arms crossed, as if I was solely responsible for our mess. And maybe she was right.

"We go to bed and try again tomorrow night," I said. "I'm too weary and distracted to timewalk tonight. The same measures put in place to protect me also disturb my concentration so we've got to come up with a better plan. And this time, no one comes into Pompeii with me. I go in alone, as in solo. Everybody stays outside the gates until I signal you."

"I meant now what about Noel, but since you're on the topic, you seriously want to go into a deserted site by yourself with him on the loose?" Peaches demanded, swinging around. "Are you nuts?"

"Sonny assures me that she can take care of Noel, that she knows his patterns better than anybody." I shrugged. "Anyway, what choice do we have? Without Interpol taking this seriously, our hands are tied. Why aren't they taking this seriously?" I turned to Rupert.

"They are seeking Evan, of that much I am certain, but otherwise they refuse to provide details now that I am officially no longer in their employ." Rupert looked exhausted. Worry was taking its toll.

"Anyway, tomorrow night I've got to get into Pompeii and timewalk with Flora if I'm ever going to find Livia's cache and free Evan. We've just run out of time."

"What if she can't locate him, what if one of Noel's minions is in contact with one of Sonny's—a mole in ewe's clothing?" Peaches demanded. She was fixed on those sheep analogies, for some reason. "Don't look at me like that, Phoeb. I still have no intention of letting you go back a few centuries without me by your side. You almost blacked out when you sensed this Flora, if it even was Flora, the other day. Imagine if that had happened while you were away from us?"

"But I can't concentrate if you're around," I told her. "You know that. I don't even know why that Pompeii thing even happened the way it did. It never has before when I'm not actually standing in an ancient site. Anyway, I need to regain that intensity somehow. Going in alone is the best chance I have. I can't risk not having it work this time," I protested. "It must. The stakes are getting too high. If Sonny knows Noel's habits, then Noel must know hers, too. I figure it will take at least a couple of days for him to piece together where we've gone. We still have time."

"Perhaps this is how it must be," Nicolina said wearily. "We will keep the perimeters well-guarded and Phoebe will have her phone with her at all times."

I had considered putting it on Do Not Disturb, something I chose not to mention.

"That's not enough," growled Peaches.

"This Baldi woman doesn't seem too happy about the plan, either," Nicolina added.

"Nor me," said Seraphina, stabbing her chest with her thumb. I was convinced that the woman's fierce expression had solidified into a permanent scowl.

Rupert cleared his throat. "It is, indeed, a great concern that Noel is once again roaming free with the local constabulary clearly unaware of what a scourge has been let loose upon the world. While Evan was on the case, that cretinous cutthroat would never dare go about his despicable acts openly under his assumed alias—"

"The key," I interrupted gently, "is to ensure that the cretinous cutthroat does not find out that we are targeting Pompeii before we locate the cache and free Evan. Noel also has a team of henchmen on his side, remember, though Sonny seems reluctant to tell me just how many Baldinos remained loyal to Noel."

"Perhaps because her numbers are significantly lower than his," Nicolina suggested.

My thinking exactly.

"And yet Sonny did say that many centurions—I can hardly bear to use that term—remain loyal to the Baldi family, and once they learned that Noel had killed Alessandro Baldi, they were incensed." I shrugged. "I guess that's good news of a sort."

Rupert stood and sighed. "In any event, let us go to bed and sleep deeply and well in preparation of tomorrow night's continued strenuous adventures."

Which we did, though I tossed and turned, my nerves frayed by anxiety so what sleep I got was limited despite my exhaustion.

⚜

THE NEXT DAY WAS SPENT IN FURIOUS RESEARCH. THIS TIME, I VOWED TO memorize the ancient map of Pompeii to avoid having to check my phone and risk disturbing my mental state while walking those ancient streets. Even Zann's virtual tour of ancient Pompeii couldn't dissuade me.

Sonny texted me every couple of hours with something like a progress report on her efforts to track Noel. Clearly there was a definite lack of progress on that end. Though she had appeared confident that she could easily nab him the night before, it seemed as though the chill light of day had cast a different light. Still, it seemed she didn't fear him so much as found him an annoyance.

Meanwhile, Seraphina, Peaches, and Nicolina worked on identifying all the properties held by the Baldi family in hopes of locating a possible location where Sonny might be holding Evan. Presumably all those properties belonged to Sonny now.

The process turned out to be more arduous than expected. The late Alessandro Baldi alone held nearly fifteen properties spread all across Europe and the Mediterranean while Sonny held close to twelve in her own name that we could identify, including one hotel. Both siblings held villas in Naples, plus smaller houses on Lake Como, and Florence, for a start.

"It's boggling," Zann muttered, looking up from her laptop. "How rich did those bastards get? Who says crime doesn't pay? I'm trying to identify which ones have been recently occupied but, like, it's not clear at all."

"I am doubtful that this line of inquiry will garner any fruit, any more than my efforts to trace Noel's whereabouts," Rupert remarked. "I regret to remind you that my previous contacts have simply disappeared."

Both he and Peaches had been plying themselves with various teas in an effort to find one that provided stimulus without fraying the nerves. One preferred oolong, the other herbal. Somehow the tea question provided them some distraction. For me, it was a distraction I didn't need.

I stared gloomily down at my tablet screen, mentally following one ancient street after another, barely paying attention. Part of me was fixed on Evan, imaging his face when I saw him last, thinking of how much he'd object to what I was about to do. He had always said that if ever he was captured, to never ever give in to the kidnappers' demands. That might be MI6's policy but it sure as hell wasn't mine.

When finally the appointed hour rolled around that evening, we all felt more prepared than we had been the night before. My team delivered my instructions to me: I was not to let go of my phone for so much as a second; I was to report to them regularly—that's me doing the reporting not one of them posting questions, comments, or sound clips—every twenty minutes; Peaches would enter the gates with me but would not approach or even keep me in her sights. Her presence was a security measure only. If I needed her, I'd signal and she'd bolt to my side.

Or that was the theory.

We arrived at the meeting place to find Sonny hunched over her phone. Seconds later, she turned to me. "We cannot pick up Noel's trail. I have put more men on the Naples airport, sent others to watch all possible avenues that he may have taken, but don't worry, we will capture him."

"All roads?" Peaches demanded. "There must be hundreds. Don't all roads lead to and from Rome?"

Sonny turned to me with a scowl. "Very humorous, this gladiator of yours. Keep her away from me or I lose my temper. I was about to say that not picking up on the bastard's trail may be a good thing because it means he has not yet made his way to Pompeii."

"I'll take that as a positive," I remarked, adjusting my black-on-black leather shadow ensemble. I'd take anything positive I could get.

"I have contributed to the guard retirement fund yet again this night. Phoebe, you must find Livia's gold. This may be our last chance." Sonny stood glaring at me.

"Don't push her. That won't help," Peaches snarled. I sent her a warning look.

We were standing on the far end of Pompeii. On the other side of the fence stood the ancient stadium with the surrounding scrubby hills providing maximum privacy. Sonny had brought a smaller team of only four men this time, presumably because the others were off searching for Noel. Remembering Nicolina's remark, I wondered how many people this Baldi sibling actually commanded.

"I'm going in alone without distractions following on my heels. The moment I sense something, I'll message you. Where are the Pompeii guards?" I said.

"On the other side smoking cigarettes and counting their cash. Make sure you find the jewels tonight, Phoebe," Lady Baldi ordered.

"I'll intend to try," I said.

"Try is not enough," she said.

"What, do you think she's some history-on-demand channel?" Peaches sniped. "She can't just push the Play button."

Sonny looked ready to erupt.

"Come on, Peach. Let's get going." I had to get her away from Sonny. Luckily, the rest of my team was spreading out around the ancient town's perimeters based on the theory that at least one of them would likely be only a shout away. The Baldinos, on the other hand, were posted at the main access points looking for interlopers and police patrols.

One of her men stood by the employees-only gate: Sonny's sometimes boyfriend, Luca. He smiled and held the gate open for us, always the gentleman. "Have a good night, ladies," he said in English.

"Call me a lady again and I'll knock your teeth out," Peaches murmured as we strode past.

I texted Rupert as we went: *Going in now.*

He was manning operation central back at the hotel while tuned in to the rest of the team. Seraphina had fixed five cameras at different points around the Pompeian gates which streamed into Rupert's laptop. This was based on our policy never to trust anybody else's security system when we can use our own.

Rupert: *All quiet on all fronts*, came the response.

Me: *Good. I'll contact you in about twenty minutes.*

Behind us, the wire gate clicked shut. One more message popped on my screen. It was from Max: *Just heard from Noel in Rome. Heading there now.*

"No," I whispered and texted a response: *Please stay where you are. Your presence will only complicate things!*

Why would Noel contact his father after all these years if not to use him against me? Damn. I didn't have time to deal with that now.

"Well, that's it," Peaches muttered, not hearing me. She was gazing at Nicolina standing on the other side of the fence. "Sealed in time."

"Don't say that," I whispered, putting the phone away. I'd call Max later. "Given what happened in this town in AD 79, I don't want to be sealed anywhere."

"Gotcha. Do you really need the lights off, too?"

I had requested that all electrical lights be extinguished five minutes after I entered, not the most comforting idea but something I believed necessary. "Yes, we need the lights off. I should be well into the midst of the buildings before they flick the switch. I'd better get going."

"Phoebe," she whispered as I was just about to turn the first corner. "I could stay way back, not utter a word. You wouldn't even know I was there. Let me watch your back."

"No," I insisted. "Stay there, Peaches. This is the only way I know to up my chances of having a timewalk event. It has to happen tonight."

I heard her mutter, *"Shit,"* as I strode away.

Moments later I was strolling down the cobbled streets thinking of Flora coming to live in this town with the sole purpose of carrying on the protection of a stash of priceless jewels, Cleopatra's jewels, while raising the next would-be empress.

Flora, in fact all of Vesta's priestesses, must have been committed to Livia's plan across the generations. Otherwise, why keep the jewels hidden, why not sell them or trade them for favors or whatever a Roman empress and mother of an emperor might do, or a retired Vestal Virgin, for that matter?

Livia had plotted her own succession plan. She believed that a man ruled better with a strong woman at his side, an adviser, a trusted partner. Maybe the emperor's power could not transfer to a woman openly but Livia planned to pass the magic diadem to another wife, one who would work her powers of persuasion behind the scenes. With the help of Vesta's priestesses, she planned to have this girl schooled in the art of behind-the-throne power plays. It was a brilliant if tenuous succession plan. The only thing fueling the conviction that it could happen was the belief in Cleopatra's magic diadem.

I was just turning a corner onto another main thoroughfare when the lights went out. I froze, trying to adjust my eyes to the sudden darkness. Damn, maybe that wasn't such a good idea, after all. Above all else, I would not use my phone light until I knew where the cache lay. Artificial light would only spoil my concentration.

I squeezed my eyes shut and reopened them. Overhead the sky shone luminous like a sheet of deep blue enamel accented by a sprinkling of silver stars. A single burnished orb of a moon glowed off to the right. Tonight I needed that luminescence, the spotlight of the ancients.

Though the moon was waning, it still shone a strong clear light. Breathing deeply, I stilled my mind while fingering my Pythia key. I had to forget about modern technology and use the guiding light of the ancients. Standing perfectly still, I breathed steadily, filling my lungs with air. At first, it was still my rational brain that dominated.

Cleopatra's diadem was the key offering made to Livia, the Egyptian queen claiming that it would bind any man to its wearer's will. Certainly, Cleopatra appeared to have bound men to her will with Marc Antony, and Caesar, and perhaps it could be argued that Livia had, too, with a husband for whom she could not bear heirs. No wonder Livia believed the magic.

She must have considered the diadem to be a kind of love potion with benefits. What if the empress believed that this magic diadem secured her continued marriage to Augustus and that the object must be passed to another woman to help her rise to power, too? Such an anointed woman would have no trouble claiming the attentions of a powerful man. Could it really be that strong a belief to drive all these women forward?

Yes.

A current of something that felt very like electricity zipped down my spine. It was true, it was all true!

My phone pinged in my pocket. Annoyed, I pulled it out to read the message from Rupert: *You have exceeded your twenty-minute check-in time. It is now twenty-five minutes since you entered Pompeii. Please send me a status report.*

Me: *I'll be fine, Rupert. Please let me work in peace. I'm putting my phone into airplane mode but I'll leave the perimeter alert engaged. Exchanging messages every twenty minutes is no better than having a crowd in tow. I'll contact you as soon as I get some answers.*

He wouldn't like that but what choice did I have? Already the glimmer of insight had fractured. Now I had to start all over again.

I hesitated briefly. Had Evan said that the perimeter alert only functioned when Do Not Disturb was activated or when it was in airplane mode? I couldn't remember. I mean, I'd never had to use the feature in combination with another before. Engaging Do Not Disturb took several steps and I only had time for one. I flicked on airplane mode and shoved it into my pocket.

Back to the beginning. One step after the other, I continued on my way but those tremors of connection had simply vanished. *Damn. Damn. Damn!*

Focus, Phoebe.

My mind plucked away at the original thread. Even if I now understood something of the power of Livia's hidden cache and Flora's conviction to guard its ultimate benefactor, I was no closer to understanding the where. The empress, her husband now gone and her son ruling from a villa in Capri, must have purchased this place in Pompeii secretly. Tiberius had been so incensed with his mother that he reportedly undid all the measures regarding women owning property when he came to power. If not for the sanctity of the Vestal Virgins, the villa would have passed to other hands long ago. But who was this treasured girl?

I turned another corner and entered a wider road, as in a dual chariot way. Augustus was a known womanizer, though not on the scale of Julius Caesar. Apparently, he had bedded the wives of his publican friends and highborn supporters. Maybe there had been a pregnancy along the way. Would one of those children have been marked by Livia as a powerful contender for a woman behind the throne?

No, I reasoned. Those children had parents and presumably any wise husband under the Emperor Augustus's rule must have felt obligated to turn the other cheek, much as Livia had with her husband's infidelities. Augustus demanded unblemished morals from his wife but not from himself—the eternal double standard.

I sighed. What other female contenders might have existed? Augustus had a daughter, Julia, from his first marriage and he forced Livia's son, Tiberius, to divorce his existing wife to marry Julia to strengthen Tiberius's succession rights. All accounts say that Tiberius had been happily married at the time, that he did not want to divorce a beloved wife and be saddled with the head-strong and rebellious Julia. Tiberius also was not particularly interested in being emperor. That was more his mother's idea than his.

So where did that leave me? Nowhere. If it was true that Livia entrusted Cleopatra's diadem to the Vestals to hold for another woman, that still didn't tell me where the hiding spot was located. Yes, it was somewhere in Pompeii, but even had Pompeii still been intact and me living in that same era, it would be challenging to find. Now that it was buried under six feet of pumice and ash, where would I even begin to look? I had seen Flora inside her hiding spot but had no idea where that place was located. I needed to follow in her foot-steps, I needed to—

Something like a skirmish sounded from far over the ancient streets. I paused, listening. What was happening? Footsteps, someone shouting. *Shit!*

I reached for my phone at the same time that someone knocked me to the right and another grabbed me around the arms while still another gagged me. I saw black-clad figures as silent as the dead. My phone dropped from my hands without switching into protection mode. A bag was pulled down over my head.

Gagged and bagged, I was thrown over somebody's shoulder.

❧ 15 ❧

It was almost predictable yet it was a testament to my desperation that I had proceeded, anyway. Bouncing along at a rapid pace, all I could think of was how badly I had misjudged my phone's capacity. Evan hadn't yet perfected all the features to work together in sync, only some. I couldn't keep those details straight because I rarely used them together. And I never read his copious instructions, anyway.

Peaches would kill me. Yes, I had just been kidnapped and that's where my mind went. Actually, thinking of other things was my personal anti-panic mode.

After several silent minutes, I felt as though we were descending downward, me being jostled at every step. Finally, we leveled off and I was lowered surprisingly gently onto a floor, my back against a wall.

The hood was pulled off and I sat staring into a deep-red frescoed room lit by portable spotlights propped on the floor. Oh, my God! I was in the Villa of Mysteries! It was one of the most fully restored and recognizable of all Pompeian villas: incredible painted interior walls vibrant with mythological scenes and that "Pompeian red" background. Vaulted ceilings overhead with only one exterior door and scenes of a sexual nature made me think this must have been a bedroom.

I pulled my gaze away from the surrounding art to find my three captors standing by as if waiting for somebody. Of course, I knew which somebody they were expecting and seconds later the bastard appeared. Honestly, part of me knew I would encounter him that night, one way or the other. It was a bit like expecting to catch a virus at some point no matter how hard one tries to avoid the inevitable.

"You bitch!" Noel burst into the room with the energy of a newly released caged animal. "How could you betray me like that? Damn you, always conniving and scheming behind my back! We had a deal!" He was standing over me, expression murderous, shaking his finger as if I was a naughty child.

In my gagged state, I could hardly launch a proper defense, but me betraying him, seriously? Besides, he sounded like a walking stereotype of the deluded male. If it ever came up in conversation, I might suggest he dredge up a few original lines.

He whipped off my gag and crouched in front of me now, stroking my cheek as if calming a beloved pet. "Why, why do you always have to behave this way, Phoebe?" he whispered softly. "Why can't I just trust you for once? We had a deal, but instead you screwed me over by joining forces with that Baldi bitch. What did she promise you, tell me!" He gave me a shake.

I wet my lips, searching desperately for an answer that might penetrate this man's twisted thinking. "I, ah...you weren't around. The police captured you so how was I to know that you were even still in the picture?" I wouldn't mention Evan in case it set him off. "She offered me half of the cache." That at least was true.

He leapt to his feet and started pacing back and forth while his henchmen watched. "Of course the bitch did, but I would have given you so much more, don't you get that? You could have shared everything if you'd stayed by my side, become my wife, my partner, my empress, but no, you're too damn fickle for that."

I couldn't counter his thinking without playing into his distorted brain. "But you didn't offer me anything," I protested, sounding convincingly wounded even to myself. "You just threatened and threatened. That's all you do these days. When did we get like this? It used to be different in the old days."

"In the old days?" He swung toward me. "Back when you sold me out to the feds?"

No, back when you lied your way into my trust and had me do your dirty work. Then I sold you to the feds and not a minute too soon. "I didn't sell you out, you got careless. How did you even know I was here?"

He laughed and threw up his hands, the light bouncing off the red walls casting a devilish glow over his sharp features. "How? How? I'll tell you how."

He snapped his fingers at one of the minions, every one of them short and muscular like human pit bulls.

One scrambled over with a laptop in hand, which Noel proceeded to flip open onto a live screen. It took a few seconds to get what I was seeing: Rupert's worried face as he spoke into a phone on one hand while frantically working the keyboard on the other.

"God, no," I whispered.

"Shocked, I see. So Sonny failed to mention that when I captured Evan, I captured his laptop, too. In fact, Boy Toy was working on the thing when we jumped him in Sicily. Oh, yes, he put up a valiant fight, no doubt about it, but no amount of brawn can match a stun gun. Brought him to his knees instantly. All we had to do was truss him up like a side of pork and take him for a bit of a ride while I commandeered the laptop."

"Shit!" I muttered.

"Yeah, big bag of doggy-doo type shit. After my tech guys figured out how to deactivate the tracker, I could just sit back and tap into your network and watch the whole show like on prime-time TV. Once I got released from jail, I caught up on the action, including every nasty thing you said about me behind my back. But I knew about Pompeii before that. The Baldi bitch had letters she told me about long ago."

Hell, he knew all about our plan, practically our every thought. I almost didn't want to ask: "And where is my team now?"

He took back the laptop long enough to tap the keyboard. Then I was watching a clip of a woman looking a lot like me with her face covered by a sack being pushed into a car by a band of masked men.

"Chasing them all the way back to Rome," he said, thumbing at the screen. "They think I've kidnapped you out of Pompeii so we'll lead them on a wild-goose chase to keep them occupied while we finish up here. And we will finish up here tonight, Phoebe. Oh, and Peach, well, we ambushed her and I had her punished for all those names she called me. Anyway, we have work to do so let's get to it."

By then I was trembling so much I doubted I'd ever be able to stand let alone invoke another century. "Is she badly hurt?" I whispered.

"Who cares?"

"I do."

He wrenched me to my feet. "Forget about her. So, we'll just keep your hands bound so you don't try anything. Now stop talking to me and start communicating to your ghosts or whatever the hell you do. And don't scream or I'll have to gag that pretty little mouth of yours again."

He pushed me out of the room into the atrium. "But your art sniffer dog here doesn't work like that!" I protested.

"Shall I throw her a bone?"

"Where are the guards?"

"Forget about them, too. They are off planning their vacation homes for all I know. Sonny overpaid the scum. I would have just shot them and saved myself the trouble. That crew won't be returning to work anytime soon." Outside the villa, he pulled me to a halt. "Which way, right or left?"

"I don't know," I whispered, gazing up at the stars.

"Oh, come on, babe, don't try that crap with me. I'm a patient man only up to a point. Tell the truth for once. You must have had some insight before we interrupted you. Where's Flora?"

Hell, he must know about the Vestal Virgins, too. "It was just starting, but every time my phone interrupted me I lost the thread. Honest to the gods, Noel: my events don't work on demand. I need time to pull the threads together, time to encourage the past to communicate."

He pulled me back against him and spoke softly into my ear. "Time, babe, really? You know who doesn't have time for your games right now?"

I squeezed my eyes shut, wondering if I could back kick him where it hurt, but there were three others just waiting for me to make a move. Couldn't risk it and end up gagged again or worse.

"Take a look at who doesn't have much time," he said.

My eyes flew open onto the laptop screen that one of the pit bulls now held before my face. Rupert was sitting gagged and bound, perspiration beading his brow. I struggled against the restraints. "Noel, no! He's not as strong as he used to be. He's got health issues. Leave him alone!"

"Find Cleopatra's jewels and I'll let him go." He turned me around to face him. "I will release him, Phoebe. That's the truth. I don't care about the old man, one way or the other. He's a has-been. Get me what I want."

"But I can't, not like this!" Panic hit me now. "I'm telling the truth, Noel, my gift has never worked that way. Surely you've learned that much about me by now?"

He hesitated, searching my face. "Well, that's just too damn bad." He said something to one of the other minions that I didn't catch but which sounded a bit like *On to plan B*. Suddenly, I was facing front again, being steered along through the villa garden and out onto the road.

"Where are you taking me?" I asked.

"For a little stroll," he said. "If you can't arrive at the loot's hiding place, then we'll give you a little help."

Did he really think that an escorted stroll around the streets of Pompeii would somehow loosen time in my head? But at least he was off the idea of hurting Rupert, which brought some comfort.

We marched down the deserted streets, Pompeii seeming even emptier and more silent than ever before. I had no idea what time it was, but by the moon's position, I guessed maybe close to two a.m.

I worried about Peaches, fearing that she was badly hurt and that my action was the cause; I worried about Evan and Rupert, and hell, I worried about just about everyone. So much angst crowded my heart at that moment I thought I might throw up. There was no way that I was going to experience a timewalk in that state. I was so closely fused to the present that nothing could get through.

We passed my phone lying in the street. Of course it wouldn't communicate my location. Airplane mode muted all signals. I should have used Do Not Disturb. Why hadn't I remembered that? *Because you're human*, Peaches's voice rang in my head. Yes, Peach, I hope you still feel that way when you see how badly I botched this up.

"Nice move, babe," Noel remarked as he urged me along.

He knew that I'd flicked on that feature. With Evan's laptop, he knew everything, everything! I stumbled but Noel was quick to catch me.

When I was shoved into the amphitheater minutes later, I realized that my captors had something very specific in mind and that I was the only one who didn't know the details.

"Do you want me to sing now?" The joke came out with as much bitterness as I felt.

"Not sing exactly but certainly perform. The amphitheater is a good place for you to begin your—what did you call it again, timewalk?—to begin your timewalk. Here, have a seat, babe."

He pushed me down on one of the stone benches where I sat, my heart pounding in my ears, planning my getaway. I looked over at the four men. One had a little crossbody satchel and kept his back to me, fiddling with something. Maybe if I leapt off the bench and knocked him down, kicked out at the others and bolted...then Noel would kill Rupert. Shit!

Before I had formed my next thought, the bag guy swung around. Now I could see clearly the hypodermic needle glinting in the moonlight.

16

They were going to drug me! That realization evoked such a twist of panic in my gut that I jumped up and screamed, "No!"

One of them slapped a hand over my mouth while the bag guy approached me with the needle glimmering in his hand.

"Just a little mind-altering drug to act as an incentive to knock that clever brain of yours into gear, babe," Noel said, stepping forward. To one of the pit bulls, he added: "I'll hold her arms, you grab her legs. Ricco, make it quick."

Suddenly Noel was behind me tugging my jacket down over one shoulder while the other pinned my legs. I bucked and struggled in an effort to avoid the inevitable while Noel held me tight from behind. "Keep struggling, babe. It makes me so hot," he whispered.

The prick in my arm was over in an instant but Noel kept on holding me. "It won't be too bad, Phoebe. You might even enjoy it." His voice had taken on the seductiveness of a lover. "Just relax and savor the ride. Not everybody gets to go back in time on a night of such historical significance."

Time slipped by. I have no idea whether he held me for minutes or seconds. None of that mattered. What mattered was the intensity of the stars overhead and that blazing hot moon. I was vaguely aware of the man nuzzling my neck but had no idea how I got from there to standing in the middle of the amphitheater gazing upward. Nothing made sense, not the four shadow men following me everywhere or the strange-colored sky.

"Flora," someone said.

I turned at the sound of my name but the voice had no substance, only shadow. Like smoke, the smoke that seared the air. And the screams, those I could hear all over the town. Something was wrong, something was very, very wrong! I began to run.

Why was I even out this time of night? I never left the sanctity of the villa after dark unless in the company of my slaves or visiting Vestals, but all around me were screaming strangers running for safety, but from what? Then I remembered. I was still searching for that wayward girl.

From the sky. That burning moon wasn't the moon at all but Vesuvius boiling over. Had we angered the gods?

Jupiter, forgive us! Have we grown too complacent in our wealth and excess? Hermes, lend me your wings so that I may reach my Juno in time! But then I thought that praying to the goddess Juno would be best so I could ask that she intercede on behalf of her namesake.

"Mistress," a man cried from somewhere to my right, "do not return home. Leave your belongings. Come with us to the shore. We must escape by boat!"

"No!" I cried. "I must find Juno!"

So I ran and ran down the streets, the people storming in the opposite direction in a surge of panic like the stampede of terrified animals I had seen that day in Rome. Now the air was so filled with choking smoke I could barely breathe.

Into my villa I ran, shocked to see the door hanging open and the servants nowhere in sight. Not even Lucius? Scrambling past the frescoes, I cried with all my breath: "Juno!" I called, but my voice had hardly any strength so choked was it by ash. I prayed by the grace of Diana that Juno had gone, gone to safety with one of her nurses, maybe with Aurelia. I hoped with Aurelia! Aurelia would keep her safe. My prayers had been answered. Praise the gods!

The villa had been abandoned. Now all I had to do was retrieve the jewels and keep them safe until we were reunited, Juno and I. That fixed in my head, I ran through the atrium, past the tablinum, toward the garden, stumbling so many times, somebody lifting me up so many times. Why did I trip so often? What was wrong with me?

The smoke was scorching my eyes and nose, the air filling with a thick, black dust. *Oh, Diana, please protect me!*

I reached the culīna, everything scattered where the servants had left it— bread cooling on the table, a pot of milk for Juno's night drink. I ran to the back of the room to the oven, panic throbbing in my heart. A sudden horrible thought struck: what if I could not reach the jewels? Because now it was as if a black wall had risen before me. Screaming, I beat the barrier with my fists.

"Flora," a shadow man asked in a language I could not quite understand. "How can we help? Tell me where it is." He repeated the question in a very bad form of my tongue.

Maybe these shades had been sent by the gods to help me and could not speak my tongue? Yes, that must be it. The goddess protects. "I must reach inside the bottom of the oven floor, lift the center brick. Deep beneath the sand, I have hidden Juno's treasure, but I cannot reach it." I stared into the blackness ahead. Why couldn't I reach it? "Because the oven is too hot." Yes, that must be it. Nothing else made sense and everything seemed to burn about me.

And then I saw her, the shape of the girl crouching in a corner. "Juno!" I cried, running toward her. "Where are Aurelia and Lucius?"

"They are gone!" she sobbed, scrambling to take my hand. "You told me to hide here in times of danger so I came. I am so happy to see you! I am sorry to have run off but I was so frightened."

We embraced. "Oh, dear child. I had hoped you would run away from Pompeii, not remain." I squeezed her tight.

By now the shadows were speaking among themselves—strange accents, stranger language, Latin but not. This must be the language of the gods. Overwhelmed, I fell to my knees in supplication, one hand still gripping Juno's. "I do not have a sacrifice to offer but I promise I will make one as soon as I am free. Please help keep my girl safe!"

"We will help," said one shadow man, touching my shoulder.

Another was making fire burn from a strange stick he held. The gods had such miraculous tools! Smoke and searing sounds followed while I crouched against a wall, staring ahead at my mistress's garden, now nothing but pale images behind a wall of darkness. I could not breathe! Fire burned my chest! I tried to shield my girl but suddenly my arms were empty!

The gods were digging, pulling out chunks of thick black stone. *Chink. Chink. Chink.* Such strange sounds all around—an odd screeching noise far up in the air.

"Hurry!" whispered the shadow who had touched my shoulder. "That's the cops!"

Cops, what were cops? But I was beyond understanding, my breath screaming to escape my chest yet grateful to have the gods help me to find the treasure and protect the girl. Mistress Livia through my priestess sisters were wise to put her trust in me. Had I not sworn to protect Juno and bring her the diadem upon her marriage? Was I not fulfilling my vow?

And then it was as though the smoke both cleared and overwhelmed me all at once. I couldn't breathe, I couldn't stand! No! The last thing I remember was gazing into a painted room where a garden grew on the walls forevermore, hoping that soon I would meet my sisters again on the other side and that we would dance together in the gardens of the gods.

❦ 17 ❦

I was strangely comfortable, not anxious, just restful, lying on a narrow bed in small a room—table, shelves, bathroom in one corner, another door opposite that. I appeared to be wearing baggy white jogging pants with an oversized hoodie—not my style at all. I thought I could see my own clothes folded on the chair across from me but it was hard to focus in the blue dark. The curtains were drawn and the floor rocked. Rocked...

Slowly, I sat up, realizing that I had no idea where I was or how I got there. Every inch of me felt raw and sore. A quick peek down my shirt proved that I had been cut and bruised all over. Had I fallen? And why were my wrists and ankles bound? The last thing I remembered was the sight of a needle glinting coldly in the moonlight... *Shit!*

Bounding off the bed, I ran to the door, stumbled, righted myself, and hopped over to try the latch—locked! Damn. I knew I was on a boat and that boat must belong to Noel. I was studying the electronic mechanism locking my ankles and wrists when the door swung open. Backing up, I fell against the bed.

Noel entered with another man at his heels, both of them dressed in white linen pants and shirts, looking like a pair of Mediterranean playboys. "How's my golden girl?" He grinned at me.

"What the hell happened?" I demanded. "Did you drug me, you shit-faced, assholean, double-decker pisshead?"

"Whoa!" He threw up his hands, that smug grin never wavering. "Nix the inventive adjectives, babe, because I'm so happy with you right now that I'm prepared to forgive every injury you've ever inflicted on me. You're a bloody miracle. You led us right to it! I had no idea that your skills had developed to this extent."

"I led you right to what?"

"Cleopatra's jewels, of course. My little sniffer bitch sniffed like a dream, slipped right into Flora's head and led us to where her villa had once stood, babbling in tongues the whole time."

"Not in tongues," said the other man in Italian. "Actually, the street form of parochial Latin. Ricardo filmed the whole thing."

"Right you are." Noel shut the door behind them. "This is Dr. Justinian Bianchi. He's a historian and my expert on all things Roman."

"Where Flora hid the cache was brilliant," Bianchi told me. A middle-aged man with a louche bearing and a lean aesthetic build, he seemed the very opposite of Noel's usual minions.

I swallowed. The last thing I could afford to do was piss off my captors. I needed to bury my rage and play along with Noel's fantasy world long enough to escape. I just hoped to hell I had the stomach for the game. "Are you saying that I channeled myself into Flora?"

"You did, babe." Noel stood there, still smiling.

I could remember nothing. Had I really walked in the shoes of a woman who had died in ancient Pompeii? That was not something I'd ever craved. My idea of timewalking was to view the past as through a porthole, not to channel another life. "Did Flora die horribly?"

"Don't you recall?" Bianchi asked, peering at me as though I were a specimen in a petri dish.

"No...I...must have suppressed everything," I said. That was true but I knew it would all be waiting for me to remember sooner or later.

"Interesting," Bianchi mused, tapping his chin.

"Didn't catch much of that, either." Noel shrugged. "I was more interested in retrieving the stash but I recall you writhing on the ground in the end, if that's what you mean, kept calling out for the goddess Juno. Got cut up pretty bad. You shrugged off your jacket, yelling that it was too hot. Ricco gave you another injection in case you suffered physical trauma from the ordeal. You can watch the clip later if you want. We have it recorded."

I tried to smile. "Wouldn't that be like watching myself die?"

"Only you were already dead for almost two thousand years, babe, and it wasn't even you. Don't forget that little reality." He appeared so pleased, clearly congratulating himself for my job well done.

"I think I have the reality pretty clear. You drugged me, right?" I was trying to keep my tone matter of fact instead of accusatory.

"I did, just a small serving of hallucinogens to nudge along your time-walking skills," Noel said. "And it worked, damn but it worked."

"Amazingly," agreed Bianchi. "I have heard that what you did last night was incredible to witness and I hope someday to watch you timewalk in person."

Sure. I'll sell tickets. "Where did Flora hide the cache?" I whispered. Why didn't I recall that much?

"In the floor of a forno, or bake oven," Bianchi replied. "A brilliant solution, really, as the tufa used at the time had amazing heat-resistant properties and the layer of sand beneath the bricks furthered the protective surface. The Romans were brilliant engineers. When the pumice and ash covered the oven, the contents remained as pristine as the day they were buried."

I turned to Noel. "May I see them?"

"Of course, babe, but first we need to have a little chat." He turned to Bianchi, who immediately exited without another word.

In seconds, Noel was sitting on the edge of the bed beside me, arms around my shoulders. "Babe, you are something else, I'm telling you—a real miracle woman, *my* miracle woman. Now's your chance to join forces with me. I promise, together we'll have it all. Forget what that Baldi bitch offered you because I'll give you more. Together we can have all the ancient treasures imaginable and, with your gifts, all the personal stories that accompany them, too. Think about it: you're a source of living provenance."

I licked my lips. It was all I could do not to shrug his arms off me. It was as if his touch seared my skin. "What did you have in mind?"

"You and me together again. When I undressed you and tended your cuts and scrapes last night, it brought back all those tender moments we spent together. Remember how good we were?"

Oh, my God! He undressed me, touched me while I was out cold! My skin crawled. I wanted to retch so badly at that moment that I could hardly get the words out. "There's this little matter of my friends—you beat one up, held another at gunpoint, and kidnapped another. How am I supposed to take that, Noel?" I had to remain calm, rational.

"With a dose of pragmatism, my love. Think of what you did to me and let's call us even. Of course, I did what was necessary this time because we have become adversaries over the years, haven't we? But it needn't be like that going forward. We could be on the same team again, the winning team, as it happens. Return to my arms, my heart, my bed. We were so great together. All you have to do is be my partner."

Partner? He was nuts. I squeezed my eyes shut. *Play into the game.* "May I think about it?"

He got to his feet suddenly. "Sure, think about it but don't take too long or try any tricks or Rupert dies."

I knew it was only a matter of time before the threats began anew. "Is he safe?"

"Perfectly. Busy napping, at the moment, I believe."

"And Peaches?"

He smiled. "I may have overstated the battering we gave her since it seems she got up and walked away."

A part of me sagged with relief. And Evan must still be safe with Sonny, or so I desperately hoped. Hope is what I clung to. "Now may I see Cleopatra's hoard?"

He fired a few terse words into his phone and, just as quick, two henchmen arrived to pick me up, literally. They pulled a hood over my head, and carried me into another part of the ship.

I counted the number of steps my captors took—up one flight, down another, fifty-four altogether. After the last flight of stairs, we walked another twenty paces. I heard a door open.

Noel kept saying: "Careful, careful. She's our golden girl" every few seconds. Minutes later I was gently lowered into a chair, handcuffed to the armrest, and the hood removed. I blinked into a large cabin where the sunlight beaming through the same curtains as mine that turned everything that deep aquatic blue.

Noel switched on an overhead light. We were now alone.

"My stateroom," he said, sweeping his hands toward one mirrored wall, the low glass tables, a king-sized bed on the dais, and the seating area that faced a marble surround in which burned an electric fire.

"Cozy," I said, not voicing the real adjectives that sprang to mind.

As he strode toward the fire unit, I sponged up the room's details, taking in everything—the clothes draped across the chair back, the books on the side table, the laptop propped open on a desk against the mirrored wall. My attention swerved back to the laptop reflected in the mirrored wall. That was Evan's laptop. I'd recognize his steel-encased version anywhere, and there it sat open and engaged for Noel's spying pleasure.

When Noel looked over his shoulder at me, I had my gaze fixed on him. "You've made yourself very comfortable here, I see. Is this where you've been living while on the run?"

"I'm not on the run, babe. I have a new identity: Peter Buck, British investment broker earning my millions by computer and phone. The Italians love me, and if they ever stop being so obliging, I'll just switch to another identity. Can I help it if I look like a certain art thief who disappeared months ago?"

He turned around again and flicked a switch above the marble hearth surround. A painting slid down to reveal a wall safe. While he entered the combination, his back shielding his actions, I scanned the desk again.

The mirrored wall reflected other objects including a cell phone—a cell phone! Was that Evan's? Rupert had told me that Evan's devices had gone dark but did not enter self-destruct mode. Evan, that brilliant man, had been experimenting with another phone prototype. Was that it? Did it play dead when in enemy hands but remain in a kind of stasis?

When Noel turned toward me, he was holding a green nylon backpack, which he carried to a table near my seat.

"The original container had perished," he told me. "Looks like it might have been leather. This is pretty unassuming considering what it contains but will do nicely."

I wet my lips. I was about to see Cleopatra's hoard and briefly feared that the sight of the precious items might plunge me back into Flora's head. I wasn't ready to go anywhere near there yet. Maybe I never would.

Noel lifted out the contents, great fistfuls of gold and pearls, inlaid bracelets and lapis lazuli neckpieces, a glowing pile glimmering in the overhead light. He lowered the bundle onto the table. I stared, too overwhelmed to speak. Those pearls were huge, many irregularly shaped but no less astounding.

"Something else, isn't it? Cleopatra's jewels. God, I've never seen anything so gorgeous. Look at them, babe, look at those pearls. Feast your eyes on what you found for me."

He lifted up a strand of huge natural creamy orbs as big as marbles, still luminescent after all these centuries. "These were strung onto a thin gold chain or the strand would never have emerged intact. Imagine the queen wrapping them around and around her naked body in gleaming coils while Caesar or Marc Antony watched, roping them between her legs, across her breasts, everywhere. I can picture these against your white creamy skin, Phoebe, you wearing them for me. You could be my queen."

I swallowed, pushing back the revulsion.

He stepped toward me, holding out a gleaming fistful. "Want to try them on?"

"I'm a bit indisposed at the moment." I rattled the cuffs against the chair arm.

"Yeah, you are, aren't you? We'll have to save this pleasure for another time." He stroked my cheek with the pearls before turning away.

Something clattered to the table, then onto the floor. He quickly retrieved a pearl the size of a marble. "There's more loose in the bag, mammoth things. Whatever they used to string them with disintegrated. Cleopatra treasured pearls almost more than gold since Egypt commandeered so much precious metals in its territories but pearls were harder to locate."

I knew that and I guessed he knew I knew it but obviously the man needed to hear himself talk.

"Look at this bracelet, a masterpiece of inlay for which the Egyptians were famous." He held up an arm cuff, brilliantly executed in lapis, turquoise, and carnelian embedded in the gold.

I stared at the glistening hoard, trying to distinguish a diadem amid all that luster. Noel just kept talking.

"In no way does this cache fully represent the splendor of Egypt. Bianchi says that by then Augustus had already claimed most of the queen's riches for himself and that this hoard would have been considered plain by comparison."

"Cleopatra sent the empress her plainest offerings because the queen did her research," I said. "She knew that Livia wasn't into conspicuous displays. She chose her gifts carefully with her most toned-down offerings." Why was I even talking to him? And where the hell was that diadem?

"Oh, I see what you're looking for," Noel said suddenly.

My gaze shot to his.

"You're looking for the magic diadem that supposedly binds men to a woman's will." He chuckled softly and began gently moving aside the strands of pearls to pluck out something at the bottom of the pile. "Is this what your heart desires?"

Out came a filigreed gold band inset with turquoise, lapis, and carnelian, a simple but no less stunning gold diadem. Holding it aloft, he said: "There's a Roman contemporary sculpture reportedly of Cleopatra wearing this exact diadem. She must have worn it during her procession through Rome at Caesar's side—not too showy, actually rather subdued, still enough to denote her a queen, in this case the queen of men."

He leaned over, lifted my matted curls, and placed it on my head, tucking the two golden comb extensions behind my ears so that the jeweled band rested securely over my brow. I couldn't quite suppress my shiver. I didn't want to wear that thing.

"A bit covered by that unruly mop of yours but it suits you, Phoebe," he said, stepping back. "After all, you already command my heart. Let's see if you can experience Cleopatra's life behind those big blue eyes of yours."

Hell, I was terrified of sensing Cleopatra across the centuries and equally sickened by the thought of ruling anyone, though I could make an exception if I could rule this bastard.

"Do you feel anything?" he whispered.

Revulsion? "'Fraid not," I whispered. "Should I push a button?"

He let loose his machine gun laugh. That rat-a-tat-tat howl of mirth I once used to find so charming and now so...not. "Too bad. Maybe it takes time but nothing a little hallucinogenic encouragement won't fix."

He pulled up a chair to sit in front of me. Leaning forward, he stroked my cheek again. "Think about it, Phoebe baby. You could timewalk through the streets of ancient Alexandria, visit the greatest library of the world, read all those ancient scrolls now lost to humanity. Together maybe we could find the mausoleum of Antony and Cleopatra. Imagine the treasure that must be buried with them?"

"You mean while I'm drugged?"

"Maybe. If we're careful and ensure that you have at least a few weeks between episodes, I'm certain we can keep addiction at bay, but would it really be so bad living part-time in the ancient past with me to come home to? We were so good once. Consider the possibilities, babe."

"I am," I said, surprised to find my voice so steady. "But let's talk about our deal first. You said that if I found Cleopatra's jewels that you'd release Evan. Since he's not in your custody now, I want to swap Rupert for him. Let him go, then we'll talk."

He threw back his head and fired laughter toward the ceiling, leaving me thinking how I hated even his Adam's apple. "Oh, shit, that's a good one! God, you're a wily little bitch, aren't you? Is he all you think about? As if you're in a bargaining position." He slapped his thighs in mirth before leaning forward again, close enough for his eyes to be directly in line with mine, for his breath to mingle with mine. "Only, you're not in a position to bargain, are you, babe?"

"If you want me to preform for you, maybe I am."

He shook his head. "You're going to perform for me one way or the other. You forgot a few details such as that you didn't locate the cache for me willing-ly," he whispered. "And you struck another deal with Sonny and screwed me over instead. You have to prove yourself first. No deals with me, Phoeb, not yet. And if you try anything, the old man is dead." He pulled the trigger on an imaginary pistol.

"You sure know how to woo a girl back."

That provoked another grin. "Get into my bed and I'll woo you back soon enough."

I squeezed my eyes shut. I wasn't doing a great job of playing along and I knew it. In truth, there was only so far I was willing to go.

"But it doesn't have to be that way, as I said." His tone was softening. "We could strike a new deal: if you work with me collaboratively like the good old days, I'll let Rupert go."

"Am I supposed to trust you?"

"Don't have much choice, do you?"

"What about the others?" I asked.

"They'll never be part of the arrangement. The agency has to go, all of them: the snotty countess, her rabid little assistant, Peaches—especially Peaches—all must be eliminated, and, of course, your boy toy up on the mountain."

"The mountain?"

He thumbed toward the front of the cabin. "Well, cliff, then, where we're heading now—Capri."

I just stared at him.

A slow grin crossed his face. "Oh, I forgot to mention that I know where Sonny is keeping him. Fool bitch thinks she's the only one who can pick up critical information during a roll in the proverbial hay. She's got Boy Toy tucked away in the basement of her chic boutique hotel on Capri, a place she once whispered to me would make the perfect place to hide somebody. Boy Toy's at her clifftop oasis and we're going there now to get rid of him once and for all. With a little luck, I can have you watch in my viewing room on my big screen. Would you like that, a ringside seat?"

The door flew open and another man in white popped his head in and said something in Italian that sounded like: "Boss, we have trouble."

"What now, Carlo?" Noel demanded, half turning.

The man's gaze landed on the hoard before swerving to the laptop. "Best see for yourself, sir."

Noel jumped up and dashed over to Evan's laptop. "What the hell?" In seconds, he was back at the table scooping the treasure into a bag and stuffing it into the safe. As the steel door clanged shut, instantly the Mediterranean seascape scene slid back into place over the fireplace.

Turning, bossman tossed a key fob to Carlo. "Take her back to her room and join me on the bridge pronto." He then bolted from the room.

That left Carlo and me alone in the cabin. A thickset man, he had quick dark eyes that seemed to take in everything in an instant.

"You there last night?" I began in my best conversational Italian. "Was it as incredible as Noel says?"

Carlo said nothing. Instead, he stood studying the cuff that secured my wrist to the chair arm. I saw his dilemma immediately: once he released the cuff from the armrest, one wrist would be free to move and so would I, though in a reduced state since I was still hobbled. He must have thought I might disarm him before he could snap on the other cuff. Moving me from place to place was obviously a two-man job.

"I'm flattered but don't worry, I'm not going anywhere. I can't very well swim with my legs bound, can I?" I asked.

He snorted, released one wrist from the chair arm, and clamped it to the other at once. I just carried on looking at him, the picture of compliancy, not making a move. "If I'm going to be working with Noel and your organization, I hope we at least get along." I got to my feet. "Shall we go?"

"You need hood!" he snapped, pushing me back to sitting.

"It's behind you on the chair." I indicated with my cuffed hands.

He located the hood and, while he went to fetch it, I spied something miraculous on the cabin floor—a single glistening pearl beneath a table on the far side. I blinked to ensure myself that I didn't just wish it there but it was real. Careless, Noel. "There, on the floor under the table. Noel dropped one of Cleopatra's million-dollar pearls!"

Carlo swung around, seeing it, too, and immediately fell to his hands and knees scrambling to retrieve the orb. *Throw a dog a bone...*

At that moment, I lunged to my feet. In three hops, I reached the table. Leaning forward, I slid the phone down into my stretchy pants with my cuffed hands while simultaneously throwing my full weight crashing into the table, taking everything with me to the floor.

There I lay, trying to push the phone deeper into my joggers before Carlo reached me.

When he flipped me onto my back, I looked him straight in the eyes. "Explain to Noel that this is an unfortunate accident and I won't say a word about the pearl."

❧ 18 ❧

Whatever emergency occupied Noel kept him away from me far longer than I expected. Carlo was clearly in a panic. He had taken his attention off the captive for one second and disaster had struck but so had a huge bonus. He was swearing all the time he was steering me hopping down the hall back to my cabin.

"Look," I told him in what I hoped would be comprehensible Italian. "I tripped, okay? It happens. My feet are bound, see? So, I got up, the boat rolled, and I went flying."

"Right into the laptop?" he hissed. His English was better than I thought.

"Yeah, sure. The desk is right in front of the bathroom door. Accidents happen, okay? You still have the pearl, right? Must be worth millions."

"Shut your mouth!" he ordered.

All around me I sensed tension and alarm. The crew were dashing past, men were shouting to one another. "Are we under attack?" I asked hopefully. The boat was definitely in motion.

Soon enough, I was shoved into my cabin. The door clicked locked behind me and, in seconds, I had the hood pushed off my head and stood panting in the center of the floor. The first thing I did was seek out the cameras. I knew Noel would want to keep an eye on me and yet no surveillance devices were immediately visible. They were there, I just couldn't see them.

Damn. I lurched across the rocking floor to the bathroom, flicked off the light with my cuffed wrists, and slid down to sit on the floor. Partially shielded by the bathroom door, I felt down my jogger legs for the phone. How long would it take for Noel to know that it was missing? He'd be fixed on the laptop at first, which I hoped to God was shattered, but knowing Evan, it was probably made out of some indestructible something or other. At least I knew that the screen had cracked.

The phone had slipped all the way down to my ankles in those baggy man-sized joggers and had caught above the cuffs. I needed to activate it somehow, if that was even possible. Each of the agency phones was designed to recognize another member but this was a prototype. Who knew if it would respond to my voice?

"Phone, activate. It's Phoebe!" I whispered toward my ankle while trying to lift the cuff elastic long enough to allow the phone to drop out. No response. Maybe it wouldn't recognize my whisper and I needed to use my full voice instead? "Phoebe here!"

I heard the cabin door click open just as the phone toppled to the floor.

"Where the hell is she?" Noel's voice.

"Here!" I had grasped the phone between my palms long enough to shove it under the bathmat.

"In the bathroom," a man said in Italian.

"Here, I said!" I cried.

The door flew open and the light flicked on as I fell backward onto the floor on top of the phone.

"What the hell?" Noel barked. He stood with two minions behind him.

"Look at me!" I wailed. "I'm hobbled on a moving boat and can't even go to the bathroom without falling all over the place. How do you think that makes me feel, Noel? Is this how you treat your wannabe queen?"

And then I cried, damn convincingly, I thought, cried so hard that something kicked in and soon the waterworks turned on for real.

The two men were helping me to my feet to stand before Noel, his reddened face boiling with anger mixed with something else—shock, realization—oh, my God, did I see *guilt*?

"Is this how you plan to treat me, Noel? Look at me!" I'd play that for all I was worth. Shaking my cuffed wrists in front of him, I cried: "I can't move, I can't walk. I fell into your table and cut myself but what do you expect? I was trying to get to your bathroom." And then I just collapsed into heaving sobs. Damn nice touch, that.

Whatever Noel planned to do with me seemed to have corroded under my tearful accusations. Was there something in men's nature that was triggered by the sight of a woman's tears, even someone as damaged as Noel?

"Shit! I don't have time for this." He jerked his head at the guy beside him and tossed him the cuff fob. "Pasquale, unlock her wrists and let her go to the loo. Wait outside the bathroom door and don't leave her for a minute, understand? Once she's out, cuff her again, get it? And keep your gun on her. Don't fall for any of her tricks."

"Yes, boss."

And to me he added with a finger stabbing the air between us: "If I find that you deliberately tried to sabotage that laptop, Rupert is dead!" And with that he left the room, taking the other minion with him.

I lifted my wrists to Pasquale, who pressed the fob and released the cuffs, his other hand keeping the gun pointed on me. He indicated the bathroom with a jerk of his head.

Turning, I hopped in, leaving the door ajar. One look in the mirror nearly froze me in shock. Yes, I looked a total mess, scratched up from the night before, bandages plastered here and there from my dramatic writhing, eyes puffy, hair in a snarl of matted curls, but what startled me more was the glimpse of the diadem gleaming beneath my mop. That almost made me laugh. Nobody had even noticed that I was wearing my crown?

Flipping up the toilet seat, I shimmied down the joggers while leaning far enough forward to fetch the phone from under the bathmat. From that angle, Pasquale could see nothing and appeared to be averting his head in some gentlemanly fashion.

The phone was pulsing red. With my heart pounding in my ears, I pressed my palm against the screen and instantly a photo of Evan and I in Paris embracing in the midst of a selfie duo came into view. That almost made me cry all over again but I pulled myself together and texted a quick all-points bulletin to the team:

On a boat with Noel, who has Cleopatra's gold. Heading to Capri where Sonny's keeping Evan. He plans to kill him, her, and all of you, too. Bring reinforcements. Meet me there.

It was now 9:15 p.m. I checked the map and found that we were zipping across the Bay of Naples, presumably heading toward Capri in a somewhat circuitous route—probably diversionary. Were we being chased?

I then tapped the "OA" map. The Offices Abroad app connected us to all the central agency devices online and indicated where they were located. Rupert's laptop showed that his computer was still in Pompeii but presently offline and that his phone had self-destructed two hours ago.

I added a quick text: *Find Rupert! Noel has him!*

That left me only time enough to run the bug scanner, which I didn't expect to work given that I was not standing in the actual room. But I was wrong. This device was so sensitive that it pinpointed the cameras and listening devices present in my cabin, all five of them, including the one located over the shower head—the shower head, seriously?—all without me having to get to my feet. It then offered me a Deactivate Yes/No option. I chose No since I needed whoever monitored the system to think everything was on an even keel.

Before I slid the phone into the jogger pocket, I scanned the icons on Evan's screen. There were so many of them, most unfamiliar to me, but I instantly identified those I needed.

I finished my business and flushed the toilet, ending my session by splashing cold water on my face and tucking the diadem deep into my hoodie's spacious front pocket. Let the games begin. Noel was heading for Capri and so was I. Seconds later, I had hopped back into the cabin, looking suitably miserable. "Can't I at least have my legs free?"

Pasquale quickly clicked the cuffs back on. "No."

"Do I get to eat?" I asked. Sounding whiny was my technique du jour.

"There," he said, pointing to a table beside a padded bench that I hadn't paid much attention to until then. It appeared that I had been offered a ciabatta sandwich and a salad with water and wine. No cutlery. Soon, Pasquale had left me alone.

For the rest of the evening I went about eating and resting as the picture of the subdued captive. Of course, Noel knew me better than that but apparently he was too preoccupied to pay me much attention. Meanwhile, I was plotting. I realized that if I lay on my side on the bunk, face to the wall, I could slide out the phone and shield it with my body. Now that I knew exactly where the cameras were located, it was easy to find the blind spots.

The first message from Nicolina came in while the phone was still in my pocket: *Phoebe, we have been seeking you everywhere. Now we have fixed your signal. Are you on Evan's phone?*

I summarized the recent events.

A message from Peaches popped onto the screen as I typed my response to Nicolina: *Shit, woman, see what happens when you leave my sight for a millisecond? Are you okay?"*

Smiling, I replied. *Battered but fine. What about you?"*

Peaches: *Battered but fine, too.*

Me: *I timewalked in Flora's shoes and led Noel right to Cleopatra's gold. Much more to say but not now. Any idea how many men Sonny commands?*

Peaches: *Not enough.*

Nicolina's response came in: *On our way to Capri now. About two hours away by car. Will try to get helicopter. Sonny has not been in contact since Pompeii. Police almost rounded up her team. Has Noel harmed you?*

Me: *Not yet. He wants me to be his sniffer bitch so I'm in my kennel. Status report on Rupert, please.*

Nicolina: *Rupert has disappeared. We returned to the hotel but he had gone, his phone left behind.*

Me: *Noel has him! He says Sonny has Evan holed up in her boutique hotel on Capri somewhere and we're heading there now. He plans to eradicate the agency starting with Evan. Got to go.*

I wanted to check the map for everyone's position but the door was opening.

"McCabe?"

With the phone safely tucked back down into my hoodie, I rolled over.

"Yes?'" I murmured. "Who is it?"

"Carlo. Noel says to check on you. What do you need?"

I sat up, taking in the massive bruise that darkened the man's cheek. "I see you got into trouble for my accident." I shrugged. "Too bad. Accidents happen, right?"

His eyes were pleading. If Noel knew that he had pocketed that pearl, Carlo would be a dead man. And he had pocketed the pearl, no doubt about that.

"I need to get out of these baggy clothes and back into my own and a shower would be much appreciated," I told him.

Carlo spoke into his phone and then shook his head. "Boss very busy. Will not grant shower until he can...supervise." The man's face was deliberately blank but I sensed so many emotions firing there, the least of which was hate for Noel.

"Supervise? Why not now?" I asked.

"Too busy."

"The approaching-Capri kind of busy?"

"We reach Capri now, yes, and wait for later."

So Noel was planning an attack but needed to wait until everyone was sleeping before making a move. What did that bastard have in mind?

"So," I said softly, "in the meantime, he asks what I need but won't give me what I want: a shower, a change of clothes. Why are you even here, Carlo?"

He hesitated, eyes searching my face. I knew exactly why he was there.

"Weren't those jewels amazing?" I said. "Cleopatra's gift to Livia, no less. A single pearl must be worth a fortune, don't you think, like as in millions?"

Carlo's swarthy complexion turned ashen.

"So I need a shower and a change of clothes. Maybe you can convince your boss to at least let me get comfy."

"I will ask."

Our eyes met. We had just agreed to something, though I had no idea what. As he turned to open the door, a key fob dropped to the floor. "Maybe nobody watches," he said, stirring his index finger around the room. In seconds, the door had shut and he was gone.

Maybe nobody watches? Was that a hint or should I take that verbatim? It didn't matter. I took a chance. Hopping up to the door, I scooped up the fob and pressed the button to release my ankle shackles and another to release my wrists.

Moments later, I had flicked off the light, snatched up my clothes, and quickly changed into my undies, top and leggings, though pulling what was left of my leggings up over my scratched and cut legs hurt like hell. The last thing I did was to shove the diadem down deep into my stretch leggings just over my stomach where you could only see the outline under my shirt if you looked hard enough. Though I love the idea of going into battle crowned like a queen, I couldn't risk losing the precious object.

Outfitted in my black midnight-prowling ensemble with a strange semicircular shape outlined over my abdomen and my superphone in hand, I was ready to get down to work.

❧ 19 ❧

The phone had the locked door opened instantly. Outside, along the deserted corridor, I was surprised to see the number of cabins stretching toward the stairs—at least thirty doors. If the ship accommodated that many men, I was in trouble. Hell, I was in trouble, anyway. The phone was showing forty-five percent power and I was going to need much more than that for what I had planned.

Keeping close to the wall, I crept toward the stairs, flicking off lights whenever I encountered a switch. Most yachts this size managed their lights on a central control box somewhere near the engine room. Briefly, I had thought about cutting the boat's power but decided against it since it would alert the crew to trouble too soon.

By the engine's vibrations, I figured we were on a steady cruise. I checked our location on the map app—we had left the Bay of Naples and were now on the other side of Capri on the Tyrrhenian Sea following the island's rocky coastline. We had to be zipping closer to Sonny's hotel by the minute because now the boat was cutting back speed. Would they drop anchor somewhere offshore or head for port?

Though I had never been to Capri, I knew it to be a steep and gorgeous island notorious as a leisure destination by the rich and famous. I only wish I was feeling the holiday mood as I inched toward the stairs. All I cared about just then was finding out what was going on.

Voices sent me ducking into an empty cabin. Men were running down the hall. I heard a door open directly across from me, sounds of entering and exiting, before the footsteps pounded back up the stairs.

After everything had stilled, I stepped out to study the door across the hall. When I had it opened, I was staring into a long narrow room where guns of all descriptions hung on racks on either side. Boxes labeled DANGER in multiple languages sat stacked on the floor along with cartons of ammunition. A bloody arsenal! How could I have forgotten that Noel had inherited an arms-dealing empire and that antiquities was just one of his money-grasping enterprises?

I backed out of the room faced with the ugly realization that the bastard could be planning to blow up that hotel and take every poor occupant with it. Shit! I broke into a sweat and posted a hasty text about needing reinforcements ASAP. The authorities had to take this seriously. In the meantime, I might be the only one in the position to stop this atrocity or at least slow it down.

Slipping up the stairs, I found myself in a carpeted area that I suspected housed the lounge and dining rooms. Nobody was in sight. Seconds later, I had exited from a side door onto the deck where I scuttled along the edge to the left, keeping low and silent, heading for the prow. The master cabin had to be up front, away from the engine noises, affording the best possible views.

Crouching down with my back to the wall, the open water visible over a low railing beside me, I waited for my heart to settle. A row of curtained windows ran behind my back, light pushing a cool blue hue into the night. Several curtains had been pulled back, making it tricky to spring past them without being seen.

On my hands and knees, I inched along until I could peer into one window while keeping hidden. Inside of what looked to be a large dining area, men—I counted thirty-six within my line of vision—stood listening to someone directing operations up front. I couldn't see who was talking or how many more men might be present but I had no doubt that some kind of maneuver was being discussed with Noel at the epicenter. Most chilling was the sight of assault rifles leaning against the opposite wall, boxes of explosives stacked nearby. Shit! I pulled back.

My best bet was to scramble toward the other side, which I did by retracing my steps. There, while crouching by a lifeboat station, I caught my first glimpse of a sentry prowling the deck toward the stern. There had to be more.

Keeping low, I scuttled around to the starboard side where it was blissfully dark. All the curtains here were solidly closed with no lights on in the cabins beyond, but what startled me was the island of Capri rearing on my right-hand side. I just stared, struck by the lights pricking like stars on the cliffs far overhead. We were that close? There appeared to be little in the way of development on the shoreline. Everything was way up on the promontories. How did Noel plan on getting up there?

Pulling out my phone, I pinched open the map. There it was, the little road jackknifing down the cliff to the hotel's dock and private beach nestled in their own secluded cove, my location showing as a red pulsing dot offshore. The hotel, Sonno Degli Dei or Sleep of the Gods, was marked by a little flag at the top of the cliff. Okay, then. The hotel was exclusive, claiming its own little piece of paradise. Seclusion in this case equaled vulnerability.

The map of the surrounding area showed more cliffside hotels scattered all over the island but this one was noted by its apparent privacy. The only way to reach it was by boat or by a twisting road reminiscent of the Amalfi Coast. If reinforcements were going to arrive in time, they'd better come by helicopter.

I set the phone on stun and crawled up to the prow of the ship. If I guessed right, there'd be a set of stairs leading from the deck directly to the master cabin. I reached it undetected and then softly padded down the steps just as one of the two sentries standing at the foot of the stairs saw me and reached for his phone. My taser brought him to his knees in seconds. Guy number two met the same fate, his eyes terrified by the sight of the phone.

Leaving the two apparently dozing on the floor, I stepped over them and deactivated the locked cabin door. I doubted the safe would open that easily and I'd never used one of Evan's apps on a complex safe combination lock before.

Dashing into the cabin and straight to the hearth, I flicked the switch, sending the painting sliding away and revealing the safe. I knew nothing about safes. I stared at the apps crowding onto Evan's phone screen, most of which were probably still in the development stage. Crap. He had ten grouped under "Openers" alone. They could be bottle openers for all I knew.

I tapped the key icon I'd just used, a basic all-purpose open-upperer. Nothing happened. I tried another, this one designated by a metal box-like icon that looked promising. Immediately red text flashed on the screen: *Line screen up with safe.*

I felt the engine idling down beneath my feet as I held the phone up before the safe. Meanwhile, what appeared before my eyes was like an X-ray of the safe's mechanism, all intersecting steel and what looked to me like mechanical whirligigs. None of it made sense to me. Was I supposed to manipulate something based on that? No way. I didn't have the time or the knowledge. The boys in white would be manning their stations soon enough and I needed to get to shore first.

My gaze scanned the other opener apps. None of them looked either promising or familiar. I took a chance and pressed the icon shaped like a fire-cracker, or at least I thought that's what I was looking at. Another diagram popped onto the screen, this one offering me nothing but a big red button. Big red buttons I could handle. I tapped it. The screen began flashing STAND BACK. *Shit!*

I was about three yards away when the explosion knocked me off my feet and had just pushed myself off the floor and was scrambling back through the billowing smoke when the fire alarm went off.

Terrifying seconds followed when I thought I had blown up Cleopatra's jewels as I clawed through the bits of contorted steel looking for the nylon backpack as the sprinkler system engaged. Finding the bag safely enclosed in a steel box inside the safe walls was like a gift from the goddesses. All I could do was snatch it and run.

And run I did. It was a mad dash up the stairs with men rushing toward me from all directions amid smoke, sprinklers, and screeching alarms. Fire alarms on a ship laden with explosives caused massive panic. It took a moment before I realized the men were more interested in reaching the life rafts than finding me—except for one.

A guy was running straight for me. "McCabe—jump quick!"

I turned and leapt over a deck hatch and ducked behind a rope housing while ripping off my leather jacket and shrugging on the backpack. He was right behind me. It was Carlo wearing a life jacket.

"What's going on?" I asked as I kicked off my sneakers.

"Arsenal will explode in forty-five seconds. Jump!"

I shoved the phone deep into the pocket of my Lycra leggings hoping that Evan had the waterproofing perfected. Then in full view of the bridge, I jumped.

The cold water shocked my senses as I sank. I knew that carrying a few pounds of gold on my back would weigh me down but I had no idea by how much. My head broke the surface with barely enough time to inhale before sinking again. In those flashing moments, I glimpsed men leaping off the boat, others manning lifeboats.

The next time I made it to the surface, Carlo threw the life preserver over my head. I clung to the thing, relieved that I had support for my burden. Then, with one hand on the preserver, Carlo began kicking us to shore.

Why was he doing this? He had to be after the gold.

The distance of at least fifty feet may as well have been fifty miles. Waves slapped my face and nose, every second one coming with crushing surf. Now I could see the shore approaching rapidly. It must be nearing high tide and a current was pushing us along.

"Duck now!" Carlo ordered.

I went under just as an explosion seemed to tear the sea apart. For a moment I seemed to be lost in a churning mass of dark water. The life preserver escaped me in the blast but by now my feet were hitting sand, yet it was still a struggle to remain upright.

With water blurring my vision, I spun around looking for the dock and found that we'd been washed off to the left. Down I went again, only now my head was about a foot underwater when the ship blew a second time.

❧ 20 ❧

This explosion was big enough to create a mini tidal surge that whipped the sand out from under my feet at the same time that it temporarily blocked my ears. I couldn't seem to right myself. Several moments of gasping and choking up water followed before I felt myself being lifted up from the surf by an arm. We had made the beach!

"Run!" Carlo urged.

Behind me, I saw lifeboats rowing to shore, men shouting, the ship nothing but a flaming mass blazing in the little cove.

"How did that happen?" I coughed out a lungful of water.

"I detonate," he said, urging me forward.

"You detonated the explosives?" No time to wait for an answer. All I had energy for was running for cover. Soon the beach would be crawling with men.

Carlo seemed to know where he was going. He led me through a forest of closed beach umbrellas and past rows of recliners, heading toward the cliff. I had no breath left to ask him anything but fished the phone from my pocket and gripped it tight. This guy *had* to be after the jewels.

The beach was a small white arc at the base of the cliff with nothing but rows of umbrellas, deck chairs, a closed snack bar and surf house crammed side by side against the cliff wall. One narrow road lit by occasional lamps switch-backed up the cliff toward the hotel. No stairs.

Behind us, the first lifeboat reached the shore, the men leaping over the side into the surf. Once we were spotted, they could overwhelm us in minutes.

145

Meanwhile, Carlo had ducked behind the snack shack, me on his heels. There, lined up in a row, stood six luggage buggies ready to ferry guests and baggage up the hill with the keys left in every one. We jumped into the first and the beast lurched toward the road.

Nothing more than glorified golf carts, these things were not designed to go fast or to go far, yet this one puttered uphill at a better clip than I expected. Carlo sat in the driver's seat, me beside him shivering while leaning forward still wearing the backpack. So far, he hadn't mentioned what I carried but he must have known. I kept the phone close just in case he tried anything.

But the phone remained cold in my hand. No amount of switching buttons brought it to life. I stifled a stab of fear and checked over my shoulder. We had only traveled up to the first switchback with at least three more to go. Meanwhile the road was narrow, dizzyingly steep, devoid of guardrails, and frankly terrifying. And now it was filling up with buggies puttering up behind us on the one-lane track and men jogging along behind.

"Can't you make this thing go any faster?" I demanded.

"Not Lamborghini," Carlo called with a laugh.

Why in hell was he so damned amused? Even in the half-light, I could see that he was enjoying this.

"I must have picked slowest one," he added.

"Why did you blow up the ship?" I asked.

"Sick of that bastard," was all he said. "I want to see him go down, maybe take over. I know you stole jewels."

"Not for your benefit."

He grinned. "We will see."

Was this another mutiny? But I didn't have time to ponder Noel's leadership problems just then. The diadem was digging into my belly and I worried that I might bend the pure gold. I needed to get that thing out and into the backpack without Carlo noticing before I punctured myself or worse.

I looked over my shoulder again. There was no passing lane on this road and yet one buggy was leaning on its horn while trying to squeeze past the one ahead of it. Too far away to see who was vying for the lead but I guessed it might be Noel. I tried to lean back to lessen the digging into my skin but the backpack nixed that idea.

So, what was going on back there? Why not just order the guy ahead to stop and commandeer his vehicle? Because, I thought, the guy ahead wouldn't obey orders, that's why. It was every man for himself now and they were all after a fortune of priceless jewels. Me, in other words. Boss dog had lost control.

"They're gaining on us," I said.

"Blow them up with your phone," Carlo suggested, sending a toothy grin in my direction.

"And drain the battery? I may need all the juice I can get before the day is out." If I told him the truth, he might try to grab my backpack and toss me over the edge.

While the buggy kept inching along and those behind us picked up speed, I was desperately seeking other options. If I got out and ran, how far would I get on this narrow ledge with the gold bouncing along on my back?

I shook the phone. "Activate!" I commanded. The phone remained cold.

"Not working?" Carlo shot me a worried glance.

"I have it on power preserve. In two minutes it will be back to full strength," I lied, but I desperately needed that thing now. Evan waterproofed all of our phones so what was I missing?

"Shit!" Carlo spiced it up with a few Italian variations. "We need your phone!"

Since when did he become a "we"?

I looked up. A set of headlights was heading toward us from above. "Who's that?"

"Probably Sonny Baldi or one of her men." And he let rip a suite of vicious curses. No fan of Sonny's, either, but Sonny could be my ally, or maybe not.

I stared ahead. The car was no luggage buggy but some sleek white convertible with a driver completely at ease with the jackknife turns. If he wasn't a resident at the Sonno Degli Dei, he was certainly a regular visitor.

"Blow up car with phone," Carlo ordered, "and then hit them behind us. Do it now!"

"Issuing commands already, Carlo? Stop the buggy."

He slammed on the brakes but only because the car had just arrived blocking our path. Out jumped Luca, Sonny's sometimes boyfriend, all relaxed-man-about-Capri, only with an assault rifle in hand instead of a glass of vino.

"Phoebe, get into the car," Luca ordered, aiming the rifle at Carlo.

Carlo pulled out a gun of his own and stood up, leaning over the buggy's windshield. "You back off, Luca, or I shoot her."

The *her* he was referring to was currently slipping from the buggy to the sports car, guessing that these guys would do anything to ensure that the art sniffer dog kept wagging her tail. No one would shoot me and at least one of them might even briefly believe I was doing what I was told. I pulled open my leggings front and retrieved the diadem, slightly wonky but fine otherwise.

147

With no time to place it in the backpack, I stuck it on my head under the matted curls.

No surprise, Carlo did not take a shot. Meanwhile, the first of the buggies arrived at the scene.

"Drop the gun, Luca," Noel cried. "You know damn well that I have more of my men up at the Sonno. I've infiltrated your whole organization!"

Well, damn. I slipped into the driver's seat, rammed the stick shift into reverse, and put my foot on the gas.

I'd just leave the boys to work it out among themselves while I shot up the hill backward.

❧ 21 ❧

Luca had left the key fob in the console. Nice. Still, I didn't plan on reaching my destination in reverse. My intent was just to put some distance between me and the warring boys. Surely one assault rifle against a herd of Noel's waterlogged troops would buy me enough time to get to the top? Or so I hoped.

The sight of me zooming backward must have startled the men because I heard nothing behind me at first. My gaze was fixed on the back windshield as I negotiated the first turn. I eased the car around that hairpin bend with sweat beading my forehead, knowing that one miscalculation could pitch me straight over the edge. There was enough light posted at every turn to see the road but otherwise it felt like every inch might bring me closer to death. I took it slow, at least in the beginning.

I could feel them watching, making it harder the way parallel parking with an audience spoils concentration. But I managed, and once I had the car back on the straight and narrow again, I picked up speed, which seemed to signal a commotion below. When I heard machine gun fire, I braked long enough to risk looking through the front windshield. The buggies were on the move again amid bullets peppering the pavement. Well, damn.

And they were gaining fast. Every time I slowed down to make a turn, they were making up the distance. Two more switchback turns ahead. I'd never make it. Slamming on the brakes, I eased forward, turned the steering wheel hard before reversing the car into the cliffside in a crunch of mangled steel, jammed the stick into park, and left the car straddling the road on an angle. Then I jumped out and tossed the keys over the edge.

I was halfway up the next length, my lungs burning, when I turned and tried to activate the phone again. Still dead. All I wanted was a little explosion now that the buggies had just reached the car.

I had no choice but to bolt on foot the rest of the way, the backpack weighing me down while the boys scrambled over the car and took off after me. They might not be able to drive the buggies to the top but they could sure as hell outrun me. Two more switchback lengths to go and my legs felt like lead.

Almost there but what then? If Noel's men had infiltrated the place, what defense did I have? Looking up, I could just see a figure standing backlit on the patio above. I trudged on, only slower now.

"Phoebe?" the figure called down. "Is that you?"

I stumbled to a halt. "Max?"

"Stay there! Peaches is coming down."

A headlight appeared over the edge zipping down the hill toward me. The bike reached me in seconds, Peaches's long leather-clad legs unmistakable. I climbed onto the back and gripped her waist as she whipped us back up the road.

"I'm so glad to see you!" I shouted.

"Yeah, me, too!" she cried back.

Behind us the boys were shouting and trying to blast out the back tire. We reached Max standing with a pistol in hand on the patio.

"Max, run for cover!" I cried. "And why are you even here?" I added.

"Phoebe!" Max tried to embrace me, backpack and all. "Thank God you're all right. Who are those guys?"

"Art thieves, wannabe warlords, gunrunners..." I gasped.

Meanwhile, Peaches had dismounted and was striding up to the top of the drive with her phone in hand while I shimmied into the driver's seat to brace the bike. Soon she was sending stun bolts at the first men to arrive at the top.

"How many are there?" she called back.

"Maybe thirty," I replied.

"And they're after you, as usual? Good thing we arrived when we did," Max said, watching her. "You can't hold them off against bullets!" he called as a shot ricocheted by her feet.

"Not that I'm not glad to see you but why are you here?" I asked Max again.

"Noel told me to meet him here but when I arrived the place was deserted, apparently evacuated after this big explosion in the cove. Peaches picked me up after I parked the car below while I was running up the drive. The guests were escaping downhill in their pj's."

"Max, that's Noel chasing me down there. The man's a criminal. How many times have I told you that?"

Max looked over his shoulder again. "My son's back there with that lot?"

"He's the leader of that lot, or was until they mutinied. We've got to get out of here. Peaches can't hold them off for long."

Bullets were pinging off the pavement when Peaches came bounding over to us. "Find cover fast! You and Max take the bike and I'll hold them off."

"No bloody way! If my son's back there, I've got to help him. He may need me," Max cried. "You two take the bike."

"Talk sense into him, will you?" Peaches demanded, trying to shove Max toward the bike.

"Max, you've got to hide," I said. "Noel isn't who you think he is, I'm telling you. He probably planned to use you for something by calling you here."

"Go, both of you!" Max told us. "I mean it. I'm staying."

Peaches shoved her way into the driver's seat, swearing like a storm trooper.

"Max, stop! Peaches, we can't leave him!" I even thought about jumping off the bike to stand by his side.

"Yes, we can," she called as she revved the engine. "We're here to rescue Ev and Rupe. Max just made his own choice."

And then we were zooming across the flagstones, me so conflicted I wanted to scream. "Peaches, that's my godfather!"

"Yeah, and somewhere is your lover and friend, plus members of the team's lives are at risk. How many reasons do you need to move? We got to make tough choices sometimes, Phoebe. Anyway, this one isn't yours, it's mine. Now where in this ritzy place do you think Sonny stashed Evan?"

"I don't know but Noel claims to have infiltrated here, too. He says that he knows where she hid him so we'd better find him before he does. Have you heard from Sonny?"

We had zipped down a flagstone path and lurched to a halt.

"Not a word since Pompeii. Something's up there but who knows what."

"And Rupert's still missing?"

"Far as I know."

"Noel says he has him, too. Any idea when the others might arrive?"

"They were almost to Rome when we got your message while I was still poking around Pompeii. Haven't checked the map recently. I ran into Max on the drive up. He said he heard from Noel. True?"

"Apparently."

The hotel entrance was brilliantly lit and shockingly empty. Even the automated glass doors were gaping wide, yet not a single person was in sight.

"All the guests evacuated?" I asked.

"Yeah, I passed a couple on the hill. They said there was a huge explosion in the cove and that the manager told everyone to leave."

"The manager," I mused. "Maybe that was Sonny?"

"Said it was a man. Let's hide the bike and get inside."

"That could be Luca, then. He ended up driving down toward the cove to fetch me but I didn't trust him any more than I trust any of these guys."

We ditched the bike and her helmet behind an ornamental hedge, me still thinking that maybe I should just check on Max for a second, but Peaches never gave me the chance.

"Set your phone on stun," she ordered as we slipped back up the drive into the foyer.

"Can't."

She shot me a quick look. "What do you mean you can't? Why don't you have that phone out?"

"It's not working," I said, taking in the polished marble flooring, brilliant blue chairs, and surround-view glass walls. Where in a place like this would somebody hide a person—in the basement?

"Not working? That's Evan's superphone. How can it not be working?"

"Maybe it wasn't waterproof enough. I swam to shore. Listen, I hear voices. Come on, we'd better hide."

We were crouching behind the reservation desk when she held out her hand for the phone. I dropped it into her palm, watching as she pressed a side button three times, causing a little water drop icon to appear on the screen followed by an animated pulsing squirt. Soon her palm was wet.

You never read the instructions, she mouthed as she wiped her hand on her jacket.

We heard a man enter the foyer calling in Italian: "Check every corner!"

I retrieved the phone and set the stun app to low. Back in business! Instantly, Peaches plucked the phone back again and tapped a different app. "This is power-packed, like a Mensa smartphone," she whispered. "Ev told me all about it. Better than any other new generation of agency phones. Let's see what it can do."

On her feet in a flash, she glanced at the screen briefly before zapping the five men that appeared with a sweeping arc of light. "Holy shit!" she exclaimed as they fell, rifles clattering to the floor. "Did you see that? It's like a ray gun."

"Did it kill them?" I asked.

Peaches was peering down at the phone whistling while I ran over to check one man's pulse. "Out cold," I said, "but still breathing."

"So are these Noel's dudes?" she asked, leaning over and whipping up an assault rifle to study. "Russian rifles."

"If they're dressed in wet white like these guys, then they were on that boat, that's all I know. Otherwise, Noel's crew appears to be in mutiny, including the guy who helped me escape. Every man for himself type thing."

I retrieved the phone from her hand, almost needing to tug it from her grip.

Peaches stared at me fully for the first time. "You sure are rocking the wet T-shirt look, woman, and what's that on your head?"

I felt my forehead. "Oh, forgot I was wearing it—Cleopatra's diadem."

Her eyes widened. "You're wearing Cleopatra's diadem?"

"I am, and look, men are already falling at my feet." I grinned. A little humor was needed just then, trust me. I removed the band of jeweled gold—a little bent but not too misshapen—from under my tangled mop and passed it over. "Do you mind placing it in the backpack with the fortune of pearls and jewels?"

Wonder glowed in her eyes as she took the diadem from me and zipped open my backpack. "Wish I had time to try it on. Bet it would look dynamite on me."

"Bet it would, too." I felt her tug on the zipper. "All secure?"

"Wow, look at that treasure. I think my eyes are popping."

"We'd better get going." I started striding down the corridor, leaving her to trot behind me still zipping the pouch. "That loot is why I'm suddenly so popular with this lot."

"Well, damn." She grinned, matching my stride. "I may just forgive you for all your harebrained ideas yet." Then she sobered. "But only after we find Evan and Rupert."

"Right." We were walking toward the hall leading away from the entrance. Just thinking of Evan delivered a punch of anxiety. "Do you think Evan may have packed in a few extra X-ray capabilities into this thing? It could be useful."

She caught up with me. "I remember him saying something about locating the blueprints of almost every building by using a feature that links to any related web source at lightning speed. Here, let me see." The phone left my grip yet again.

"Here it is. Look. Every hotel built anywhere has associated blueprints, most of which have been added to a digital databank somewhere. See, Ev figured out a way to link into all of them with this feature here." She tapped an icon shaped like a red house. In seconds, she had pinpointed our location on the group map. "You tap settings, click on this box, and ta-da! It goes and retrieves the info you want."

I peered over her shoulder at the diagram. "That man's amazing and I had forgotten that the Greeks first settled Capri and the Romans loved it, too."

"Yeah, and this hotel is built over a cave system. Look." She pinched open the screen. "And they now use part of it as a wine cellar."

"That must be it." We exchanged glances. "Let's go," I said.

By the diagram, it looked as though the caves were deep in the cliff with an interior set of stairs carved right into the living rock, the entry near the kitchen. Both of us kept our phones in hand with the perimeter warning alerts active, expecting to meet resistance at every turn.

We almost made it to the kitchen entrance when Evan's phone started beeping seconds before Peaches's did.

"Hold it right there," a man commanded.

We slowly turned. Two men were striding down the hall toward us from the foyer, each holding a rifle.

"Carlo and Luca," I said. "What a surprise. Are you two best buds now?"

Carlo smirked while Luca appeared his usually relaxed and debonaire self except for the bloodstains and dirt smears on his striped linen pants.

"Drop the phones, ladies, and then pass over the backpack," Luca said, ignoring my question.

Peaches turned to me. "Is he serious?"

"Drop the phones, now!" Carlo snarled.

"Wow, so manly but no can do," Peaches said. "See, as soon as I drop this baby, the intruder alert goes off and that will trigger a spray of radiation particles in all directions rendering everyone dead in seconds, except for us, of course. If you try to take it forcefully, the effects are even worse. I'm talking nuclear." None of that could be true but hopefully the boys would buy it.

Certainly Luca looked concerned but Carlo only waved his gun. "Then we shoot you and take backpack that way."

"She said that idea was even worse. Weren't you listening?" I asked.

"Disastrously worse." Peaches picked up the tale. "That will cause both phones to explode and this whole place will blow up, including you two cutie pies. Hey, didn't you used to work for Sonny?" She was gazing at Luca.

"Yes, and Carlo here worked for Noel," I said. "Looks like there are flaws in everyone's loyalty programs these days." To the men, I added: "Where's Noel?"

"Locked up in the beach shed with his daddy," Carlo told me with a smirk. "We put him there, like we'll put you if you don't do as we say. We are in charge now."

"And Sonny?" I was looking at Luca.

Luca shrugged. "Sonny is taking a rest, poor darling. Like Carlo says, I'm in charge now."

"I thought you two were a team?" Peaches asked, looking at Carlo.

"Shut up and move!" Carlo ordered.

"You just don't get it, guys." Peaches aimed her phone toward the men's feet, delivering a bolt strong enough to blast a hole in the marble floor. They leapt backward amid a spray of flying stone chips. "Drop the guns, boys, or I'll blow up your legs next."

That convinced them. In moments they had lowered their rifles and raised their hands.

"Now you move," she ordered. "You'll accompany us to the wine cellar."

The men strode ahead of us, sending wary glances over their shoulders every few seconds.

"Why the wine cellar?" Luca asked.

"That's where Sonny's hidden Evan, right?" I asked.

"Wrong," he said. "She has taken him somewhere else."

I hesitated. "Where?"

"How would I know? There is no need to go down to the wine cellar, I'm telling you."

Peaches and I exchanged glances again.

"So, why don't I believe such an honest, loyal guy like you?" I asked. "Let's just take a look, shall we?"

"You are wasting time! We should be killing off the rest of Noel's men. You have those phones," Luca continued.

"Stop talking, Luca. You're pissing me off," Peaches remarked.

We continued down the hall, past doors labeled Steam Room, Pool, Massage, through a bar, and into a long, multiroomed kitchen with Peaches periodically checking her diagram along the way. "There should be a set of stairs off to the right."

When we reached the stairway, we ordered the men to proceed in single file ahead of us, Luca first, then Carlo.

"You have jewels on your back," Carlo said so casually you'd think we were sharing a chat over coffee. "I helped save your life."

"Thanks for that," I acknowledged. "Only I wonder how long your helpfulness would have lasted once you got hold of my backpack?"

Carlo seemed to be pondering this as we descended deeper and deeper into the heart of the cliff. "I am a fair man. We had a deal," he said.

"We had an understanding. You helped me escape if I kept quiet about that pearl you pocketed. I kept up my end so we're even."

The stairs started out as wide polished marble steps complete with safety treads at first but soon narrowed to roughly hewn stone.

"You could share Cleopatra's jewels with us and then we all work together," Carlo suggested.

"Yeah, that's a likely scenario," Peaches remarked. "Keep moving, bozo."

Only by now the stairway was winding and narrowing to the point where we could no longer keep both men in our sights. When Carlo suddenly fell backward, nearly knocking me off my feet, Peaches shoved us both aside to chase the escaping Luca down the steps.

22

I kicked Carlo back from me and ordered him on his feet, the weight of the backpack nearly knocking me off balance. My phone slipped out of my hand and Carlo turned and lunged for it.

"Carlo, don't—"

But the idiot touched it, letting out such a curdling scream followed by a whimper so intense that I almost felt sorry for him.

"Don't be a baby, Carlo. You probably have first degree burns but you'll live." I snatched up the phone and pointed it toward him. "Now move it! Peaches," I called. "Are you all right down there?"

"All right," she called back.

"Turn around and keep moving," I ordered Carlo, which he did while nursing his hand as if it were a wounded kitten. "And don't try anything else or I'll push one of the superbuttons."

When we reached the bottom, Peaches was flexing her right hand while a bruised and surly-looking Luca slumped against the wall.

"What happened?" I asked.

She winced and made a fist. "I punched him, bastard made me so mad. Sometimes I just feel like using the hands-on approach. Get up, bozo."

Bozo struggled to his feet, one hand rubbing his jaw.

"Take us to the wine cellar now and no more tricks."

Luca stumbled obligingly along with Carlo sulking away behind him.

"Pathetic," Peaches said under her breath.

We were walking along a rough-hewn corridor lit by modern lamps when I heard a sound like a sigh coming someplace up ahead.

"Evan?" I called.

Our pace quickened, Peaches hurrying the boys along by zapping them with low voltage charges.

When we arrived at the source of the sigh, we were shocked to see an arched barred room that seemed to imprison racks and racks of wine along with the haggard woman staring out at us.

"Sonny?" I gasped. She looked like hell, all frizzy blond hair and smudged makeup beneath puffy eyes but her legs were stretched out on a wine crate with empty bottles stuffed with cigarette butts all around. She appeared surprisingly relaxed.

"Phoebe, you have come to rescue me? No need," she said with a shrug as she climbed to her feet. "I'm actually not locked in. I only let that idiot think I was while I kept out of the way."

"What idiot?" I asked.

"That one." She pointed to Luca. "He thought he was holding me prisoner but I always keep an extra key hidden where it counts."

"I only did it for your own safety, my love," Luca began.

Sonny waved a dismissive hand. "Don't start. I'd have you executed if I didn't think you'd end up in jail anyway."

"Where's Evan?" I demanded, not interested in a lover's quarrel.

"Not here," she said, flipping one hand around behind her. "Come, I will take you to him now."

"Sonny, don't! He's your collateral," Luca said.

Both Sonny and I ignored him.

"She does not take me seriously," the man griped. "I make suggestions and she does what she wants, always. This time I had it up to here." He pointed to his forehead. "I tried to lock her up only to teach a lesson." Then he broke into Italian directed at Sonny that sounded like some kind of ardent protestation of his devotion mixed with a plea for forgiveness.

Sonny just rolled her eyes. Soon she was strolling from the wine cellar while Peaches ushered in the two men. Sonny slapped Luca's face while exiting. "Idiot," she hissed.

Luca nursed his cheek. "My love, you know I only did this for your own good, so we could have a life together. Forgive me."

The bars clanged shut behind us and Peaches applied the lock.

Carlo gripped the bars with one hand and waved his other in the air. "I need a doctor!"

Peaches gave the men a passing glance. "Are those two for real?"

Sonny folded her arms and stood gazing back at her ex lover. "He adores me but he is so tiresome. Does anyone have a cigarette? I just smoked my last."

"We don't smoke, I keep telling you that," I said. "Now, where's Evan?"

Sonny sighed. "Follow me but I'm warning you: that was one long night."

"Ours was no picnic, either," Peaches told her.

Sonny began treading unsteadily toward the stairs in her bare feet while we followed behind, Peaches keeping her phone aimed at the woman's back.

"You don't need that," Sonny said.

"Yeah, well, I'll decide what I do or do not need."

Meanwhile, I was checking our group map. "Nicolina and Seraphina are almost here." And to Sonny: "Is Evan unharmed?"

"I see you brought the jewels," was her response.

"What does that have to do with anything?" I asked.

"Because I said I would give you Evan if you brought me the jewels."

"She has the jewels on her back!" Luca called from behind us.

Sonny shouted over her shoulder: "Don't drink all my Barolo, you bastard!" Then to me she added: "Evan is fine but resting. Noel gave him a battering even while the man was out cold—coward. Had him drugged, too. He has a druggist on his payroll now, or that is what I call him, a man good at giving injections."

"Yes, I encountered him," I told her.

"Where have you hidden Evan?" Peaches demanded, turning to face her. "Tell me before I shake your teeth out."

Sonny's gaze never left my face. "I don't talk to her, I talk to you, understand? Tell her to back down."

I shot a quick look at Peaches, who turned away in disgust.

"Evan rests upstairs in my finest room where we brought him after I rescued him," Sonny told me as we climbed the stairs. "If he could walk, he would be free to leave anytime he desires. God, I am so thirsty. I must drink some water and then coffee soon."

"You released him?" I asked as I climbed up behind her.

We reached the top of the stairs. "Do you seriously think we'll believe that?" Peaches exclaimed.

Sonny turned, her mascara-smudged gaze fixed on me. "We made the bargain, you and me, Phoebe. This does not involve your gladiator there." She thumbed toward Peaches. "I have kept my word, now you keep yours. When Noel ambushed you in Pompeii, I sent a message to my men to release Evan. I knew that Noel would figure out the wine cellar thing and try to kill your man at the first opportunity. He had infiltrators working here but I already knew which bastards were which. They have since been disposed of." She shrugged. "You might say I had them fired." She paused as if briefly considering that statement. "Well, *fired at* might more correct."

"And on that basis you released Evan?" I asked.

"Luca and I argued about this in Pompeii, had a big fight, him telling me that I was too weak to do the things necessary to run my father's organization. He wanted to kill Evan to show strength. I disagreed. Sometimes the weaker move is in fact the strongest. Ah, good. There is still water available." She had just spied a guest commode against the wall where a silver bucket sat stacked with bottled water.

"So you argued and Luca...what then, he bundled you up and dragged you here?" I was gaping at her by then. Sonny had turned to gaze down at us from two steps overhead.

"You heard him. For my own protection, he said. Have you heard anything so foolish? He had bought out one of my other men. Luca took me back here and thought he had locked me up but Evan had already been released. You see, I keep my promises. Now you keep yours."

"No bloody way!" Peaches erupted. "We don't negotiate with criminals, do we, Phoebe? Tell her."

"Criminals?" Sonny asked, eyes never leaving my face. "I do despise labels, don't you, Phoebe? We are all so much more than the labels others give us."

"There is the little matter of verification, Sonny. I have yet to see Evan. How do I know you're telling the truth?" I said.

She nodded and began to climb again. "I take you there now. Once you confirm my words, we talk again."

This whole discussion left me reeling. I had agreed to the deal, of course I had, but I was being coerced, wasn't I?

The corridor was surprisingly empty when we reached the top and followed behind Sonny—no Noel wannabes, no damp men in white running around shouting orders.

"Where did all the bad guys go?" Peaches asked.

Lights were flashing through the lobby's sweeping glass windows which looked out over the patio. Something red pulsed down in the cove beyond and there were sirens screeching from the bottom of the hill out front.

"Looks like the police have arrived," I said.

"So maybe they ran away?" Sonny plucked up a bottle of water from a guest refreshment table. She downed it in seconds. "I am so thirsty!" she exclaimed. "Too much wine. I will pay for that later, I know, but what else do I do down there? Come, we had best visit your Evan before the police tie us up with questions. This way." She was heading for an elevator.

Peaches and I followed behind her, my gladiator obviously disgruntled. "The cops are going to nail her, too," she whispered.

"No, they won't," Sonny said, catching her words. "I have done nothing illegal."

"Are you bloody kidding me? Isn't kidnapping not an offense in Italy?" Peaches demanded.

Sonny addressed me. "Did I kidnap you, Phoebe? I do not think so. If I recall, I invited you to lunch. There were no guns or force used."

"You told me that if I didn't come, Evan would die," I protested.

"And so he would have had I not intervened." Sonny caught a glimpse of herself in the floor-length mirror behind the guest console and grimaced. "Either Luca would have killed him or Noel, so that was the truth."

"And the man with the gun you showed me who would apparently shoot Evan in key places if I didn't comply?" I was incensed by now.

She shrugged. "So there, I lied. Okay, not nice but not a crime, eh? The man was nowhere near Evan. Come, let us see your man now. This way."

We followed her to an elevator, Peaches widening her eyes at me. I wasn't sure what she was trying to convey. Probably *Do you believe this?*

"One other thing, Phoebe. I rescued your Rupert, too," Sonny remarked.

Now we both gaped at her. "You rescued Rupert?"

"But of course. I knew that Noel held him hostage at your hotel but I sent my team over to free him. Maybe I briefly thought about using him as an extra bargaining chip, I admit, but then decided not to. Consider it another proof of my goodwill."

Peaches just stared at her as if unsure whether to snort or shake her molars loose as the elevator climbed three floors.

"So, if you rescued Rupert, where's he at?" I said, more than a little exasperated by that time.

The elevator door whispered open. Sonny pointed. "Is that him? I have seen pictures."

We gazed down the hall at the gentleman who appeared to be ambling in our direction. It did look like Rupert, though a very worn version dressed in a white terry hotel bathrobe. Rupert objected to hotel bathrobes in principle— too bulky at the waist.

"Oh, there you are, Phoebe and Penelope. I am very relieved to see you at last indeed. This has been a most long and arduous evening and not one I wish to repeat anytime soon. Did you hear the explosion in the cove? I could not find the management so ushered the guests out at the first opportunity but I believe the coast guard have arrived now."

I ran up to him and nearly hugged the breath out of him. "Rupert, how did you get here?"

"Why, one of Sofonisba's men released me, of course. I thought you knew?" He peered over my shoulder. "Is that the lady herself?"

"It is," Sonny said, coming up beside him and extending her hand. "Pardon my appearance, Sir Rupert, but I have just spent many hours locked up in the wine cellar, much as you have been kept hostage, though I admit that the wine helped pass the time. Terrible thing, though. I was forced to down several bottles of my best vintage. I hope you've been well cared for while I was away?"

Rupert appeared momentarily confused. "Oh, very well, thank you, um, yes. Your staff took very good care of me and my son—"

"Where is he?" I cried.

Rupert turned. "Where is who, Phoebe? Please do be specific. I—"

"Your son, Evan, where's Evan?"

"Why, down the hall to the left. Phoebe, the lad's not conscious yet, though he fades in and out. He's doing much better. The doctor expects him to make a full recovery—"

But I was hardly listening. I arrived at the door of a spacious guest room where the bed lamp illuminated a sleeping man, one whom I nearly fell upon until I realized the poor guy was truly unconscious and that a bandage bound his chest and one hand. I gripped his other. "Evan?'

He turned his head and whispered: "Phoebe..."

I could have cried had I not been too aware of an audience looking on.

"He needs to rest, Phoebe," Rupert was saying. "Noel gave him quite a battering, leaving him with a few cracked ribs and a broken finger. We won't mention the other wounds he inflicted upon him but I am quite certain the lad will heal there, too."

"Phoebe?" Evan whispered.

I placed a finger on his lips. "I'm fine, I'm fine. Don't speak. Just rest."

"Where's...Noel...?"

"Locked up." I leaned over and kissed his cheek, thinking that I would soon start sniveling or worse if I didn't pull myself together.

"Locked up where?" I heard Sonny ask behind me. Reluctantly, I pulled myself away from the patient after one more longing look to assure myself that he truly was alive and somewhat well.

Rupert took my arm and drew me out into the hall. "Yes, where have you secured that scum, Phoebe?" he asked.

"He's locked up with Max..." Oh, shit, I just remembered that. "Down in the beach canteen. We have to get down there and let Max out, dispatch Noel to the authorities."

"The beach canteen?" Sonny asked. "What idiot put him there?"

I met her eyes. "Luca, maybe?"

She threw up her hands. "That man cannot do anything right! The canteen is linked to the hotel by a tunnel and an interior elevator that leads to the kitchen. Luca is not involved in the operations of my hotel so doesn't know this but Noel does."

"No bloody way!" Peaches exclaimed. "I'm not letting that bastard get free again." She took off toward the elevator, all but Rupert following.

"I'll just wait here with the lad in case Noel accosts him," Rupert said. "I have your phone, Phoebe."

"Good," I called back.

Sonny, Peaches, and I stepped out into the lobby, Peaches so eager to get to the beach she almost pried the doors open when they failed to part quickly enough. In seconds, she was dashing down the hall.

"Take the elevator at the back of the kitchen for the quickest way down to the beach," Sonny said. To me she added, "Now, Phoebe, let's you and I go to the lounge and pour ourselves a coffee. I keep a carafe brewing for guests twenty-four hours a day. We can discuss our deal before the police get involved."

Peaches was retracing her steps toward the kitchen when she overheard that remark. "You're not seriously going with her, are you, Phoebe?" She turned to glare at me.

Sonny continued speaking as if she hadn't heard. "We can take our mugs with us up to the upper patio for our chat. It's best that we avoid the police for the time being so we can complete our business, yes?"

"Phoebe?" Peaches was glaring at me, her expression as much a warning as demand.

"Just get Noel, Peach, please," I told her. "Go!"

23

The sun was just breaking the horizon over the Tyrrhenian Sea when Sonny and I walked up the outside stairs to a small patio perched at the highest point on the property. It was such an intimate setting with tables and chairs pulled together beneath a vine-covered pergola that, for a moment, all I could do was pause long enough to inhale the view. If one could skim past the flashing lights in the cove or the equally frenetic pulse of those just visible at the far edge of the hotel, it would be perfect. I just needed one pure moment to loosen the coils in my stomach. So far, nothing was working.

I was torn in multiple directions: I wanted to remain by Evan's side; I wanted to hunt down Noel; I wanted to be reunited with my team—yet a single piece of crucial unfinished business drove me to join Sonny that morning.

She seemed so relaxed. With a fresh cigarette burning between the fingers of one hand and her mug in the other, it was as if she was ready for a pleasant tête-à-tête between friends.

"Aren't you worried that the police will round you up and toss you in jail, too?"

"Why would I?" She smiled while taking a seat and stretching her legs out on an empty chair across from her. I pulled up one of the chairs on the opposite side of the little wrought iron table. "I have done nothing wrong. I assisted you and your friends against a notorious art thief. I have stolen nothing."

"You are now head of an arms cartel," I protested while deliberately keeping my tone as even as hers. I took a sip of the rich strong coffee. Hell, I needed that.

"Not true." She drew on her cigarette and blew smoke into the dawn. A transparent halo hovered briefly overhead before being dispersed by a breeze. "My father was head of an arms cartel and then Noel and my brother followed him. I was never involved in such things and there is no proof that I was. I am not interested in running guns and perpetuating wars, though I admit to using my influence to assist the Ukrainians. Do you blame me for that?"

She knew I wouldn't.

"Nor can I be accused of any crime regarding you and your friends. I helped you to escape," she continued.

This woman was formidable in a thousand subtle ways and I knew she had an angle I couldn't swallow. "You have the reproduction of a piece of priceless art on your yacht which could prove that you're holding the original contraband should I encourage anyone to search it," I pointed out.

"Ah," she said, still smiling. "There is no law against owning a reproduction."

I stared at her. "So," I began, "you think you've covered your bases and now you'll try to tell me that you taking Cleopatra's jewels is somehow not a crime."

She dropped her feet to the pavers and swung around to fully face me. "I will not take Cleopatra's jewels. You will give them to me."

"Then I would be committing the crime."

"Nobody yet knows what you have in your possession except Noel and a few criminals who none will believe, am I right? Besides, had I not set everything in motion, those jewels would still remain buried."

"But I found them."

"*We* found them with Noel."

Would I ever win that argument? She was right. "And why would I let you take anything, our pseudo deal notwithstanding?" I demanded.

"Because, Phoebe," she began, the smile now changed into something more feral, "if you do not, countless ancient treasures will remain buried in time, maybe forever."

"Oh, please."

Sonny flicked her hand impatiently. "My father was an obsessive collector of books, scrolls, and manuscripts with the wherewithal to steal, sequester, and hold on to them in a manner that no legal entity could ever do."

That brought to mind my vivid memory of her father roaming around the

Medici collection with an intent to use them for his own purposes before we stopped him. I believed her.

"I am speaking here of, among others, papyri from Herculaneum, which when deciphered reveals unbelievable secrets including possibly the lost tomb of Cleopatra and Antony, scrolls from Alexandria—yes, do not look so shocked; they were not all destroyed—the lost paintings hidden by the Nazis. Also, my father blasted into the foundations of the ruins of an old chapel and found a trove of manuscripts and incunabula belonging to the Knights Templar, and I personally know of a man who holds a vast collection of African art that may lead to a priceless treasure. I now have access to this ancient legacy and all that they contain."

Stark disbelief must have registered on my face. "Then why didn't your father move on these treasures if they were so incredible?"

"Because he's not a timewalker like you, Phoebe, and neither am I. He might have some of the clues—those I chose to disclose, that is—but not the ability to locate them. He couldn't even read these sources himself. He needed me and his handful of scholars for that. Mostly he'd allow a few to access a tiny portion of his library at a time. Only I was given the full access. He trusted me, not them, but maybe that was his mistake. I told him little. I read, studied, and waited."

I swallowed more coffee hoping against hope that it might help clarify this murky situation. "Waited for your opportunity to come out from under your father's, brother's, and Noel's thumbs, you mean?"

"In a way. I watched and waited. All these men wanted this rich source material to track down antiquities and other valuables for their own ends—to get wealthier, to buy and trade guns and other contraband. They did not care about the objects themselves. That's not what I want. I want to find history; I want to hear the voices that time has left behind, to know where the recorded stories end and the human ones begin. I only gave my father enough clues to keep him going. The rest I kept secret. Until now."

"Are you trying to tell me that you don't want these ancient treasures for yourself, that's it's all about hearing these human voices?"

"Of course not. I must stay alive, pay my staff, enjoy the lifestyle to which I've become accustomed. I'm saying that I don't want and need it all. I am not greedy. For every timewalk you take that leads to treasures based on information and source material I provide, you will take half for your museums and art galleries. That is half of what you would never otherwise have for your institutions. But that's only part of what you care about, too, isn't it, Phoebe? You also want to hear those lost voices speak the way I do, only in your case they speak in your head."

I hesitated. "I'd rather they didn't speak through me. It's terrifying...to carry all those voices in my head now that I can hear them more clearly."

"Yes, I understand," she said softly. "That must be so difficult."

It was more than just difficult, it was heartbreaking and thrilling all at the same time. I took a deep breath. "You know that the agency's mission is to find the ancient lost and the stolen and return them to their original owners or to humanity as a whole. For me personally at the heart of it all, I want to know that the ancient and the beautiful or simply informative remain in the hands of the many not the few. I want to know that everyone has the opportunity to see for themselves those objects that have shaped what it means to be human." Something like a tremor was coursing through me which I couldn't quite contain. Maybe it was the sudden jolt of caffeine.

Sonny leaned forward, propping one elbow on the table. "I applaud you. So I ask, how often does it happen that the governments all agree quickly who gets what and to what museum?"

I met her steady gaze. "You know how fraught international law can be."

"I do. Take Cleopatra's jewels, for example."

"In the case of Cleopatra's jewels, which were found on Italian soil, Italy will make the strongest case for ownership, but since Cleopatra was an Egyptian queen, that nation will demand that the jewels return to Cairo. Egypt has been very aggressive over the looting that Britain, in particular, has made on her treasures across the centuries, and they have little tolerance for any new and improved version. In this case, Cleopatra provided a gift to a Roman citizen, making the ownership clearly Italian. Maybe."

"Providing one has the proof." She took another drag of her cigarette. "I have letters from Livia to the Vestal Virgins, you do not. I have the provenance. See my point?"

Decades of legal wrangling in international courts, all of which might ensure that Cleopatra's jewels may never find their home for a long, long time. Even the right to release photographs could be prohibited due to copyright wrangling. Unless the objects came with a clear path to ownership to prove history and ownership, the bounty I carried on my back may as well remain buried under a brick in Pompeii. Yes, I saw her point.

"Listen, Phoebe, I am suggesting a partnership equally beneficial to us both. I provide the clues, you timewalk, and together we discover lost or stolen antiquities. We share everything. We cooperate every step of the way. It is not possible that you will find these treasures without me or I without you. Together we will hear the past speak in the most powerful manner, and for everything we uncover, we share and I give you the source material to cut through the legal red tape. This will ensure that these treasures will be seen now, not later."

It was a bargain so tempting, how could I refuse? At the same time, how could I accept? "Only your deal means I enter an agreement with a thief, call yourself what you will. Your intention is to keep part of these treasures for yourself, to sell or to hold at your discretion. You're asking me to willingly relinquish ancient art and antiquities, which goes against everything I stand for."

"But if you do not enter an agreement with me, neither you nor the world will ever see these ancient sources. But if you make a deal with me, you take half of everything for your museums and art galleries, items which you would not otherwise have access to. How does this go against your goals, Phoebe? I would even share with you the locations of the paintings my father stole and name those who bought them. In short, I offer you everything your agency could ever desire, a feast of the ancient lost and stolen." She tapped one broken nail on the table. "All yours, all ours."

I stared at a far point on the horizon, unable to speak.

"Show me Cleopatra's jewels, Phoebe. Tell me about Flora. Surely you owe me that much."

I returned my gaze to her. I needed time to think. She didn't appear to have a gun, at least I had yet to see her carry one, but she'd had plenty of opportunity to pick something up as she trotted off to fetch coffee. Damn. I pulled out Evan's phone long enough to see the red battery warning. The phone did not have enough juice left to defend an ant.

"You don't need that, Phoebe. I will not attempt to take anything that you do not agree to give me."

Slowly, I shrugged the backpack off my shoulders and unzipped the top to lift the strand of pearls, the cuffs, the inlaid collar, the gold, the jewels, the diadem, leaving the hundred or so loose pearls in the bag. We stared at the glistening hoard as the sun rose higher, gilding gold upon gold, the light fracturing the jewels into bright shards of color, the whole pile sparkling and mesmerizing in its splendor.

Sonny caught her breath. For a moment she didn't speak but got to her feet, eyes wide with her hands pressed against her mouth, cigarette forgotten. She flicked the butt away seconds before burning her fingers.

"Oh," she gasped. "Cleopatra's very own." She ran her fingers over the glossy mound, tears in her eyes, hesitating briefly over the diadem, which I had sat on top. "We are gazing at history, Phoebe. Women, maybe much like ourselves, held these very pieces and dreamed of a better world, maybe for themselves, maybe for others." Her gaze lifted to me. "Tell me about Flora."

I knew we would come to this and it was all I could do to speak of the woman whose death now seemed as real as if it had been my own. The memories had returned slowly like the replay of a damaged video track with Flora's very thoughts burned into my mind. "She was trying to protect a girl," I whispered, "a girl whose life and education had been entrusted to her by the Vestal Virgins of whom Flora had once been part. Livia initiated the plan, the Vestals carried it out. After several generations, they identified a girl to rule the world. Her name was Juno."

"Juno," Sonny whispered. "This girl was named Juno?"

By then it had all unfolded in my mind, a deep knowing that had begun in Pompeii and snaked its way into my memory, a past that was not my own. Not a comfortable knowing, not an easy knowing to bear, and yet by now I felt the burden was more of an honor than a curse.

"Who was this Juno?"

"Flora never knew exactly the circumstances of her birth but believed the child was of noble blood and stolen from her mother as a baby. The mother may have even relinquished the child willingly if the Vestals insisted."

"Yes, the Vestals were a powerful group. I could see them holding such sway."

"The girl was raised by Flora in the villa that had been long ago bequeathed to the Vestals by Livia herself. Cleopatra's jewels were to be Juno's dowry and the diadem her assurance to rule all men," I said.

"A child who," Sonny said, picking up the story, "was raised in Pompeii with Flora under the guidance of a cult of sacred priestesses."

"And they had her educated by scholars and tutors to become a future power behind the throne," I added. "Livia and the Vestals planned for this girl to be the next Livia, ruling with skill and vision. They believed absolutely in the power of Cleopatra's diadem."

Sonny whistled, turning to look at the golden circlet gleaming on the pile. "And did Juno survive Pompeii?"

I lowered my gaze, tracing the table's wrought iron curlicues with my finger to keep myself anchored in the here and now. Those delicate black coils weaving in and around as if within its own universe could be a symbol for time itself. "No," I whispered. "She died with Flora. I can't bear to go back there again, never, never again."

Sonny was beside me in a moment, her hands gripping my shoulders. "Stay with me, Phoebe. You now must control this powerful gift of yours and not allow it to control you. I know someone who can advise you. Maybe I'll take you to him someday?"

I met her eyes. "Thank you but I don't need help and I'm not going anywhere at the moment. I'm learning to find my way." Though it took everything I had, I remained fixed in time.

"Good." She dropped her hands. Turning, she picked up the diadem from the top of the jeweled pile and held it to the light. "So Livia and the priestesses believed that Juno would control the world with this?"

I watched her carefully, saw how her fingers trembled as she held the gold band aloft. "Yes. She believed that it held the power necessary to control men and, through them, the world."

"Sad, isn't it, that women believed that they could only rule from behind a seat of power and never on it?"

"In Cleopatra's case, she had ruled her domain from on the throne but even she could not hold her power against the force of Rome."

"Rome was a very male power like most forces throughout history. But Livia had believed this diadem was the key," Sonny whispered.

"Yes, but I suspect Cleopatra knew better, which is why she passed it on to Livia," I said.

The sun was high enough now that I had to squint to see her.

"Do you believe this diadem can bind men to the woman who wears it, Phoebe?" she asked.

"Of course not. If women are going to rule the world, they need to step out from the shadows and be heard as a powerful voice in their own right. Women have gone unheard long enough. We need to be united, even when our opinions differ."

"I feel the same. Take the diadem with you as your half. Let other women see what lengths women had to go to rule their worlds, the price they had to pay." Sonny smiled sadly as she lowered the crown back to the pile, lifting instead a richly inlaid jeweled golden cuff shaped like a snake. "I would like this."

"I haven't agreed to anything," I said.

"Yes, you have. I see it in your eyes. Now, you choose something and then I will, and so it will go until we have divided the treasure."

"No," I said. "Those objects are priceless and don't belong to either one of us. Instead, take the loose pearls, which must be worth millions. Those are marketable and easily fenced, enough to keep your enterprise afloat. Everything else comes with me. That's the deal, take it or leave it."

Our eyes met across the gleaming pile. I counted the seconds as the sun rose higher in the sky.

❧ 24 ❧

Peaches was just striding down the stairway when I exited from the kitchen door.

"Peach!" I exclaimed. "Tell me that Max is all right and that Noel is in custody!"

People in various uniforms were dashing around everywhere—what looked to be emergency personnel, medical professionals, and plenty of police interviewing someone near the lobby entrance.

She turned and stared. "First tell me that you didn't just make a deal with the devil."

I drew her by the arm into a coat vestibule. "I don't believe in devils. Where's Noel and Max?"

"You believe in angels so why not devils? And I have no idea where that bastard and your goddad are. The canteen was empty when I got there. Looks like Noel escaped through the tunnels and took Max with him. I combed through the place until the police arrived and insisted on taking over. They ordered me to keep out of the way. They think that by having dozens of dudes searching the grounds they'll find that bastard better than I can but it's not that easy. At least Nicolina and Seraphina are crawling around the rocks searching, too."

"Calm down." I raised my hands as if she was the only one getting excited. "There aren't that many directions he can escape from without a boat. It's either down the main drive or through the cove and both are blocked off. Even the tunnels are dead ends according to that diagram."

She peeked out into the hallway before pulling back and giving me that look-that-could-not-be-denied. "Tell me what happened between you and Sonofabitchi."

"I am carrying Cleopatra's jewels, including the diadem. Here, you take them. They are wearing me down."

She helped me shrug out of the backpack and peered inside. "Answer my question."

There is a price to be paid when someone knows you too well. "I struck up an arrangement. In return for clues and provenance that could lead us to missing sites that might otherwise remain lost in time or even destroyed, she receives part of the proceeds."

"Proceeds? What in hell does 'proceeds' mean?" she asked, shaking the bag. "You mean like part of the priceless art and antiquities, treasure in other words? Are you kidding me?" I'd never seen such disbelief mixed with so much fury.

"How could I do anything else, Peach? If it weren't for those letters, I would never have had enough information to timewalk in Pompeii, would never have found Cleopatra's jewels. When Sonny waved terms around like 'Templar's gold' and mentioned paintings still missing from the Nazi thefts and other priceless masterpieces thought lost forever, how could I just let that go? I couldn't."

"It could all be a ploy," she pointed out.

"This one wasn't."

"So you did make a pact with the devil." Her words were tight with anger.

"Stop with that devil stuff. Besides, neither one of us are angels. There is no black and white in the world we live in but only a thousand shades of gray and a million colors in between. I learned that much when I ditched that law degree. In this case, the ends justified the means."

"Tell the international law world that."

"Any argument on ethics has more than one side, depending on what you stand for. What do we stand for if not for retrieving lost and stolen art and returning those riches to their rightful owners? What I agreed to today does that only on a much larger scale than I ever could have imagined."

"But at what price?" she demanded.

"There's a cost to everything. You know that. Please stay on my side in this, Peach."

"I'm always on your side. I'm just hoping Evan will get past this one. He technically works for the law, remember." She fastened on the backpack and turned away. "Come on, we've got to find Max and Noel."

At that moment, a stretcher bearing Evan flanked by two medical personnel was passing in front of the coat vestibule, Rupert trailing along behind.

I was beside them in seconds. "Will he be alright?" I asked, touching Evan's arm. He appeared to be down under again, deep in whatever land the painkillers sent him.

"Phoebe, I am certain that they will take good care of him," Rupert assured me. "As soon as we have finished here, we will proceed to the hospital to see the lad." Rupert gently held me back. "In the meantime, we must let him go while we take care of business. The police have been asking questions to which I simply do not know the answers, but that officer speaking to the doctor over there is the capo, I believe. He says he would like to speak to you as soon as possible."

I caught Peaches's eye over Rupert's head.

"First, we've got to find Max and ensure Noel's in custody," I said. "Then we'll talk to anybody they want."

"Don't tell anyone that you saw us, Rupe," Peaches added as we took off down the hall.

I heard Rupert calling after us: "Nicolina and Zann are looking for him, too." Uniformed personnel were darting everywhere. At any moment, one of them might try to physically stop us.

"I think the top cop just spotted us. Follow me!" Peaches led me to the stairway to the right of the elevator and bolted upward.

"Where are we going?" I asked.

"The one place I haven't checked yet. There's a series of little viewing trails and lookouts around the point that I saw on the hotel diagram. Thinking that maybe Noel could be holed up someplace out there. He'd know the property well enough since he'd been with Sonofabitchi, right?"

"Right," I puffed. Admittedly, I was running out of steam by then. "He could be dashing around here dressed up like an officer...for all we know," I said between breaths. "There are enough uniforms crawling around here to get lost among."

"I know how wily that bastard is," she whispered.

"I'm more worried about Max. What if Noel's hurt him?" I said, almost not daring to utter the thought.

"Do you believe that Noel would actually hurt his own father?"

"Yes, and so do you. Shh! I hear voices."

We paused long enough to hear the footsteps overhead.

"Let's get off on this floor," she whispered. The hotel only had four stories, the top opening onto a roof garden. We bolted through the door to the third level. "We'll take the fire escape the rest of the way," she told me as she headed for the end of the hall.

"Peach, do you understand why I did what I did?" I asked as we burst out to a set of exterior metal stairs that climbed the back of the building. The property had been built flush with the cliff, which flanked it in the early-morning light. For a moment we stood in silence getting our bearings. Soon we were heading down.

"Not now. Look!" Peaches said with a hiss.

Not now made perfect sense. Below us on one of the upper patios Nicolina, Seraphina, and Zann could be seen running for one of the stone stairways heading down. We headed after them, Peaches sending a text while we sprinted in their direction.

By the time we reached the bottom level, our team had disappeared and no one was answering Peaches's text.

"They're chasing somebody," I said as we dashed across the pavers and down the next stairway. This part of the property appeared to climb the cliffside in interconnecting patios, one being where Sonny and I had held our meeting. No sign of Sonny now or anybody else, for that matter.

At the top of the next stairway, I paused. "Look!"

Below us, two levels down, five officers stood at the edge of the main terrace where the road jackknifed down to the beach. Beside them, also looking downward, stood the rest of our team. A helicopter buzzed overhead. One of the officers had a megaphone and was demanding something in Italian of somebody below. I didn't have to see him to know who it was.

My heart was in my throat as we sped down the steps and ran over to join them.

"What's going on?" I asked as I arrived beside Nicolina.

"Phoebe." She said my name and placed a hand on my arm without looking at me. There was no need to respond. I saw what everyone else did: a man standing on the road below, one arm over the shoulders of an older man with his gun pointed at his skull. It shocked me.

A part of me still couldn't believe that Noel would be so heartless as well as so desperate to use his own father as a hostage. Maybe I still held out hope that something like a heart beat in that scarred chest if his.

Max, on the other hand, was staring bleakly ahead while his son held a gun to his temple. I could only imagine what it felt like for a father to finally face the truth of what his son had become. Both were bruised and battered but my godfather had a black eye as well as a swollen lip. I worried about his heart in more ways than one.

"Put the gun down and your hands up," the officer blared. "Release the hostage immediately. You cannot get off the island. It is surrounded."

"You're going to get me an airlift out of here or the old man is dead," Noel cried, shaking Max for emphasis. He shot a quick glance over his shoulder to where a line of armed officers blocked the road down to the beach.

"We do not negotiate," the capo insisted. "Release the hostage now."

Peaches leaned over and whispered. "If you keep him busy, I'll dash down through the kitchen and sneak up behind him from the beach." She'd never get past the officers and we had no idea just how twitchy Noel's trigger finger might be. He was cornered and frantic.

"There's no time. Stay," I hissed. "I need him to focus on me."

I broke from the others and strode down toward the drive, ignoring the officer shouting for me to stay back. Peaches remained where she was but I knew she'd have her phone ready to level at Noel, which she could no more risk than the snipers lining up to take a shot. One false move and it would be Max who went down. I had to keep Noel busy.

"Noel, are you seriously using your own father as a shield? Is that what you've become?" I asked as I strode down the hill.

"Stay back, Phoeb, darlin'," Max called, his voice choked with emotion. God, I couldn't bear to see him looking so beaten. "This is my battle."

"No, it isn't." I stopped a few yards away and stared at Noel. "It's mine. It's me you want, isn't it, Noel? As usual, you have to get to me by using someone I love so I'll make it easy for you. Here I am. Take me instead." I spread my arms.

Noel emitted one of his machine gun laughs, only this one fired short. "You've got to be bloody kidding me, sniffer bitch. I don't want you, not anymore. You're nothing but grief—always have been. Don't know what I saw in you in the first place. Get away from me or your goddad gets it in the head." He jammed the gun into Max's temple. Both of them were the same height but Noel had a wiry strength after so many years on the run while Max had long ago given up his gym pass.

One of the officers above called down: "You are surrounded. Place your firearm on the ground and raise your hands."

"Noel, do as they say," I pleaded.

He glanced quickly to the patio above. "Nope. I told you before, babe: I'm never going to die in some prison somewhere. If they won't let me leave with my hostage, then what do I have to lose?" A wolfish grin crossed his face, one filled with more pain than mirth. "I may as well die here and take whoever I can down with me, right? Might keep me company in the great hereafter."

God, he was ramping up. "Then take me. Look, Noel. I'm unarmed." I threw Evan's dead phone to the ground and held up my hands. "See, nothing to defend myself with. You can take me knowing that I have no special powers for protection for once."

His cheeks were sunken, his expression tense and ragged. Whatever demons drove this man were in full control of him now. Surely he'd like nothing better than to take his rage out on me?

"A bit late for that, isn't it, babe?" he said softly. "You had your chance—*we* had our chance."

I couldn't afford to have his anger diffuse, either. In his case, a cold realization could be as deadly as mad desperation. I needed him to turn his anger on me. "Okay, so once again I've whipped the treasure out from right under your nose, didn't I? It's in the hands of the authorities now waiting to be returned to where it belongs. You put your little sniffer bitch on the scent and she went and retrieved the loot again but not for you, Noel, never for you." I took a step forward. "You've lost again. How many times is it now?"

He shoved Max off to the side, nearly toppling the older man, while I stepped forward with my hands raised. The moment Noel reached out to grab me, I lodged a swift kick to his groin, causing him to double over and drop the gun, which Max snatched off the ground in a stumbling grab.

Now Max clutched the pistol barrel in both trembling hands. "Stop right there, son, or I shoot," he said.

Noel looked up at him as he slowly straightened. "You can't pull the trigger, Dad. You just don't have it in you."

"But I do." I whipped the gun from Max and turned it on Noel.

"You can't, either, babe," he said.

But he was wrong.

25

No, I did not kill him. I'd been told over and over again that under the circumstances it may have been better if I had. Avoid the trials, the courts, the chance that he might wiggle out of his conviction. None of that mattered.

Yes, I cared about ending the years of terror he'd inflicted on me, my friends, and the world, but killing anyone was not in my DNA. I did pull the trigger, aiming to the left of the heart he no longer possessed and watched him drop. There was a certain satisfaction in that and relief, too. Because I'm not that good a shot, I could have easily missed and killed him dead, but I didn't. No blood on my hands.

As Noel collapsed, Max ran to his side, and I relinquished the gun to the police. After that, I was ushered into custody. What followed was interview after interview, some accompanied by agency members and some solo, me explaining the whole torturous play of coercion and interaction to one authority after the other. Most were sympathetic, others grilled me as if I were the criminal, but I was getting used to that.

I explained how I found Cleopatra's jewels based on a letter Noel Halloran possessed. No, I had not actually read the letter myself, I told them, since we couldn't read the badly damaged ancient script. It was at this point that I fudged the truth, de-emphasizing Sonny's role in lieu of Noel's. That was surprisingly easy since Sonny herself had emerged looking more heroine than criminal and I simply turned up the volume on the storyline.

Generally, my tale went that Noel had held Evan Barrows captive, threatening to kill him, and it was on that basis that the agency began the search for the jewels. After that, Noel kidnapped me and forced me to locate the secret hoard.

It seemed so straightforward up to that point but I could no more explain how I'd actually found the cache than I could any other of life's mysteries. I just did. My mind works that way, I said. To me, a woman named Flora became the key player in a running dream that I found both enlightening and frightening.

So, I told the truth (mostly) and, by now, I had enough of a reputation with Italian Interpol and the antiquities divisions that they heard me out. Whether they could quite get their heads around this woman who claimed that she could pluck away at the strings of time until something lost and ancient spoke to her is another matter entirely. I could hardly believe it myself.

In the end, the authorities had little choice but to accept the reality of the impossible or, at the very least, the unlikely. Fact was that I laid a pile of ancient jewelry at their feet along with the letter sealed like a scroll that apparently granted convincing provenance that those jewels had once belonged to Cleopatra, the last Ptolemaic ruler of the Egyptian dynasty, given to Livia Empress of Rome as a hoped-for bribe.

The diadem alone rendered everyone speechless. One rapt antiquities expert who had been called in to verify the finds could barely speak when he brought up the picture of the presumed statue of Cleopatra wearing that same circlet. The diadem was the clincher. As for the pile of loose pearls, no one knew about those. As I said, I fudged.

In any case, my most difficult hearing was not before the police but the Agency of the Ancient Lost and Found, my friends, and my godfather, the latter having flown back to London in a state of shock. Our reckoning would come later.

"I know that my arrangement with Sonny Baldi puts us squarely in the crosshairs of a legal and ethical dilemma and I—" I began.

"Call it for what it is: a deal," Peaches said. "You made a deal with this woman before clearing it with us." She appeared slightly less angry than she had back on Capri but her anger had a way of going underground for a slow smolder before erupting all over again. Madam Vesuvius.

"I did and I'm sorry that I couldn't involve you in that moment. It was one of those flash decisions. Either I called Sonny out to the authorities or accepted the opportunities she offered in the name of accessing more of the world's lost treasures sooner. I made the choice and stand by it, but if you decide not to stand with me in this, I understand." I'd be desperately hurt, but really, who could blame them?

We were sitting in the lounge of Nicolina's Naples hotel room where we awaited visiting hours to begin in Evan's hospital. I'd been with him most of the previous day and had yet to tell him the details. He was still too groggy with the effect of drugs and a lingering concussion. That was my excuse, anyway.

Nicolina spoke first. "Is there anyone in this room who has not crossed the legal line? I do not think so." She gazed at us each in turn. "We all have. That is how we all came together, yes? You, Peaches, were once a guerrilla in the Jamaican jungle; Zann, you broke into a building in Florence and discovered the Botticelli; I will not even begin to list my transgressions but they are many. We are not angels."

Rupert, who had been sitting studying his hands, cleared his throat. "Yes, to some extent I would argue that in our line of work regarding retrieving the lost and stolen, we have, indeed, all encountered matters of some legal and possibly ethical uncertainty. I assure you that as a prior Interpol agent, I did knowingly and with the full understanding of my superiors perform tasks that were clearly illegal as well as possibly unethical, depending entirely upon one's point of view."

Blazing relief and gratitude filled my heart. "Thank you," I whispered. "I really don't know what I would have done if you had decided to stick to the rules."

"We have never stuck to the rules," Zann commented. A second later she added: "Have we?"

It was only later as we were crossing the street toward the hospital that Peaches strode up beside me. "Your Sonofabitchi sure knows how to push your buttons, doesn't she? Have you heard from her since Capri?'

"Not a word," I said. "I figured she'd get in touch once this whole business settles down. Why?"

"This." She passed me a piece of paper. "She emailed this to me so I had it printed out."

"What is it?" I asked.

"It's an article published in a popular online art mag talking about the widespread poaching of African artifacts. She underlined the part where it named some bigwig collector in Santa Fe who apparently owns a wooden carving that may lead to a lost hoard of African art. She added a line saying that she has more information based on a nineteenth-century journal in her late father's collection."

I stopped dead center of the street. "African art?" I broke into a grin. "And you say that she knows how to push *my* buttons? Looks like she knows where to find yours, too."

"I'm not falling for it."

"I'm betting you will," I said, turning away to continue crossing the road. "Didn't you once complain to me that the poaching of African art is nothing less than the cultural raping of an entire continent? Maybe we now have the opportunity to undo some of that wrong."

"But at what cost?" she wailed.

"There's always a cost."

She clutched my arm to hold me back. "But who's going to pay it, Phoebe? Do you think Ev will go along with us partnering with an art thief?"

I gazed past her to the hospital knowing that today I must tell him the full story, no matter what the consequences.

"I don't know," I whispered. "I can only hope there's enough between us to get past this. Maybe he can love me without loving every single thing I do."

"*We* do," she corrected. "It's the Agency of the Ancient Lost & Found who agreed to go with you in this. All of our necks are on the line."

"Sometimes you have to stick your neck out to improve the view. Come on, let's go."

THE END

Ready for another Adventure? Book 7 is in Pre-order now: The Zambezi Code

The Agency of the Ancient Lost & Found

Book Seven

The Zambezi Code

JANE THORNLEY

AFTERWORD

I'd be the first to admit that I had Cleopatra all wrong. Yes, I knew she had been a brilliant and strategic queen who used every tool in her arsenal to ensure that Egypt continued as a sovereign domain. Despite her feminine wiles, her brilliant mind, her audacious spirit, she is remembered for "bewitching" two Roman generals. This is a queen that lost the battle in the gender wars in history a long ago but she needs to be remembered for more than that.

Cleopatra truly did try to bribe Livia with a cache of jewelry according to contemporary accounts. That Livia hid them from her husband with the intent to ensure that a woman would one day rule the known world is entirely the work of fiction...yet, maybe she dreamed of doing just that. How could intelligent, educated Roman women not consider the imbalance in the social order and scheme of ways to right the wrong?

As for Phoebe's growing psychic abilities, that's only partially fictive. Most of us know or have heard of those who have the gift. Exploring the possibilities is part of the fun.

ABOUT THE AUTHOR

JANE THORNLEY is an author of historical mystery thrillers with a humorous twist and just a touch of the unexplained. She has been writing for as long as she can remember and when not traveling and writing, lives a very dull life—at least on the outside. Her inner world is something else again.

With multiple novels published and more on the way, she keeps up a lively dialogue with her characters and invites you to eavesdrop by reading all of her works.

To follow Jane and share her books' interesting background details, special offers, and more, please join her newsletter here:

NEWSLETTER SIGN-UP

ALSO BY JANE THORNLEY

SERIES: CRIME BY DESIGN

Crime by Design Boxed Set Books 1-3

Crime by Design Prequel: Rogue Wave e-book available free to newsletter subscribers.

Crime by Design Book 1: Warp in the Weave

Crime by Design Book 2: Beautiful Survivor

Crime by Design Book 3: The Greater of Two Evils

Crime by Design Book 4: The Plunge

Also featuring Phoebe McCabe:

SERIES: THE AGENCY OF THE ANCIENT LOST & FOUND

The Carpet Cipher Book 1

The Crown that Lost its Head Book 2

The Florentine's Secret Book 3

The Artemis Key Book 4

The Thread of the Unicorn Book 5

SERIES: NONE OF THE ABOVE MYSTERY

None of the Above Series Book 1: Downside Up

None of the Above Series Book 2: DownPlay

SERIES: TIME SHADOWS

Consider me Gone Book 1

The Spirit in the Fold 2 (companion to The Florentine's Secret)

Made in the USA
Monee, IL
03 May 2024

57947422R00107